The Bright Season

The Bright Season

a novel

by *Melanie Lageschulte*

The Bright Season: a novel
© 2019
by Melanie Lageschulte
Fremont Creek Press

Kindle: 978-0-9997752-7-1
Paperback: 978-0-9997752-8-8
Hardcover: 978-0-9997752-9-5
Large-print paperback: 978-1-952066-08-5

Cover photo: PhotoliveX/Shutterstock.com
Cover design by Melanie Lageschulte

Web: fremontcreekpress.com

Also by Melanie Lageschulte

* 1 *

It was already too hot, and it wasn't even ten in the morning. Melinda swiped her forehead with one thick chore glove, willing to add more dirt to her face in exchange for removing some of the sweat smothering her brow. Her straw hat was a ratty old thing rummaged from the farmhouse's back porch closet, but she'd been smart to grab something with a wide brim rather than her usual canvas cap. With no trees nearby to offer even a hint of shade, she kept her back to the sun's searing rays as she studied the pasture fence.

"Another one! This is the tenth hole I've found today." Her shoulders sagging from discouragement as well as the heat, she tossed her tool bag and roll of wire to the ground. The moment she crouched to study the gap, she heard an ominous hum and felt a sharp pinch on the side of her neck.

"Get away!" She swatted at the mosquito but it was too late, a welt already rising on her skin. "I can't believe they're out at this hour. And there's no puddles around, since it hasn't rained for a solid week. Where are they coming from?"

Probably from the other side of the fence, where endless rows of corn marched across the fields surrounding Melinda Foster's two-acre farm. The plants were less than a foot tall on this first day of June, their stalks still thin and their leaves delicate, but there were thousands of them, and their neat rows harbored a system of shadowy tunnels. As she reached for the pliers, Melinda wondered what other critters were, right at that moment, traveling through those secret spaces.

Did birds land inside the cornfield's depths, seeking a patch of shade? Squirrels and chipmunks surely made use of these hidden routes, as they were seemingly everywhere in this part of northern Iowa. There would be mice and rats, too, and ...

A rustle echoed under the corn leaves, just off to the right, and started in her direction. She gripped the pliers tighter, her muscles tensed for whatever might appear out of the field's shadows.

"Stormy! Don't scare me like that!"

Relieved, she dropped the pliers into the ragged weeds at her feet. The potential predator was simply one of her friendly barn cats, and the rusted tool would have been a pathetic defense against any set of gnashing teeth.

Stormy blinked his green eyes at the sudden change in light, then stepped smartly across the dirt path that buffeted the field from the fence. He expertly slipped through the wire grid and rubbed his gray-tabby cheek against Melinda's sun-browned arm. With greetings out of the way, he plopped into the weeds and rolled over, requesting a tummy rub.

There was so much work to do, but she couldn't resist taking a little break. Stormy purred with delight and stretched his white-capped paws toward the cloudless sky.

"You were trespassing, mister. Horace and the rest of the Schermanns sold off those fields ten years ago, long before you were born. Where's your partner in crime? When I find you, Sunny isn't often far behind."

She stared into the rows of corn, expecting to see a flash of fluffy orange fur, but found only more shadows and silence. If Sunny wasn't with Stormy, he was probably off on some other adventure, either in this field or within the windbreak of trees that bordered the west and north sides of the farm. Her boys were now brave and affectionate, an about-face in temperament from the shy, skittish strays she'd discovered in the barn when she arrived last summer.

Horace had guessed the cats to be just a few years' old, and they'd appeared only a few weeks before he joined his brother at the nursing home in Elm Springs. Melinda had arrived soon after, expecting to leave her jobless life in Minneapolis behind just long enough to help Aunt Miriam run Prosper Hardware while Uncle Frank recovered from a heart attack. But she'd decided to stay, and the cats had, too.

"Now, you listen to me." She shook a warning finger at Stormy. "I don't want you boys running around in the corn! You stay in the yard, OK? And whatever you do, don't let me catch you out on the road." The ribbon of gravel that ran past her acreage saw only a few vehicles a day, but many drivers had the foot to the floor.

"And that includes the pasture across the road, too." One of Sunny's ears flattened with annoyance and he rolled over, turning his back to her commands.

"There's probably snakes in that overgrown grass, since there's no sheep over there this summer. We had company last year, didn't we? But things got way out of hand. I guess that's why they say good fences make good neighbors."

Between the sad state of Horace's fences and an equally worn-out section on the other side of the gravel, Melinda had come home one September afternoon to find several of her ewes romping with the flock from across the way. There had been a ram in that group, and the resulting lambs were one reason fence repair had become such an important, and endless, part of her new life.

Stormy's eyes were closed, and he was already deep into that slumber cats can accomplish in one twitch of a whisker. Melinda was about to break off a length of wire when she caught a different movement out of the corner of her eye.

Her dad was coming back from the barn with more supplies. Roger slipped the substantial roll of wire over one of his tanned forearms and used his other hand to unlatch the pasture gate. Hobo darted around Roger, his sort-of-shaggy brown coat glinting in the sun, then made sure his friend was still behind him. He barked at something he thought he saw in the cornfield, then rushed across the dry grass toward Melinda, the white tip of his tail waving in greeting.

Hobo had also started life as a stray, a lonely pup who'd appeared under the lilac bushes in the front yard a few years ago. Horace and his brother Wilbur, who were lifelong bachelors, had taken Hobo in, and the dog had made this farm his home. Melinda had been both humbled and relieved when Hobo finally made room in his heart for her, too.

"Hey, buddy!" She got to her feet and braced for the onslaught of affection coming her way. "Now, don't jump up! We've been working on that, remember? Maybe someday you'll learn some manners."

"Oh, I doubt that. Farm dogs do as they please." Roger rubbed Hobo's ears. "And that's how it should be. He behaves himself when he's in the house, at least."

Retired from the communications company in nearby Swanton, Melinda's hometown, Roger liked to get out on the golf course to keep up his "farmer tan." As a former country boy, he also loved to drive out to Melinda's acreage and help cross off whatever was on her to-do list.

"Here, I found that other stash of wire in the grain room. I hope this will be enough." He crossed his arms and evaluated the pasture, which stretched east of the barn down to the road, then south and west toward the surrounding cornfield. "I can see how this all became too much for Horace. Fixing fence is slow, dirty work, and there's plenty of it out here. I'm amazed he made it into his early nineties before he had to give up the farm."

"He's a tough old guy," Melinda said affectionately as she snapped off another length of wire. She motioned for Roger to hold the fence steady so she could weave the new piece through the grid. "I'm barely forty, and I couldn't do this for more than a few hours at a time, crawling around, especially in this heat."

"Notice how I offered to just be your go-fer? I don't think I could get low like that anymore. If I tried, you'd have to call Doc and Bill to get me upright." Bill Larsen was Prosper

Hardware's only other full-time employee. He and John "Doc" Ogden, one of two veterinarians based in little Prosper, were part of its volunteer emergency crew.

"I'm not going to risk it. You stay right where you are."

She grimaced and tried to bend the wire to her will. But it was stronger than it looked, and its ends pressed into her palm right through her gloves. With his free hand, Roger reached into the canvas bag at his feet, pushed aside the sunscreen and bottled water, and fished out a pair of pliers so big they almost looked deadly.

"Here, see if you can twist it with this. I hope we can get a few more sections done before we have to quit, and that's probably only another hour. Good thing we started early. I can't believe this heat, and this early in the summer, too."

She crisscrossed the wire again, gripped the new pliers tight, and turned as hard as she could. It finally caught. Roger began to laugh when she rocked back on her heels.

"What?" Melinda pushed her hat's floppy brim aside and squinted up at her dad. "What's so funny?"

"When you moved back here, did you ever think you'd be doing this? Fixing a rundown fence in this blazing heat? You were so excited to have fresh eggs and take over Horace's garden. Remember those pretty floral gloves you bought?" He shook his head. "You weren't exactly planning to become a sheep farmer."

"Yeah, it's not very glamorous, that's for sure." She waved her fingers, her thick cotton yellow gloves dulled by layers of dirt.

"That fancy pair only lasted a week before they ripped. Hey, looks like we're going to have company."

A chorus of "baaas" began as soon as the sheep rounded the last corner of the barn. Ten ewes fronted the flock, while the last two ambled along behind the seven lambs. They were too far away for Melinda to read the numbered green tags in their ears, but one of the latecomers had to be Annie, Horace and Wilbur's former bottle baby who never wanted to go anywhere fast ... unless it was her idea.

"They were all east of the barn when I went in for the wire," Roger explained. "Several of the ewes ran in to see what I was up to. When they ran back out, I wondered if they'd watch to see where I was headed."

The sheep's hustle across the pasture made Melinda want to laugh and cringe at the same time. She adored her ewes and lambs, and their devotion touched her heart. But she wished they wouldn't run anywhere in this heat, even to meet up with her. Their faces and legs were black, and their cream wool was incredibly dense. Next year, she'd contact the shearing company earlier so she could get her girls' annual salon appointment set for some time in May. Just a few more days, though, and the ewes would be as cool as the lambs were in their nubby charcoal coats.

If only she could make a magical phone call and bring a soaking rain to her pasture and garden. The sheep's supply of grass wasn't growing back as fast as it should, and it took a daily march with the hose to keep her vegetables thriving.

Shadowed by the sheep, Melinda and Roger moved down the fence to the next gap. This one, at least, was minor and easily repaired. Melinda had just squatted before another weak spot when her straw hat suddenly jerked backward.

"Hail, Caesar!" Roger gently pushed the largest lamb away. "That straw's not for eating. Let that brim go, now, so Melinda can fix your fence."

"He's going to his new home next week." She rubbed Caesar's dark ears. "I'm going to miss him, but John will give him a great life. And while he's cute and harmless now, that's going to change once he grows up. I'm not willing to deal with the attitude, from him or any other buck."

Caesar was twice the size of the other lambs, and the only male that was still intact. Neighbor John Olson, a veteran sheep farmer, had purchased Caesar to sire a separate flock to benefit his sons' college funds.

"So, no more lambs then?" Roger gestured at the other youngsters, who no longer clung to their mothers and liked to run together. At three months old, they were gaining fast.

Even Little Clover, the youngest of the triplets, had nearly caught up to the others.

"No way. My first lambing season was by accident. And it's going to be my last." Melinda snapped off another length of wire. "I know I shouldn't keep them all, but I can't stand the thought of selling any more of them."

Roger was quiet for a moment. "Well ... there's no hurry, I guess. Just see how it goes." He picked up the tool bag and shifted it down the fence. "In the meantime, you've got quite the crew. Makes this place feel like a real farm."

An obnoxious bellow sounded from somewhere in the pack, and one of the ewes barged toward Roger. Hobo, who resting a few feet away, got to his feet and began to bark.

"Annie, stop that!" Melinda waved her straw hat, but was ignored. "Dad, be careful!"

"Oh, she just doesn't want to be left out." Roger rubbed the ewe's forehead, which was just what she wanted. "Caesar's so full of himself, isn't he? It's not right for him to get all of the attention."

Melinda cut more wire and eyed the next hole. She'd need to break out the monster pliers again. "So, you talked to Mark last night? Which weekend is he coming home?"

Her brother lived in Austin, Texas. Their sister, Liz, was in Milwaukee with her husband and their two young sons. Mark hadn't been back for over a year, and Melinda couldn't wait for everyone to be together again.

"Last weekend in July, I think." Roger took a long swig from the bottle of water and passed it her way. "The same one as the Foster family reunion. It sounds like he wants to bunk out here with you."

"Well, I don't know where I'll put him," Melinda sighed. "If Liz and her family stay here, I'll be at capacity, just like at Christmas." But then she smiled. "What's the point of having a farmhouse if you can't fill it with the people you love? It'll be fun. This is going to be a wonderful summer!"

✳ 2 ✳

The fireflies were flashing their greetings by the time Melinda reached for Hobo's leash and her sneakers. The farmhouse was blissfully cool and quiet, the silence broken only by the hum of the air conditioner and an occasional grumble from Horace's vintage refrigerator.

Grace and Hazel were stretched out on the floor of the living room, right where the narrow oak boards met the scrolled-iron air register. They were six months old now, their kitten cuteness slowly transforming into adult-cat elegance, but neither seemed to mind how the blast of refreshing air tousled their long-haired coats.

"Don't bother getting up, girls. Going for a wind-blown look, Grace?" The regal calico barely opened one eye, then yawned. Hazel stirred long enough to stretch her brown-tabby frame and put her white front paws right on the metal grate.

"Hobo and I are going for a walk before it gets dark. Down to the creek, where it's dusty and there's wild animals lurking about. Not your style, I know; and I'm glad."

Horace had served as Hobo's doorman, but Melinda's work away from the farm didn't allow her to do the same. Adding a dog door from the kitchen to the enclosed back porch, and a second out to the stoop, solved that problem. She worried Hazel and Grace would follow in their doggie dad's footsteps, but neither showed any interest in the outdoors. Instead, they enjoyed the house's sweeping views from several favorite perches, including the back of the cream-colored sofa in front of the living room's picture window. The screened-in front porch, which allowed them to safely smell and hear everything going on outside, was as close to nature as they were willing to get.

Hobo wasn't with the kittens, but Melinda knew where to find him. Tired from supervising evening chores, he was dozing on the antique bed in the downstairs bedroom. Horace always let Hobo sleep on the crazy quilt his mother, Anna, stitched years ago, but Melinda always made sure at least one fleece throw protected the heirloom from Hobo's stray hairs and sometimes-dirty paws.

The rattle of the leash jolted Hobo awake. He gave a happy whimper and was up in a flash, his toenails clicking on the wood floors. He bounced with excitement while she hooked the lead to his collar.

"You ready to go down to the creek? You're acting like you never get to go, but I know you do." She tried to pat him on the head, but he was already dragging her toward the back door. Hobo had the freedom to visit the waterway on his own; it was the chance to explore it with Melinda that had him so excited.

It was a still, humid evening, a soft haze already blanketing the low-lying sections of the rolling fields. Other than the crunch of Melinda's sneakers on the gravel, there was only the chirp of crickets and the croak of an occasional frog from the thick grass along the lane. The day's bright light had faded to a gentle blue, and she rejoiced to see a cloud line advancing from the west, the dropping sun setting its base aglow. She hoped for rain, and not just for the relief it would give her garden and pasture. There was nothing more soothing than falling asleep to the pitter-patter of drops on the farmhouse's steep-gabled roof.

They reached the road and Hobo turned north, panting from expectation more than the heat. The farm's birds and squirrels were fine entertainment, but so many more possibilities awaited him at the waterway. A raccoon or possum might be out and about at this soon-to-be-sunset hour, or a trio of deer. Once, he and Melinda startled a crane that was wading in the creek.

"Calm down," she gasped, the sweat already beading on her arms. "There's plenty of muddy water for you to drink down there, but I forgot my bottle back at the house."

Hobo slowed his steps and she hoped that, for once, he was honoring her request. But then he started to sniff a mysterious hole on the gravel's shoulder, his best way to determine what kind of critter called it home.

Melinda's mind wandered as she waited, taking in the countless shades of green under the blushing sky. What would this summer bring?

The Foster family reunion would be one highlight, to be sure, along with having both of her siblings home at the same time. And she'd really be able to enjoy Prosper's Fourth of July celebration this year, since the planning committee's reins had eagerly been taken over by Vicki Colton. Vicki and her husband, Arthur, had created quite a stir in the little community of roughly two-hundred people. They were the town's first new residents in nearly a year, and Vicki planned to open a craft store that fall next door to Prosper Hardware.

But it was the small things Melinda looked forward to the most. Lounging in the porch swing with a page-turning book. Snapping the first ripe tomato off the vine. Gulping a glass of ice-cold tea after mowing the lawn.

And of course, spending more time with Chase Thompson. A silly grin spread across her face as Hobo once again pulled her toward the creek. She chided herself for being so giddy, but then decided she might as well enjoy this new distraction as long as it was available.

Would it last? It was hard to know, as they'd had only one official date so far. Meeting Chase for pizza and beer last Friday in Charles City had been far less painful than she expected. She was so nervous that she'd nearly invented an excuse to duck out at the last moment. Now, they had plans to meet for dinner this weekend. And she couldn't wait to see him again.

If this wasn't a relationship, what was it? A flirtation? Absolutely. They were certainly more than just friends. She and Chase had met under unusual circumstances, so why would she expect things to progress in a typical fashion?

Chase first turned his truck up her driveway a few months ago. He'd flashed his megawatt smile and tried to sell her an aerial photograph of her farm, a picture his family's company had snapped last summer. The print was beautiful, and Melinda was instantly smitten with it, but its steep price tag and Chase's hard sell quickly soured her on the deal. He returned several times, and every discount was a little better than the last, until she finally agreed to purchase the print. Only then did he ask her out, and she found herself saying yes to that offer, too.

No matter what happened with Chase, this summer would certainly be different than the one before. That season had been filled with upheaval, change and difficult choices. Sometimes, Melinda could hardly remember all the things she used to have: a vintage apartment in one of Minneapolis' best neighborhoods, a successful copywriting career at a prestigious marketing firm, and a closet crowded with the latest fashions.

She glanced at her dusty sneakers and shook her head at the hole in her heathered-gray tee shirt. Her wavy brown hair, threaded with a few stubborn grays, was rolled in a messy bun that had nothing to do with style and everything to do with trying to keep cool.

All of the lovely trappings of her past life started to fall away the day she was laid off from her job. And as the months went by, she found herself intentionally tossing aside most of what had been left.

"But I got all this in return." She looked over her shoulder at her cozy farmhouse, which was just visible beyond the leafy grove that marked the north side of the property. The crackles in the house's white exterior paint weren't visible from this far down the road. Soft gray trim wrapped its many windows, and gray-green shingles hugged its steep dormers. The barn's trademark red finish was weathered and worn, but its walls still gave off a rosy glow as the sun dropped in the west.

Hobo's ears lifted the moment they approached the waterway, where a dented, yellow "one lane bridge" sign stated the obvious. The crossing was merely a run of wooden floorboards coated with packed-down gravel and flanked by metal side rails.

The willows, weeds and volunteer trees gathered along the creek were significantly taller than those in the road's ditches, and Hobo couldn't wait to explore the undergrowth near the bridge. Melinda let out his lead so he could scoot down the embankment, then perched on the railing's edge.

A red-winged blackbird circled above, its screeches warning Melinda it had a nest somewhere nearby. The creek was lower than it had been last week, and mumbled softly as it bubbled over the rocks that lined its muddy bottom. The stream skirted the hill that marked Nathan and Angie Hensley's farm before it turned south and then west to reach this little bridge. Once it passed under the road, it made another curve to bypass Melinda's acreage.

The native grasses below her started to sway, which ruffled the feathers of an indignant blue jay in a nearby bush. Hobo soon appeared on the side of the road, and began to bark. Melinda saw a vehicle kicking up dust as it approached from the north. It slowed at the crossroads, then continued in their direction.

"Who do you think it is?"

Hobo barked again, but this time he wagged his tail. She reeled in his lead and anchored them both to the edge of the road. "Someone we know? Don't tell me you can pick out the truck from this far away ... Hey, you're right! It looks like Ed, one of your favorite people."

Ed Bauer and his wife, Mabel, were Melinda's closest neighbors, living half a mile north on the gravel. They were in their early seventies and mostly retired from farming, although Ed kept a few beef cattle as a hobby. Mabel had lived in their farmhouse most of her life, and was a close friend of Horace's youngest sister, Ada Schermann Arndt. So many people had helped Melinda adjust to country life, but she wouldn't have lasted more than a few weeks without Mabel and Ed's friendship and guidance.

The rusted brown pickup, an old beater Ed used only for farm chores, coughed to a stop and he cranked down the window. He waved one browned and wiry arm at Melinda and Hobo.

"Nice evening, isn't it? You know, I doubted Hobo would ever adjust to being on a leash like that. Horace and Wilbur didn't get around well enough to take him for walks. But he really seems to love it." He grinned down at Hobo. "Yeah, you've got the good life, don'tcha?"

"You came by just in time to see him on his best behavior. It may not last long."

"Mabel said you're going to have some company next week. Sounds like fun."

Melinda rolled her eyes. "Yeah, I guess you could call it that. A bunch of electricians storming my house and ripping into the walls isn't exactly my idea of a good time. I'll be glad to get the system updated, though. I'm just worried what they might find."

Most of the farmhouse's quirks hadn't raised red flags when the acreage changed hands. But the property's wiring was woefully out of date, and the inspector had insisted on a complete upgrade to the home's electrical system. With home-improvement season in full swing, Melinda had been on the crew's wait list for weeks.

"That's the trouble with old houses." Ed got out of the truck and leaned against it, settling in for a chat. He adjusted his worn green cap and reached toward Hobo, who wanted a pat on the head. "Who knows what's hiding in those walls? But you've got a fine place, Horace's grandpa knew what he was doing. Just needs a little upkeep, that's all."

Hobo sniffed the side of Ed's truck and tried to pull Melinda toward its bumper, his fluffy tail whipping back and forth.

"Hobo, don't be so nosy." She tightened her grip on his leash. "Well, I'm sure you're on your way to somewhere, we won't keep you. And tell Mabel to let me know if I should bring anything for supper next Wednesday. I really appreciate the invite, since my place will be a torn-up mess."

"Will do." Ed nodded, but didn't turn away.

Hobo was barking now, his front paws making prints on the pickup's gravel-dusted bumper. A hint of a breeze drifted over the truck's bed, and Melinda nearly gagged on the sudden stench.

"Ed! *What* is in that burlap bag? Is that where the smell is coming from? My God, it's awful."

He poked at the gravel with the toe of his boot, and had such a secretive look on his lined face that she became more curious than disgusted.

"What are you up to? Because you're up to *something*."

Ed stared warily down the empty road, first north and then south, as if someone might hear him. "You got that right. But promise me you won't tell anyone about this."

She gave him the side-eye and peered into the pickup's bed, trying not to breathe in the stench. "Is that a dead animal in there?"

"Yes. Well, no, it's not what you think. It's just roadkill."

She took a quick step back. "Hobo, come here! Are you working for the county or something? Surely there's an easier way to make a few extra bucks."

Ed snorted. "The county doesn't know, but you could say I'm helping them out. They don't have enough staff to run around and pick it all up. And it's going to good use." He pointed over the bridge. "Look there, to the east, in that stand of oaks. Notice anything unusual?"

She stared at him for a moment, then studied the waterway. "It's a bunch of trees, Ed. Same ones that've always been there."

Ed's voice was now hushed with excitement instead of secrecy.

"Look in the very top of the canopy, just past that little twist in the creek. What's moving around up there?"

Finally, she found it. A sizeable dark shape, shifting back and forth, with a head of white feathers. A second figure hopped out from behind the first.

"Eagles! They have a nest here? I've seen them flying over the fields a few times, but I assumed they were just passing through. It's five miles over to the river."

"I first noticed them back in March." Ed beamed and began to talk faster, eager to share his secret. "The guy who owns this land's up in Mason City, has it in set-aside acres. He asked me to walk the creek once the snow was gone, see how much tree damage there was from the ice storm."

He stepped to the bridge railing and pointed into the canopy of the largest oak. "I saw this pair flying around, and watched to see where the nest was. I think this is their first year, since it's not very large. If everything goes well they'll come back, and add on to what they've got."

"Do you mean there's ..."

"Yep." Ed nodded like a proud grandpa. "Hatched out mid-April, I'd guess. I've walked back in there a few times, but you can't see much. They're sure busy, though, so there must be a few little ones up there."

Ed turned back to his pickup and dropped the tailgate. "Then one day, I was coming back from town, and I saw a dead raccoon laying there on the side of the blacktop. And I thought, 'well, there you go.'"

He reached for the corner of the burlap bag and hauled it toward him. Melinda took two big steps back, out of revulsion as much to keep Hobo out of Ed's way.

"The stuff's got to be pretty intact and fresh, or I don't stop." He dropped the bag on the gravel, then used its long twine ties to drag it to the shoulder of the road. "I'm picky; it's not too often I come across something good. I toss it where it's easy for them to find it. They've got little ones to feed."

"Does Mabel know about this?"

"Well, she did the first time. It doesn't matter, it's not like I take it up to the house or anything. But the eagles? Sure, she's excited about them, too. It's wonderful to see them making a comeback. And to have a nest, right here in our township? Well, that's something."

Ed leaned in and lowered his chin. "No one else knows, and we need to keep it that way. Word gets out, and there'll be gawkers every night, and twice as many on the weekends. They'll trample the wildflowers, wave their phones around taking pictures and video ... No, the eaglets need to grow up in peace."

"How long will that take?"

"I think they'll stay in the nest for another month or so. Sounds like the chicks hang around for a few months after that. So, you won't say a word? If this gets out, it's all over."

Melinda nodded. "Not a word. Hobo and I better start back, the sun's almost down. We'll let you ..." She shuddered and looked away. "Well, do whatever it is you need to do."

Ed grinned his thanks, opened the truck's door, and reached for a pair of elbow-length rubber gloves. "Yep, I'm going to drop my load and head home. See you next week."

* 3 *

The steak house appeared as if by magic when Melinda rounded another curve. She'd driven over ten miles down this county blacktop, through several twists and turns, with only a smattering of farmsteads to break up the sloping fields and thick stands of trees. It had been years since she'd traveled this far north and east of Prosper, and she'd forgotten just how hilly the terrain was here. The area around Meadville, Chase's hometown, was only a forty-minute drive from her farm, but its unique beauty made it seem much farther away.

She was out of her comfort zone, too. Here she was, on a Friday night, wearing a soft blouse and a pair of heeled sandals that hadn't made it out of her closet since she moved back to Iowa last summer. Her shoes were comfortable, at least, and she'd ditched the idea of a dress and instead pulled on her nicest pair of black capris. Chase had offered to take her on a plane ride over the countryside after dinner, and a skirt just didn't seem appropriate.

At first, she'd emphatically told him no. But the more she thought about it, Melinda decided she needed to stretch her own wings a bit. Besides, he'd promised to keep the plane upright.

"No loops or barrel rolls," she reminded herself as she checked her lipstick in the rearview mirror. "And the plane has seat belts, for God's sake. It's a commercial craft, not something out of a cartoon. He flies all the time. I just have to trust he knows what he's doing."

She took a deep breath, and studied the restaurant through the windshield. "Chase was right. This place is popular. Look at all these cars!"

While the steak house was merely a single-story structure with weathered wood siding and a metal roof, the parking lot was far more substantial. And three-quarters full even though it wasn't yet six. She counted several luxury vehicles among the more modest rides as she made her way across the lot, and noticed how many of the cars had out-of-county plates. Apparently people were willing to drive an hour or two just to get here, and then happily grill their own meals when they did.

Chase had arrived a few minutes ago, according to his text, and was already inside, waiting for a table. So this place didn't even take reservations, but still drew such large crowds. Would it live up to the hype? And would this evening live up to her rising expectations? The only way to find out was to open the door.

A cool blast drew her into the cavernous space, which was cozily dim and decorated with old farm implements and metal signs. It was the sort of atmosphere offered by countless national chains, but Melinda suspected this place had been here enough decades to be the real thing. Conversation and laughter bounced across the dining area and up to the exposed-beam ceilings. A large group was right behind her, and she stepped out of the way and tried to get her bearings. Where was he?

But the minute she saw Chase, all of her reservations dropped away. He'd stopped off at his house to shower and change into jeans and a blue button-down that brought out his eyes, and his sandy-blonde hair wasn't quite dry yet. He was about her age, not married, not divorced, no kids. No complications and, from what she knew of him so far, no serious baggage. If she could drop her own and let things evolve at their own speed, this just might work out.

"Hey." He held out his hand, and Melinda slipped hers into it. A thrill ran up her arm, but she casually let go. He offered her one of his trademark "it's all good" grins. "Will be about thirty minutes, I guess. I'm glad we got here as early as we did."

"I can't believe how packed this place is." She had to lean in close so he could hear her over the chatter echoing around them. "I came around that last bend and *ta-da*, there it was."

"It's a hidden gem, for sure. All the meat is sourced from local farms, and most of the rest of the food is, too."

Their table was finally ready, and Melinda realized she was starving. The spicy, faint smoke from the grills wafted around the restaurant, and the platters carried past by the brisk wait staff were heaped with mouthwatering dishes.

"So, what's good here?" She flipped over the menu.

"Everything. But I'd recommend something smothered in barbecue sauce. They make their own. And I don't know about you, but I've had a long day. How about we let the kitchen staff grill our meat for us?"

"Sounds good to me." An impressively large table, topped with lights and crowded by lines of hungry customers, sat off to the side of the space. "That must be the salad bar. No small-town restaurant is complete without one."

"Actually, the salads are plated in the kitchen. That's just the baked-potato bar. You can load up with bacon and ham, sour cream, veggies, something like six kinds of cheese ..."

"A buffet of cheese? I think I'm in heaven."

"Well, eat up. It's all included in the price. And I'm buying tonight."

"No, you are not." Melinda snapped her menu in his direction. "Dutch, remember?"

"But you had so much farther to drive and ..." He dropped his shoulders. "OK, ma'am, have it your way. So, have you given any more thought to that proposition of mine?"

A waitress suddenly appeared with their glasses of water.

"Don't mind him," Melinda told the woman. "He just wants me to go up in a plane."

She raised an eyebrow, then grinned. "Fair enough. But you wouldn't believe the things I overhear, some nights. People like to meet up at this place, from all over. Ones that maybe shouldn't, if you know what I mean."

"Sorry to disappoint you," Chase said. "But I'm not married, and neither is she."

"In that case, you can eat with a clear conscience." The waitress pulled an order pad from her apron's pocket. "I have to say, though, the guilty ones leave the biggest tips. Anyway, on a less salacious note, we've got a few specials tonight ..."

Chase had a steak, and Melinda the grilled chicken. The potato buffet was everything he said it would be, and she was soon too full to even think about dessert. They stuck to iced tea, despite the restaurant's extensive beer and wine list, as Chase was determined to get Melinda up in his plane.

The more they talked, the more they laughed. And while neither of them was stepping out on anyone else, Melinda soon saw the advantage of meeting at such a remote location. Prosper was mostly filled with kind and caring people, but that interest sometimes veered into a scrutiny Melinda didn't have the patience to tolerate. It was tough enough to meet a nice, available guy around Prosper, but the anonymity she had enjoyed while living in Minneapolis was even harder to find.

It was likely that Auggie Kleinsbach, the manager of Prosper's co-op, was familiar with Chase's company, since the bulk of its business came from crop-spraying services. But as far as Melinda knew, none of the other coffee-group guys or any of her friends had ever crossed paths with him. She wasn't trying to hide Chase from anyone. But until she was ready to share the details, she was thankful her personal life could remain just that.

"What are you thinking?" Chase raised his eyebrows. "Something's obviously making you happy. Going to share?"

"Well, spending time with you, for one." She focused on slicing her chicken and tried not to smirk. He was obviously good at reading her emotions, and that wasn't a bad thing.

"Oh, come on now, it's more than that."

"I was just thinking how nice this is, to be on a date without everyone gawking and gossiping. No small-town politics, if you will."

"Why do you think I picked this place?" He waved his fork around. "So, how are plans going for the Fourth of July festival? Sounds like it's a good thing that other woman volunteered to lead the committee."

"Vicki's got it under control, and I'm so glad. All I have to do is handle publicity, and that's almost done. I sent the last press release out yesterday. And I think the Mason City station might send a crew down to cover the parade."

Chase shook his head with admiration. "What a score! Prosper's pride will be on full display. All the color and action of the parade, thousands of people lining Main Street ... that's about the best kind of press you can get."

He thought for a moment. "Are you sure we didn't cross paths at the U? We must have taken some of the same media classes."

Both of them had earned communications degrees from the University of Minnesota in Minneapolis, and they'd been on campus for most of the same semesters. It was sort of amazing they'd never met before.

"Oh, I think I would have remembered you if we had," she said coyly.

Maybe that wasn't true, as she'd squandered her college years falling for moody, creative types who often turned out to have big egos and even bigger insecurities. But then, didn't most people spend their twenties doing the wrong things, and learning along the way? How much better life was now, even with its ups and downs.

Their bills came, separate as requested. "I'm so full, I think you'll have to roll me out of here." Melinda reached into her purse.

"I'm stuffed, too. It's a nice little walk from the airport's parking lot to the hangar. Will do us both good, I think." He grinned. "What do you say?"

"OK, maybe, for just a few minutes ... but not too high. I get vertigo easily. This was a wonderful meal, I'd hate for it to end up all over the floor of your plane."

Chase rose to his feet but didn't rush around to pull out her chair. Melinda liked that; she didn't need any help. "We'll keep it low, then," he promised. "But not so low that we crash into a barn, or a herd of cows, or ..."

"Oh, great!" She swatted him on the arm, and he laughed. "I hadn't thought of that. Let's go see this plane."

Chase led the way to the regional airport just a few miles down the road. It was nothing more than a vast, groomed field behind a chain-link fence, a tiny building, and a hangar with room for only eight aircraft.

Although the winds were calm and the skies clear, they had the place to themselves. Nearly all the planes at this small airport were for business use, and the work week had been over for several hours already.

"There's not much to see," Chase admitted as he swiped a badge at the front gate. "Turn-around's up here, by the office; runway heads off over there." They walked slowly across the manicured lawn, enjoying the cooler air. Melinda felt like reaching for his hand, but didn't. She could sense that all of Chase's focus, if only for the next few moments, was on his plane.

"And here she is." He gestured proudly. "Not fancy, but it does the trick. Looks bigger here on the ground, right?"

"It sure does." She ran a hand over the glass-like surface and noticed the gray paint was actually silver.

The plane shimmered in the soft light beaming in from the western horizon; sunset would come on in less than an hour. "I love the logo; have I told you that? It's the same one as on your truck."

"Designed it myself." Chase beamed.

"Really? It's perfect." She stepped back, trying to see into the cockpit. There were indeed two seats in the front of the plane, just as Chase had said. She wouldn't be stuffed in the back somewhere.

"Well," he put an arm around her shoulder, "do you want to take it for a spin?" He was so eager to show her his plane, so excited to include her in something that meant so much to him. How could she say no? And it was a beautiful night.

"We'll take it easy. I'll give you the tour I give my grandma, when I take her up."

"Well, if she can handle it, then so can I. Let's go."

Chase showed her how to adjust her headgear as the plane roared to life. "Are you sure?" He punched some buttons and the engine kicked into high gear, causing him to shout. "If you don't want to, we don't have to ..."

She gripped her armrests but nodded emphatically. "I'm sure. Just take off before I change my mind, OK?"

They taxied down the runway, the nearby cornfield approaching faster than she would have liked. Just before it seemed like the plane would crash through the fence, it lifted so suddenly and effortlessly that it took her a second to realize they were off the ground and heading south.

"We'll buzz over Decorah first, then head back this way." The agile little plane tacked to the east and then quickly veered north, the stunning views sliding past. She closed her eyes for a moment.

"Sorry for that turn. You still OK?" He reached over and squeezed her hand.

She nodded and laughed. "Just a little dizzy."

"Should be straight going for a while now. Don't look down, just out. That'll help."

And there was so much to see. The forested hills and terraced fields were even more stunning from above. The highways looked like tiny gray ribbons, and tan stripes noted the gravel roads. They passed over a miniature grid that held a small town, as well as the little red rectangles that marked each farm's barn. The lowering sun filled the cockpit with a golden glow, and she could see the glittering pinpricks of the stars as they prepared for their nightly debut.

It was a stunning scene, a whole world in miniature. The plane glided so smoothly that if she closed her eyes, she

couldn't be sure they were in motion. Chase tacked a bit
higher as they reached the outskirts of Decorah, and she
didn't even mind. They floated over the town and made a
careful turn, pivoting toward the west.

"Still OK?"

She nodded, so overcome she couldn't speak. She didn't
know when she'd felt so awestruck, and comfortable and free,
all at the same time. At last they turned south and the airstrip
came back into view.

"So, this might get a bit bumpy, it's not like a big
commercial bird. Just relax."

"And don't look down?"

"Right. I'll do that part."

The airfield was rising fast. She closed her eyes as they
descended, the setting sun burning through her eyelids, then
bounced in her seat as the wheels touched the pavement.
Chase hit the brakes and they made a careful turn, rolling
back to the hangar.

Melinda clapped her approval when they at last came to a
stop. Chase was grinning from ear to ear.

"So you liked it? And you didn't even need an airbag!"

"I loved it. Oh, that was incredible! Everything looks so
different. It's not like a regular flight, not at all. You're up
high, of course, but still low enough to really see everything,
all the roads and fields and towns."

She pulled off her headgear and Chase did the same.

"So you'll go again, then?" He was eager for her approval.
"Not right away, I mean, but ... another time?"

"Yes, absolutely."

Before she knew what was happening, he leaned over the
gap between their seats and his lips were on hers. She slipped
her fingers into his hair and pulled him close.

"Well," he finally said, "that's the best flight I've taken in a
while. If you have time, I have another surprise for you."

"Really? I can't imagine how you're going to top that one."
She meant the plane ride, not the kiss, but it had been
wonderful as well. He'd almost kissed her the first time they

met for dinner, when he was walking her to her car, but hadn't. At first, she'd been relieved. But as the days went by, she found herself hoping he'd try again.

Chase rummaged around in the back seat of his truck. When he turned back, he had a sheepish grin on his face and a blanket and bottle of wine in his arms.

Melinda was amused. This evening was turning into something out of a cheesy romance novel, the kind she never cared to read. But she found she didn't mind, not at all.

"Can you grab that tote?" Chase jerked his chin back at the truck. "Sorry, there's only plastic cups, and some crackers. I hacked the cheese into cubes, but they're not all fancy."

"Sounds perfect to me." Everything had been carefully planned, from what time they met for dinner to the plane ride just before sunset, and now this alfresco picnic. Melinda was flattered, but it was clear he'd done this before. How many women had he charmed in this way? She didn't know, and decided she didn't care. It was a lovely summer night, and she was going to make the most of it.

They settled on a small rise west of the hangar. The stars were brighter now, the sun slipping below the rolling hills. A gentle breeze whispered across the grounds, rustling the flowering bushes along the fence.

Chase uncorked the wine while Melinda unwrapped the cheese and crackers. "I never get tired of these sunsets." She held her glass steady so he could fill it. "In the city, you'd be lucky to catch a glimpse through the buildings and trees."

"It's one of the perks of small-town living, that's for sure." He sipped his wine, then stared into her eyes. "I'm glad you came. It took courage for you to get up in that plane."

"Oh, it wasn't so bad." She looked out over the airfield, very aware of how close they were, their shoulders nearly touching. She turned back to face him. "You know, there's only one thing that would make this night even better."

"And what would that be?" He smirked and carefully set his cup on the edge of the blanket, out of the way.

"If you would kiss me again."

* 4 *

Melinda fumbled with her keys as she opened Prosper Hardware's back door the next morning. The lock was sticking again, but that wasn't her only problem. She was short on sleep and running late. It was Saturday, when the store was always its busiest, and four in the afternoon seemed so very far away.

Despite all this, she was surprisingly cheerful. If she wasn't careful, there would be such a dopey smile on her face that the coffee-group regulars would know she'd been up to something. As she made her way through the darkened wood shop to reach the main part of the building, Melinda tried to remember what such a make-out session had been called when she was in high school. Maybe second base?

It was a silly analogy, especially for a woman her age. But she'd felt like a teenager, there with Chase on a blanket in a dark field with a bottle of wine. Of course, they'd had to sober up before heading their separate ways, which became just another excuse to spend another hour, or more like two, alone. It was almost eleven before she'd started for home.

She felt guilty sneaking into the house just as the mantel clock struck midnight. Hobo ran into the kitchen, sleepy and surprised, and the confusion on his face had nearly done her in. *Where have you been?* He and the kittens, as well as her outdoor critters, had their supper at the usual hour before she went to meet Chase. But she'd left in such a hurry, and been away for so long ...

Melinda had hugged Hobo and offered several apologies, then braced herself for another guilt trip from Hazel and Grace. They were already curled up on her bed, together, and barely opened an eye when she came in, as if they hadn't even noticed she was gone. But as soon as she was ready for bed, both wanted to snuggle. She found herself awake for over an hour, listening to the kittens' purrs and the faint rumble of the air conditioner outside the window, wondering how she felt about everything, and what might happen next.

The heated debate on the other side of the door brought her back to the present. The coffee guys usually parked along Main Street and came in the front, as Auggie still had a key from when he worked at Prosper Hardware during high school, forty-odd years ago. And from the vehicles she'd spotted along the curb, all the metal folding chairs would be full this morning.

Given the noise, the men were discussing something with great interest. In one terrible moment, just as she cracked the door open, Melinda wondered if it was her.

What exactly do you mean when you say you saw them together?

That sounded like Jerry Simmons, Prosper's mayor and a retired principal. His objective tone had saved more than one council meeting from dissolving into a shouting match.

Well, they were at the same table, leaning in close ...

Melinda closed her eyes and sighed. Auggie. How had he been at the steak house, and she hadn't noticed him? With his dark-rimmed glasses and booming voice, he was hard to miss.

Can't two people sit next to each other? That doesn't ...

But she touched his hand. I'm sure of it!

Melinda steeled herself and started up the main aisle, making her footfalls louder than usual on the polished oak floorboards. She expected her entrance to stop the gossip, but it continued after she reached the oak showcase that served as the store's counter.

George Freitag, a retired farmer in his early eighties, adjusted his suspenders and shook his head.

"None of that means anything, how do you know something's going on?" He suddenly noticed Melinda. "Hey! What's going on with Karen?"

Uncle Frank turned toward his niece, his brown eyes alight with interest. Poor Doc, who was Karen's business partner, shifted in his chair and was suddenly preoccupied with his phone.

"What?" Melinda put her purse on the counter and tried to get her bearings.

"You know what we mean." Auggie's tone was both exasperated and wheedling. "Come on! You, of all people, should be able to help us out. We have to know!"

Melinda stared at her friends, gathered around the vintage sideboard that served as an informal coffee shop every day but Sunday, and didn't know if she was more annoyed or amused. At thirty-five and single, Karen Porter stood out in Prosper as much as Melinda did. The fact that Karen had an advanced degree and was the community's first female veterinarian apparently wasn't as noteworthy as her personal life, which Melinda knew was as spotty as her own.

Auggie looked like the cat that had caught the canary as he sat by one of the store's plate-glass windows, sipping his coffee and enjoying the commotion caused by his tidbit of news.

"It's really none of our business," Jerry finally said, more as a prompt for Melinda to speak than an effort to change the conversation. "I take it, then, that you're not supposed to say anything."

Jerry then stared at Doc, who was still checking his messages. But Melinda could tell by Doc's expression that curiosity was getting the upper hand with him, too, although he didn't want to admit it.

"Like I already told you," Doc suddenly said, "I don't know anything about Josh and Karen! If you want the scoop on Karen's love life, you're going to have to ask Melinda."

"Karen and Josh?" Melinda leaned on the counter as she digested this news. Josh Vogel had recently taken over a small-animal practice in Swanton, and he'd worked with Karen and Doc to start clinics to provide services for feral and barn cats in the area. He was single, but it wasn't like …

She began to laugh and couldn't stop, between her lack of sleep as well as her relief.

"Karen and Josh," she said again. "That's who you're talking about? About Karen?"

George frowned. "Who else would it be?"

Frank whirled around from the sideboard, where he was adding creamer to his mug, and Melinda quickly looked away. Her mom knew about Chase, as did Karen and even Aunt Miriam. But Miriam wouldn't have said a word.

"Karen is not seeing anyone, I'm sure of that." Melinda busied herself with putting her purse under the counter and reaching for the dust cloth, then attacked the oak showcase with surprising energy. "No, guys, sorry to disappoint you. Karen and Josh are just friends. She would have told me if that had changed."

"But they were at that coffee shop over in Swanton." Auggie sounded like a little boy whose favorite toy had been taken away. "And in a corner booth."

That brought knowing nods from Jerry and Frank, as if it somehow strengthened their case.

Melinda dropped the cloth and started for the coffeemaker. She might as well get a cup now, as it was going to take a few minutes to straighten this out.

"Look, it's not what you all think." She dumped a generous spoonful of sugar in an empty mug and added the brew, which was strong and black. George had been sweet enough to bring in some chocolate-flavored creamer, which he knew she liked, and she paid him back with a thankful smile as she added a shake to her coffee.

"I know Karen and Josh were meeting yesterday to go over plans for the upcoming cat clinics. There's only been two so far, but the response has been overwhelming. More than seventy cats have been helped already! They want to make them a monthly event, at least until winter sets in."

She looked at each of her friends in turn. "And if you all remember, Josh's practice is in Swanton. That coffee shop would be an obvious place for them to meet."

Auggie turned to Doc for confirmation.

"Melinda's right about the spay clinics," Doc said proudly. "The July event's nearly booked up, and we've already got a few farmers on the list for August."

"And just because they were sitting close, it doesn't mean anything is 'going on.'" Melinda set her mug on the sideboard long enough to supply the air quotes. "Josh and Karen are friends, that's all. I'm sure of it."

This seemed to put the rumors to rest, at least for now. Melinda was eager to change the subject. "So, what else is going on today?"

The men looked at each other, and then the floor.

"Well," Frank said at last, "you were off yesterday, so we hoped that … we wondered if you might bring in some treats."

George's blue eyes twinkled with anticipation. "You know, maybe some of the strawberry muffins you were talking about the other day."

"Or even some cornbread?" Jerry sounded hopeful.

"You've got some rhubarb-strawberry jam left from last summer," Uncle Frank added, "and it's almost time to make more. You know we like to eat, we can help you use up the rest of it. Or, maybe some of those blueberry biscuit things …"

"Scones." Doc pointed at Frank. "Those are amazing. And scones have less sugar than muffins, so they're healthy …"

"Are there scones today?" Bill popped in from the back. He was in his mid-thirties, with a stocky build that would probably give him a noticeable paunch as he aged. "Emily almost sent along some cookies, but I said that …" He stopped when he saw the surprise on Melinda's face.

"That's OK if you didn't," Jerry quickly added. "It's so hot, it's not a good idea to overeat. And I had a big breakfast already."

"It's going to stay hot, at least through this week," Auggie said with conviction. Along with owning Prosper Feed Co., he operated a weather observation station out of the co-op's tallest tower. "No chance of rain until at least Wednesday; you can bet on that."

"Good thing we got that shower the other night, then," George joined in. "Gave the garden a good watering, at least."

The guys were trying to get out of a tight spot, and she decided it was best to address their assumptions head-on.

"I'm sorry to disappoint you, but I didn't have time to bake anything yesterday. I spent the whole day catching up around the farm. I've been trying to mend fence when I can stand the heat, and getting the house straightened up so it'll be ready for the electricians to come next week."

"Why do you have to clean?" This from George. "Aren't they just going to make a mess?"

"Yes. But I have to move things around, give them room to reach all the outlets and such. I just hope they don't have to chop too many holes in the walls to get this done."

Auggie nodded understandingly. "Drywall's easier to patch than the lathe-and-plaster walls you've got out there. And the lines are, what, maybe forty years old?"

Melinda shook her head. "Joe Trimball's the head guy, and he thinks some of it goes back beyond that, maybe even to the late forties, when the electrical system was first put in."

Ron Schermann, one of Horace's nephews and the Realtor who arranged the sale of the farm, had recommended Joe highly. Even so, Melinda was glad to see Jerry's face light up with admiration when she mentioned Joe and his crew.

"They worked on my neighbor's house a few years' back. He'll get it done right. Which is the point, since you don't want to flip a switch and have flames shooting out of the wall. You'll get along with him just fine."

"Like a house on fire!" Auggie guffawed. He insisted Frank return his high five.

Doc shook his head. "You were just waiting for that one, weren't you?"

"Oh, it's been some time since such an opportunity has come my way! Well, Melinda, I guess you're off the hook for treats for a week or so."

"Joe thinks it'll take at least three days, or maybe more, if they run into any snags. And with a house that old, who knows what they'll find?" She reached for the broom kept by the front door and began to sweep the mat.

The electrical work would get done, one way or another. She liked to cook and bake, but it would be a while before her kitchen, and the rest of her house, was back to normal. "I know you guys bring snacks from time to time, but it's random. How about we start a rotation for morning treats?"

"A schedule." Frank nodded cautiously. "You mean, we each bring something once a week?"

"Doesn't have to be that strict." Doc quickly warmed to the idea. "How about, if you want to bring treats, just give the group a heads-up a few days before?"

"I like that." George gave his approval. "When you get to be my age, you like to know what's coming your way. No surprises."

The bell above the front door announced Vicki's arrival. It wasn't yet eight, but her smile was wide and infectious as she burst into the store. Her arms were filled with blueprint rolls and a black binder, and a canvas tote dangled from one tanned forearm.

"Hello, everyone!" Vicki plopped her stuff on the counter and pushed her expertly highlighted brown hair out of her face. "Melinda, I know the store's not open yet, but I just had to show you something before my inspector gets here!"

The guys mumbled their greetings but didn't share Vicki's enthusiasm. Her husband, the new manager at one of Swanton's banks, had a calm, relaxed demeanor that put just about everyone at ease. Vicki, by contrast, was a whirlwind of energy. She was channeling most of it into renovating the vacant building next door and volunteering for every cause little Prosper had to offer, but some people found her overeager, or even rude.

Melinda had first met Vicki through the library's book club, and soon learned there was a lot to like under her get-it-done demeanor. Vicki and Arthur's only son was off at college, and feathering their new nest in one of Prosper's largest homes wasn't filling all the holes in Vicki's heart.

"Let's see what you've got," Melinda said warmly, pushing her dust rag aside. "I can't wait to see your ideas."

Vicki beamed and reached for the thick binder. "Now, this palette for the craft shop is very preliminary but, isn't it stunning? I'm thinking a range of blues and creams. But tasteful. Nothing too flashy."

"Sophisticated." Melinda nodded.

"I'm leaning toward a soft blue-gray on the walls." Vicki flashed a ring of paint chips in varying shades. "Something neutral, the perfect backdrop for all the merchandise. I'll have the shelves the same color, so they blend in." She waved the samples at the guys, who nodded cautiously, blank looks on their faces.

"But first, we need to put up the beadboard," she told Melinda. "Very vintage. And refinish the floors. I'm hoping for hardwood under that nasty vinyl but, oh well, we can just bring some in. And then, I'm thinking some sort of print for the curtains, and for the padded chairs in the tea room. What do you think of this toile?"

"It's ... lovely." Melinda tried to hide her doubts. Prosper's Main Street had a simple charm, with several brick buildings and even a few limestone structures. City Hall, just across the way, was on the national historic register. And Prosper Hardware's pressed-tin ceiling and gleaming oak floors added to its cozy, comforting appeal.

The designs for Vicki's new business certainly matched her personal style. But was it too much for a town this tiny?

When the men stayed silent, Melinda offered an encouraging smile. "I'm sure it will all come together. It's ... like something out of a magazine."

"Exactly!" Vicki slapped one manicured hand on the counter. "Charming simplicity with a touch of country.

French country, to be exact. You know, I was thinking last night, if the tea room takes off, I might try to add wine nights, too."

Her smile dimmed as she leaned over the counter. "What's up with the boys this morning? They seem ... distracted."

"They were hoping I had muffins or something for them, but I haven't had time. I suggested they set up a rotation, take turns bringing treats in the mornings."

Vicki studied the men closely. Melinda could almost hear the gears clicking in her friend's mind.

"Do you all like to bake? Because I just had the best idea!"

Jerry shrugged. "Well, a little. My sugar-cinnamon popcorn is rather good. But my wife does, and I think ..."

Vicki hurried across the room. "We need another event for the Fourth of July Festival, something new we can turn into an annual tradition. Why don't we have a bake-off ... a pie contest? And this is the twist ... it's only open to the men!"

She pointed across the street. "We could set it up right there, in front of the library. No, wait; there's not enough room along the sidewalk. How about in the city park, near the food vendors? And we could charge people a buck or two to taste and vote, with the money going to, well, a good cause. Is there anything the town needs?"

George stifled a snicker and Jerry blinked. Prosper needed a lot of things, and none of them could be covered by pie-tasting proceeds. Even small projects strained the city's budget. It had taken a last-minute donation from Doc to fund Main Street's flower baskets, which meant Aunt Miriam didn't have to pull the cash from her purse again this year.

Auggie glared at Vicki over the top of his glasses. "Well, maybe we could fix a few potholes."

Vicki suddenly noticed the hands on the round wall clock were advancing toward eight. "This will be great! Every little bit helps, right? I better get next door. Melinda, let's think through the logistics for the bake-off. I'll add it to the agenda for our festival meeting next week."

She gathered up her blueprints and samples and, with a quick wave, darted out the door.

"Don't start." Jerry looked around at his friends. "She volunteered to chair the committee, and I'm tired of having to nag people into it. You all know how hard it can be to find anyone to take the lead in this town."

Frank nodded understandingly, as he'd joined the city council in November.

"Well, I tell you what." Auggie rose to refill his mug. "This could be sort of fun. I'd be proud to put my famous coconut-cream pie up against the rest of the competition."

Doc snorted. "You don't know how to make a pie."

"Nope. But I've got three weeks to learn, right? It's my favorite kind, so I'll start there. It can't be that hard."

Melinda thought of how a cream filling had to be cooked just right so it wouldn't curdle, and how easy it was to overbeat a meringue. Auggie was fired up to meet Vicki's challenge, but maybe he'd bitten off more than he could chew.

* 5 *

Her stomach growled as she turned east at the crossroads and headed up the hill to the Hensleys' farm. She was ravenously hungry, as Angie had requested. And excited to visit with a friend she hadn't seen much of lately.

Angie had two little girls to look after and also helped Nathan manage their large-scale farm. And now, she was eight months' pregnant with their son. To top it off, it was also her turn to organize the annual women's luncheon at the church just down the road, an event expected to draw a hundred ladies or more. Angie had called around the other night and asked Melinda, Mabel and Helen Emmerson to give their honest opinions on several dishes before the menu was finalized for next month's celebration.

Mabel's car was already parked in the yard, and Melinda hoped Helen, another retiree, would be able to join them. Helen and Will lived on the blacktop leading into Prosper and, while Melinda drove past their place daily, she hadn't seen them since Christmas.

"Come on in." Angie adjusted the topknot that tried to keep her auburn curls out of her flushed face. There were shadows under her hazel eyes. "Don't mind the mess. I feel like I've been on the run for days. We've got some late calves coming on, Nathan was up half the night ... I'd give anything for a shower."

Even with the air conditioner running, the kitchen was steaming from the wealth of food. Two slow cookers were plugged in on the counter, and a large casserole pan had just come out of the oven. Several crockery bowls were heaped with side dishes, and an array of desserts waited next to the refrigerator.

"This is quite the spread." Melinda set her purse on one of the kitchen chairs. "Please tell me the other church ladies are going to make most of the food for the luncheon, once you narrow it down. And the decorations, the program ... how are you going to manage all this?"

"Oh, you mean in my delicate condition?" Angie snorted and rubbed her lower back. "Delegation, like you said. And one day at a time. I was vice-chair for last year's event, so they didn't spring this on me. But there's still so much to do."

Mabel came in from the living room, where she'd been chatting with Emma and Allison while they watched cartoons. Her snow-white hair was curled and primped, even on this hot day.

"Helen is running a bit late, says for us to get started. And speaking of showers ... what about the baby kind? Angie, are you sure you don't want us to throw one for you?"

"No, no, that's fine. A cousin is hosting one for family. And we don't need much, at least for a while. This little guy won't know the difference between new and used for some time to come. And I'm sure both grandmas will buy plenty of cute outfits for him to model on special occasions."

She called over her shoulder to the girls. "How about you go outside to play for a bit, before it gets too hot? I'll let you know when it's time for lunch."

The front-porch door banged shut as Angie pulled a pasta salad from the refrigerator. "They are wound up today! Promise me you'll take home most of these desserts. The girls don't need any more sugar, and Nathan and I don't, either."

"I'm sure Ed will be happy to help." Mabel reached into a cabinet for a stack of plates. "This luncheon has been held for over eighty years," she explained to Melinda, "and it's not just for members of First Lutheran. All of us area ladies are invited. Angie, what's the theme for this year?"

"A bridal fashion show, wedding dresses through the decades. I can't believe how many we've found so far! And we've got some models lined up, but we could always use more." She looked hopefully at Melinda.

"Oh, no." Melinda shook her head as she set the table. "I'll eat whatever you put in front of me, but I'm not parading around in someone's gown. Besides, I'm forty now, remember? Can't you find some girls to do it?"

"Hey!" Mabel winked. "If you're not a girl these days, what does that make me? I've got thirty-some years on you, dear."

Angie set a potato casserole on the kitchen table. "Actually, Mabel, is yours in wearable condition?"

"It might be, I'd be happy to get it out and take a look. Of course, I outgrew it years ago. Having three kids will make that happen."

Melinda thought of Anna Schermann's wedding dress, which was nearly a hundred years old. Ada took it home when the family removed their prized possessions from the farmhouse. If the dress wasn't too fragile, it would be a wonderful addition to the fashion show. But she would talk to Ada before getting Angie's hopes up.

"I do need your help with something else, Melinda." Angie set out a pitcher of citrus punch as her guests took their seats. "We'll mail postcards to all the ladies of the congregation and former members, like usual. But could you hand-deliver invites to some other women in the township? I wish I had time to do it myself." She patted her growing stomach. "I'm thinking ten or twelve stops, if you're up for that. Just those who live close by. It'd be more personal that way."

"Absolutely." Melinda raised her glass. "Count me in."

"Hello, sorry I'm late!" Helen popped through the back door and tottered up the three steps from the basement landing. She was a slight woman with straight, iron-gray hair. "Oh my, look at this spread! Angie, you've outdone yourself.

Why didn't you ask us to make some of these dishes?"

"I might take you up on that yet." Angie waved to her neighbor with the stirring spoon in her hand. "We may need help making food for the actual event, given the large quantities. Once I get the menu settled, I'll have a better idea who on the committee can do what."

Mabel reached for a serving bowl filled with cucumber-and-tomato salad. "Well, I think this is the last one that'll fit on the table. We'll just have to go through the line."

"Remember to pace yourself," Angie warned her friends.

Melinda started on the left side of her plate and worked her way across, bite by tasty bite. There was a chicken salad studded with grapes and celery that Angie said could be served as-is or on split rolls. The pasta salad had a pleasant tang from a tomato-basil dressing, and a blend of sour cream and two shredded cheeses made the potato casserole rich and filling.

Next came mixed greens studded with mandarin-orange segments and walnuts, set off by a pleasantly sour vinaigrette. A simple gelatin salad was filled with fresh strawberries, and its sweetness was offset by a hearty calico-bean casserole layered with ground beef and a savory sauce.

"What do you think?" Angie asked. "Any winners so far?"

"All of them," Mabel answered. "Maybe the question isn't which ones taste the best, but which ones are the easiest to prepare?"

"And for a hundred people," Helen added.

"Well, the chicken salad is a lock." Angie sat back for a moment. "It's tradition, we have to have it. The recipe's been modernized a bit, with the addition of the grapes and a few other things. But it's basically the same; even the mayonnaise is made from scratch."

Melinda almost dropped her fork. "Homemade mayo? It's fabulous, but who does that these days?"

"I do." Angie rolled her eyes. "When I'm chair of the luncheon committee, anyway. It was a learning experience, that's for sure."

"Well, I think the calico beans balance out the cool creaminess of the chicken salad." Melinda took a sip of punch. "This is good, but can you get by with just coffee and milk, and maybe iced tea?"

"Start with those dishes," Mabel suggested, "and round it out with a couple salads. That should do it."

Helen patted her stomach. "I think I need to digest for a few minutes before we move on to the sweet stuff."

Nathan came in with the girls, and they filled their plates and went into the rarely used formal dining room, since the kitchen table was crowded with company and platters of food.

The dessert options included individual-size chocolate mousses with whipped cream, shortbread cookies with a lemon glaze, and a marble sheet cake. Church ladies were known for their pies, but Angie explained those were left off the menu on purpose. The luncheon was supposed to be a special occasion, leaning more toward a tea party than a food stand. To keep with the bridal theme, mixed nuts and homemade mints would also be offered on the tables.

Melinda told her neighbors about the pie bake-off at the Fourth of July celebration. They loved the idea, but Mabel made an important point.

"The crust is what will separate the men from the boys. How are you going to make sure they don't cheat with the pre-made stuff?"

"It'll do, but it's never as flaky," Helen warned. "You can usually tell the difference. Personally, I don't mind. It's so easy, and then I can focus on the filling."

"Sounds like I might have a few potential judges here." Melinda raised an eyebrow, and both Mabel and Helen shrugged. "Vicki wants to let the public vote as a fundraiser, but she's also looking for a few official taste-testers to hand out some special awards and break a tie if we need to."

Once they could sample no more, Angie went upstairs for a much-deserved nap. The other women sorted the leftovers and tackled the mountain of dirty dishes with an assist from Nathan.

Melinda's car was roasting inside, even though she'd cracked its windows once she got to Angie's. She blasted the air-conditioning, tried to keep the yawns at bay, and wondered how she would spend the rest of her afternoon.

The garden needed to be weeded again, but the first thing she wanted to do was take a nap. But where? Every room in her house was in turmoil.

The electricians had been delayed at their last job and hadn't arrived until yesterday. Even though it was a Saturday, they would be there until at least four. While Hobo simply decamped to the yard and his doghouse, the chaos had poor Grace and Hazel on edge. And to make things worse, the air conditioner was out of commission until the end of the afternoon.

It was a windy day, and the farmhouse's windows were wide open in an attempt to catch any cooler air that might pass by. They also broadcast the crew's considerable noise all over the yard, and the clanging and banging and shouted instructions reached Melinda before she made it to the farmhouse's back steps.

She was inside the porch, bracing herself for the racket just beyond the kitchen door, when Joe suddenly popped through.

"There you are! How was the tea party?"

In an effort to chat with the strangers who had taken over her home, she'd tried to explain where she was going. But now, she was too tired to clarify everything.

"It was good." She dropped a container of lemon cookies on the table. "I thought you guys might want a few leftovers." To her surprise, Joe barely glanced at the treats. Had he brought along an extra box of donuts that morning?

"I'm glad you got back when you did, we've been watching for you. Hey Al," he shouted over his shoulder, his voice rising above the roar of the fans blasting warm air around the house. "Bring that thing in here, will ya?"

"Oh, great." Melinda tried to find somewhere to set her purse. Most of the counter was cluttered with tools and surplus electrical wire. "This was going so well. I was afraid you'd find something bad. Whatever it is, just tell me."

"It's not like that." Joe grinned mischievously. "Wait until you see this!"

An older man in a gray tee shirt entered the kitchen with something under his arm. "This was in the crawlspace, back behind that little door in the office." Al handed her a faded cigar box. "We found it tucked between some rafters."

She held it gingerly with her fingers, squeamish about the dirt and cobwebs that covered it as well as what might be lurking inside. "Don't tell me there's something dead in here. Or a snake."

"Open it!" Joe rubbed his hands together. Both guys were smirking. She couldn't figure out why they were nearly bursting out of their steel-toed work boots.

"They're love letters!" Al frantically motioned for her to open the box. "She wrote them, and he kept them. Once they married, she must have been too sentimental to throw them out, even though she'd gotten her guy."

"Well, I think it's really sweet," Joe chimed in. "Been quite a few jobs since we found something this interesting, you know? Mostly it's just old newspapers."

"We rarely find anything of value," Al said sadly.

Melinda flipped back the lid. Just as the men said, the pressboard container was crammed with faded letters and postcards. She quickly covered them with a protective hand, as the hot air swirling through the kitchen threatened to give them wings.

"What I can't figure out," Joe mused, "is how they got in that nasty crawlspace to begin with. From our experience," he nodded with authority, "women always hide their secret treasures under a loose floorboard, or in the back of a closet."

"Not somewhere as dirty as where we found that." Al wrinkled his nose. "No one's been back in that hidey-hole for decades, I'm sure. I tried to wipe off most of the mouse poop."

Melinda eyed the cigar box's contents, trying to explore the top layers while using the lid to block most of the draft.

"Oh, wow, just look at these! I bet Ada wrote these to Henry. They were the parents of the man I bought this farm from," she quickly explained. "There's so many, they must have really been in love." She set the cigar box on the table, slipped out the first piece of paper, then closed the lid. "OK, let's see what we have here."

The paper was fragile at the corners but surprisingly bright, the ink still a deep indigo.

June 9, 1947
My dearest Horace ...

The kitchen started to spin. Joe gently pushed her into a chair. "Geez, you look like you've seen a ghost." He caught the letter before it could fall to the plaster-dusted floor.

"Who's this Horace, anyway?" He flipped the note over several times, as if it might give up its secrets if he studied it hard enough. "The girl's name's not on there, at least the ones on the top that we looked at."

"Horace lived here all his life, until just last year." She was so stunned, she could barely get the words out. "But he was never married."

The men's eyes widened with shock. "You sure?" Joe's skepticism was all over his face.

Melinda closed her eyes for a moment. "Yes."

"Is he still alive?" This from Al.

"Yes. Very." She sat there for a few more seconds, then grabbed her phone.

"Who're you calling?" Joe put the letter back and pushed the cigar box across the table, as if suddenly afraid to touch it. "That Horace guy?"

Melinda shook her head. "Absolutely not. Not yet, anyway." Her heart began to race as she scrolled through her contacts. "Not until I talk to someone else first."

* 6 *

She'd been to the living room's picture window several times already, craning her neck to see up the gravel toward the bridge. Nothing yet. The house was quiet but charged with anticipation, despite a welcome rain tapping on the roof. The mantel clock struck one, and Melinda flinched.

"They'll be here soon, I just have to wait." She scanned the room one more time, noticed a stack of newspapers behind her reading chair, and stuffed them in the wicker basket next to the couch. It was impossible to hide the in-progress mess of the electricians, but Melinda had tried to clean up as she passed the minutes until her guests arrived. Soon, she was back at the window.

"Kevin had to pick up Ada, but it's less than forty-five minutes here from Mason City. I just hope they have a chance to see the letters before Jen and Edith arrive."

Ada had picked up her phone on the third ring yesterday afternoon, and Melinda had been relieved. This wasn't the kind of thing she wanted to leave a voicemail about. Horace's baby sister was stunned into silence at first, but then talked in a rush once the shock and confusion had worn off.

She wasn't clear on all the details of her brother's personal life, especially since they were so far apart in age. There had been someone, a girl he went to several dances with, but they'd parted ways without any drama that Ada could recall. But that was later, in the early fifties. In the summer of 1947, when Horace was twenty, Ada had only been three.

Her son, Kevin, was very close to his uncle, but likely wouldn't know any more than she did. Wilbur might have, being just two years older than Horace, but his dementia counted him out. That left Edith Clayton, who was right in the middle of the eight Schermann children and the only other living sibling in Iowa. Edith resided in Hampton, which was about a half hour's drive away, as did two of her grandchildren, Jen and Dave, who were close to Kevin. Jen had quickly volunteered to bring her grandma out to the farm that afternoon.

As for Horace ... Melinda's stomach flipped over as she turned on the coffeemaker. The letters had been found just yesterday, and trouble was already brewing. Ada insisted they hold off on telling Horace, and Kevin was furious. Melinda didn't know how to help, other than bake a cheesecake, dust the house, and try to keep out of the line of fire.

But that didn't seem possible. Ada had insisted she count the letters right away yesterday, while Joe and Al still hovered over the table. There were twenty-two of them, going back to the spring of 1946. All had the same looped handwriting, and some of them closed with a signature: *Your Maggie*. And in the very bottom of the box was another find ... a black-and-white photograph of a very young Horace and a very pretty dark-haired girl.

Once she got off the phone with Ada, Melinda had extracted two promises from Joe and Al: They would get the air conditioner going before they left, as they wouldn't be back until Monday and she couldn't stand the heat one more minute; and they would not tell anyone about the letters. They quickly gave their word, and Melinda thought they would honor it.

But even so, it was the kind of story that was hard to keep to yourself: A dusty box hidden in an old house, two young lovers, a mysterious parting.

"It's like a movie," she told Hobo, who was trying to work in a nap on the downstairs bed before company arrived. "Except this is all very real, and Horace's life is at the center of it. I just hate the idea of keeping him in the dark." Hobo licked her hand, as if he agreed.

There was a knock at the kitchen door.

"Hello, we're here!" It was Kevin.

Hobo was suddenly alert, and ran ahead to reach their guests first. Ada's cropped white hair was plastered to her head, thanks to the rain, but she was so distracted she hardly seemed to notice.

"I'm glad you called right away," Ada said as she hugged Melinda. "I just hope Edith can help us get to the bottom of this. I think this is the first time in my life that I've truly wished I was older." She gestured at the kitchen table. "I would have been over there, a toddler drooling in my highchair, and none the wiser."

That brought a laugh from Kevin, but Melinda could sense the strain between mother and son. He quickly turned to Melinda. "Hey, where's my hug?"

"I was getting to that! No Jack today?" Kevin's boyfriend had helped clean out the buildings before Horace's auction, and Melinda had liked him instantly.

"Nope. He's dying to find out what happened, but this meeting is for immediate family only." He nudged her and winked, the blue eyes behind his glasses so similar to his mom's and uncles', and Melinda felt honored to be included.

"Sorry about the mess, the electricians hope they can wrap up tomorrow or Tuesday. I tried to clean up a bit."

Ada brushed off Melinda's concerns. She had farmed in the area with her husband until he passed away, and wasn't fazed by a little dust and dirt. "I've seen this place far worse. Once Mother was gone, Horace and Wilbur kept it livable, and that was about it."

"Yeah, my uncles' definition of 'clean' didn't match most people's, especially as they aged." Kevin was an instructor at the community college in Mason City, but he'd spent many weekends helping Wilbur, and then Horace, remain at home as long as possible. "It was too much for them to keep up with. Their main concern was caring for the livestock, not making the windows sparkle."

"So ..." Ada looked around anxiously. "Where is this box?"

"In here." Melinda hurried into the dining room and reached inside one of the built-in buffet's drawers. It was a relief to put the box in Ada's hands.

But Ada held it for only a second before setting it on the table, pulling away quickly as if she might get burned. The three of them were still huddled against the buffet, staring at the box, when there was another knock at the back door.

"Oh, Jen and Edith are here." Ada threw up her hands in a thankful gesture and hurried into the kitchen.

Edith was short and slight, and walked with a cane. But her eyes had the same laser-like focus Horace's did every time he arrived at the farm, seeking out what was the same and evaluating everything that had changed.

"I forget how wonderfully green everything is out here this time of year," Edith told Ada as she removed her plastic rain bonnet, revealing her tightly curled gray hair. "And those coneflowers in Mother's kitchen garden! They're beautiful." Her face lit up when she reached down to pet Hobo. "Oh, aren't you such a happy boy!"

Edith leaned toward Melinda and lowered her voice. "I hear Horace coughed up the cash to get the wiring redone. It's about time. Ada's still keeping him in the dark?"

"Yes, for now."

Melinda waved to Jen, whose dark-blonde hair was caught up in a ponytail, and wondered whose side she was on. Jen rolled her eyes; it was clear she was in Kevin's camp.

"It's just as well." Edith lowered herself to the dining-room chair whose seat had been raised with a stray cushion. She eyed the cigar box but didn't touch it. "Best we keep it on the down-low until we narrow our list of suspects."

"Grandma loves her police procedurals," Jen whispered to Melinda as they turned back into the kitchen. "Can I help?

Get everyone something to drink? Give me something to do. This suspense is too much."

"There's coffee and iced tea." Melinda dipped her head at the refrigerator. "And a margarita cheesecake."

"With tequila?"

Jen perked up so fast that Melinda laughed. "Sorry, no, just lemon and lime juice."

"I may need some alcohol before this is all over." Jen reached into a cabinet for glasses and plates. "All Grandma talked about, all the way over here, is how she can't believe Horace ever had a girlfriend in the first place. She kept on about how he's so smart, but incredibly shy."

"Can't shy people fall in love?"

"Exactly." Jen opened a drawer and pulled out forks and teaspoons. "Just goes to show, you never know all of someone's secrets."

Despite her nerves, Melinda had to smile at how easily Jen found her way around this kitchen. These Schermann relatives weren't Melinda's biological family, but they were the link to her farm's past. And Horace was so much more than that.

He wasn't just her landlord for the first nine months she lived in this house; he'd quickly turned into a mentor and a friend. Horace was quick to size up any situation and had a sharp sense of humor. His gentle, honest advice had given her the knowledge she needed to take on this farm, and the courage to embrace this new life and not move back to Minneapolis. Now, it was her turn to help him.

They were all around the dining-room table at last, but the cheesecake was still in the refrigerator because no one seemed to have an appetite. Everyone looked at everyone else, and waited. Finally, Ada took a deep breath and pulled the cigar box to her side of the table.

"This really isn't any of our business, I know." She flipped back the container's dirt-stained lid. "I just ... I really think it's best if we sort this out before telling Horace what we've found."

Kevin sighed sharply. "Mom. You know I don't ..."

She held up a hand. "We've discussed this already."

Melinda saw a need to steer the conversation toward safer ground. "Edith, do you remember Horace seeing anyone around this time? You would have been, what, maybe nine? Her name was Maggie." She pulled the black-and-white photo from the box and passed it around.

"Oh, Horace," Ada said sadly. "How happy you look. What happened?"

"She's certainly pretty." Kevin whistled. "Look at those dark curls, and that smile. No wonder he was smitten."

"He's so ... young." Melinda didn't know what else to say. The Horace she knew was a faded copy of this robust man, who had a full head of blonde hair and a confident grin.

He stood behind Maggie, his arms around her waist. They were laughing. The side of a tree was visible behind them, and a field beyond that. The snapshot could have been taken anywhere, but Melinda had that feeling of seeing a strange place that was, at the same time, somehow familiar. She looked out to the front yard, wondering, but couldn't be sure.

Edith studied the photo, then shook her head.

"Maggie ... no, that doesn't ring a bell. But someone was always coming and going at this house. Between neighbors helping neighbors and Mother being so welcoming to all of our friends ... and Horace and Wilbur were adults by then, working the farm while us kids were in our own world. They were kind to me but had their own lives, if that makes sense."

"It does." Jan patted her grandma on the hand. "I understand. I'd just hoped we might get some answers without having to snoop through Uncle Horace's things."

"I'm afraid there's no way around that." Edith pulled the cigar box in her direction. She slipped the first letter off the stack, adjusted her glasses and brought the note nearly up to her nose. No one moved.

"Oh, my, this girl was good!" She let out a bark-like laugh. "Listen to this: *You're the last thought I have at night, and the first one to cross my mind every morning.*"

Edith scanned the page, then continued on in her gravelly voice that was in stark contrast to the sentiments in the letter.

"And it gets better: *The days until I will see you again are agony, my darling. I ache for the touch of your hand, the burn of your lips ...*"

"Stop it!" Kevin groaned and covered his face with his hands. "We have no right to read these! This girl, this ..."

"Maggie," Melinda prompted him.

"This Maggie, she never intended for anyone but Horace to see these letters. Put that away!"

Edith reached for another sheet of paper. "Well, how else are we going to find her?"

"How will these letters be enough to go on?" Jen leaned toward the box but didn't reach inside. Her expression darkened. "There's so many ways this could end badly. For all we know, Maggie may not even be alive. Or, what if Horace doesn't want to see her? What if she wants nothing to do with him?"

Kevin snatched the box off the table. "I don't like this, I don't like any of it! I say we knock this off, right now, and just give the damn box to Horace!"

Melinda had never seen Kevin so upset. His voice was suddenly so loud that Hazel, who was napping on the couch, raised her head in alarm.

"You can't be serious!" Edith narrowed her eyes at her nephew. "We have to know more before we can do that. The shock alone could give him a heart attack! And he'll be mortified that anyone found them in the first place."

"That's exactly my point!" Kevin clutched the box to his chest. "Who someone loves, or doesn't love or used to love, is no one's business but their own!"

"Calm down, Kevin." Edith frowned and shook her head. "We're trying to help Horace. I don't see what all the fuss is about."

Jen looked at Melinda and suddenly, it all made sense.

Jen was closer and reached Kevin first. He was almost in tears now, and didn't resist when Jen put an arm around him and gently pulled the box away. Ada and Jen knew about Jack, of course, as well as Kevin's past boyfriends. But what did Edith know? Probably nothing.

Kevin dropped into his chair. Ada squeezed her son's hand and turned to Melinda. "You know Horace pretty well. What do you think we should do?"

Jen handed her the box. This time, she was glad to take it. A few more shoves across the table, and it might fall apart.

It was too late to put the box back where it was found, pretend it didn't exist. Maybe Ada was right; they had to know more before they told Horace. Reuniting him with his lost love might make up for intruding on his privacy. And if a happy ending was in doubt, maybe they could keep him from being hurt again.

"OK," she finally said. "We don't have enough information to go on. There has to be answers, some clues, in these letters. I say we start reading ... silently ... and see what turns up. Whatever happens, we do what's best for Horace in the end."

One by one, everyone nodded. Even Kevin.

Edith motioned for Melinda to hand her the next letter. "I agree, Detective Foster. Let's do our best to crack this case."

The house was soon as quiet as a library, the only sounds the rustle of paper and the rain drumming on the roof. Letters were passed around and unfolded, their contents skimmed for relevant information. Melinda fetched a notebook to keep track of anything useful. The reviewed letters were added to a row that soon marched down the dining-room table, with the earliest notes placed on Ada's end and the latest at Kevin's elbow.

There was so much to read, but few solid clues. It was clear that Maggie and Horace were blissfully in love, two exceptionally bright young people with an intellectual connection as well as a physical one. As for how far that progressed, it was hard to say. Maggie had a flair for words and romantic notions, but her notes were light on specifics.

The first letters, dated April 1946, were rather prosaic, filled with Maggie's likes and dislikes and how much she loved school; she was at the top of her junior class. Horace was two years older, and already farming with his family. It sounded like they met at a dance, but there was no evidence of exactly where and when.

Later notes were mostly filled with declarations of affection, but there was another, more interesting theme: Maggie couldn't wait to leave country life behind and make her own way in the world. By early 1947, Maggie's senior year, her letters were filled with plans to attend Iowa State University in the fall and become a teacher.

"Horace was valedictorian, you know," Ada said. "I often wondered why he didn't go off to college, surely he could have gotten a scholarship. I know he did odd jobs for other farmers as a teenager, and I'm sure he saved every penny. He could have been anything. An engineer, a lawyer, a teacher. Every time you turned around, he had his nose in a book."

"Maybe that was the problem," Jen suggested. "He's shy, and the thought of moving away was too much for him."

Edith nodded with admiration. "You should have seen him doing the books for the farm. Father was bright, and Wilbur, too; although Wilbur used to have a bit of a wild streak in him. But Horace had them both beat. He could calculate seed costs and price the markets' losses and gains faster than anyone, and most of the time, do it in his head."

Melinda put down the letter she was studying. She hadn't wanted to read any of them at first; but now, she wished there were more. Something that might lead them to Maggie. "There's nothing in this one that will help us. Maybe they just grew apart."

"Young love." Ada shrugged. "It doesn't always last, does it? Kevin ... what is it?"

"There's something here! This one's from later, May of 1947. Maggie's planning to go to Iowa State, but that's not all. She mentions several times that *we* are going to love Ames; talks about all the things *we* can do together at college."

Jen leaned down the table. "Could she be talking about someone else, maybe a friend?"

Ada shuffled her pile with renewed interest. "Here, this one's from the same month. Oh, my God, she had to be talking about Horace! There's things here about registering for classes, and where they would live. Were ... were they *engaged*?"

Edith gasped. "Hand me another, Melinda. How many more are there?"

"Just a few, maybe five."

Jen took the next one. "Horace had been out of high school for two years already. Would he have gone off to college that late?"

"Many veterans did, after the war," Ada said. "Horace didn't serve, he was just young enough and lucky enough to never get drafted, but Wilbur did. If Horace was determined to continue his education, and could find the money ..."

"And the grades," Kevin added. "We know he had the grades."

Edith picked up the photo again, lost in thought. Suddenly, the picture fell from her weathered hand.

"Grandma?" Jen came around the table. "You're so pale. What is it? Did you remember something?"

"I've seen this girl," Edith finally said, her voice hardly above a whisper. "Oh, my God, it's *her*."

"When? Where?" Ada gasped. "I haven't, I'm sure of it."

Edith put a hand over her eyes. "One day, when I was around eleven, someone came to the door. I was in here, hiding under the big table with a book, when I heard a car come up the driveway."

It was a Saturday. Horace, Wilbur and Henry had gone to town. The other, older children were away for the afternoon, or outside. Anna was snapping green beans in the kitchen, with little Carl scooting around her feet. Ada was probably down for her nap.

The strange car and the pretty young lady sliding out from behind its wheel grabbed Edith's attention, and she slipped into the kitchen to eavesdrop through the open windows after Anna went into the back porch.

"She had on a burgundy dress, with cream flowers, and the highest heels I'd ever seen." Edith's voice grew stronger as she remembered. "She was stunning. Her hat was beige, very chic, at a jaunty tilt that covered part of her face. No one around here dressed like that. I remember wanting to be that fashionable someday, when I was old enough."

Ada grasped her sister's hand. "Did Mother know her?"

"Oh, yes," Edith said ominously. "She didn't call her by name, though. The girl seemed friendly at first, but then she started crying. I was hiding under the window by then, so I couldn't catch it all, between her tears and Mother's low, stern tone. She rarely spoke like that, to anyone. And then the girl got angry. 'Where is he? I came all this way ...'"

Jen leaned forward. "What did great-grandma say?"

Edith looked at the floor. Then she sized up everyone around the table, including Melinda. "I'll tell you everything I heard. But it doesn't leave this room."

She took a deep breath. "I never heard Horace mentioned by name, you see, and I thought maybe there was some mix-up, or it was some girl Wilbur knew. He never married, of course, but when he was young ..." Edith shook her head with grudging admiration. "Well, he always had a least one on a string. Anyway, this girl kept crying, and Mother kept saying, 'he's not here.' And then Mother said: 'Get out of my yard, and don't ever come back. I know what happened, I know what you did. You're not good enough for my son.'"

For a moment, no one said anything. But by the looks bouncing around the table, it was clear everyone had the same shocking thought.

"Oh, no." Ada said slowly. "No. Horace wouldn't ... he's so responsible. If something had happened ..."

"We don't know for sure this was about Horace," Kevin said.

"It has to be." Jen held up the photo.

"Wait." Melinda tried to gather her circling thoughts. "Maybe Horace didn't do anything. Anna only blamed Maggie. Whatever she did, maybe she did it on her own."

"Grandma," Jen said quietly, "you have to tell us everything you remember from that day. What happened next?"

"I ran upstairs. I was terrified I'd get caught, spying on adults like that, and be punished. Kids and adults were in separate worlds back then. The whole next week, I did my chores with so much zeal that our parents probably wondered what had gotten into me. Days passed, and it seemed I was in the clear. I just put it out of my mind, I guess. Until now. And this photo ... like I said, her hat shadowed part of her face, but it has to be her."

Kevin took a gulp of his iced tea. "When exactly was this? You said you were eleven. Was that 1948, or 1949?"

"1949."

"So, two years later." Melinda picked up the final three letters and scanned them for anything that made sense, but found nothing. "The last one here is from July 1947, and it's as lovey-dovey as the rest."

"Something happened." Ada shook her head. "But what?"

"We have to find her." Jen rubbed her face, suddenly weary. "Find out what happened. No matter where it leads."

"How far are you willing to go?" Ada reached for the cigar box, tears forming in her eyes. "What if ... what if there's something we don't want to find?"

Kevin began to gather up the letters. "We're too far in to quit now. I know you're all thinking this is some scandalous movie-of-the-week nonsense, but what if it's not? Maggie came back, I believe that, but why? If nothing else, we need to clear Uncle Horace's name."

Melinda picked up the photo and turned it over. The back was as blank as it had been the day before. "A first name isn't much to go on, but it's a start."

* 7 *

When it became clear further examination of the letters would only reveal more questions than answers, Melinda packed the notes away in the cigar box and returned them to their new home in the buffet's top drawer. Then she brought out the margarita cheesecake, and her stressed-out guests attacked it with gusto. Sunday night, she soothed her worries with another generous slice, but half of the dessert still remained.

Joe and his crew would be back the next day, but she suspected the electricians might not care for cheesecake, or any treat they couldn't easily snarf one-handed. And while the Prosper Hardware coffee guys were always eager for snacks, cheesecake was probably not their jam at such an early hour, and she wasn't going back to work until Tuesday. So she cut the rest into wedges and stashed them in the deep freeze.

Monday was spent doing whatever kept her busy and out of the electricians' way: running errands in Swanton, watering the garden, cleaning the chicken coop. As she shopped and hauled and scooped, her mind stayed stuck on Horace and Maggie.

What happened between them? Was Maggie still alive? Could they track her down? How would Horace take the news, whatever it might be? And, the most-pressing concern: where was Melinda going to look first?

She was crouched by the green beans' fence, ripping out weeds, when she finally found an answer: the Prosper library. It was an unassuming, single-story building, so much the opposite of the grand city hall next door, but held a modest collection of local reference titles in one back corner. Melinda loved history and had always meant to give those titles a glance, but had never found the time. Tuesday, on her lunch break, she'd make it happen.

Nancy Delaney, Prosper's only full-time employee, served as its librarian as well as city clerk. She would be knowledgeable about the library's historical collection, but Melinda decided to go it alone. Nancy was her friend, and a discreet professional, but Melinda had promised to keep the search secret. It wouldn't be hard to roam around alone, as Nancy would either be sorting books at the library's antique circulation desk or tapping away on her other computer in city hall, which was connected to the library by a cased opening in their shared wall. School had been out for a few weeks already, and the small library might be crammed with kids and their moms and caregivers. Melinda could slip to the back of the stacks and browse without attracting too much attention.

The past was on her mind when she arrived at Prosper Hardware Tuesday morning, but the coffee guys were clearly focused on the future. A load of merchandise arrived the afternoon before, and they were distracted by the contents of two shipping containers now parked by the sideboard.

Aunt Miriam was there, too, her brown eyes dancing with amusement as she leaned against the showcase, sipping her coffee. When Melinda asked what the fuss was about, she shook her head.

"You'd think prize-winning walleye and trout were being pulled from the river every day, given how excited they are. It's like Christmas morning around here."

Uncle Frank lifted a partially assembled fishing rod from one container, and Auggie and Jerry reached for it at the same time. Bill wore a wide grin as he sorted packets of lures.

A shiny-new tackle box sat in George's lap, and he was enthralled with its cubbyholes and trays. "Look at all this room," he said to no one in particular. "Why, it's far better than mine. I think it's time for an upgrade."

As she tucked her purse under the counter, Melinda decided she'd been right to leave the cheesecake at home. The men were far too distracted to appreciate it just now.

"Well, there's a chance the stuff will sell," she told Miriam. "Summer is fishing season, after all, and Father's Day is next weekend. As long as Uncle Frank didn't go too crazy on volume, maybe it won't be a flop."

"He and Bill were so excited about their idea, I hated to tell him no. I'm glad the new store tee shirts and caps are selling so well, but that doesn't mean every addition to our merchandise line is going to be that popular."

Auggie had the first fishing rod assembled and was waving it about. "Now, that's a fine pole. But you know, the best way to make money is to carry all the accessories as well as the main products."

Miriam shook her head at him, but he either didn't notice or didn't care. Always the businessman, he was already off and running with his idea.

"I like these bobbers and lures you got in, but there's so much more to fishing," he reminded Frank. "You should get life vests, too. You're already carrying a few coolers this time of year, but I'd expand that line. Smaller ones would be perfect for holding a few beers, or even for bait."

"Hey, there's an idea!" Bill looked up from sorting lures. "Live bait! We've already got a refrigerated case."

Aunt Miriam waded into the group, sidestepping the cartons and packaging that littered the oak-plank floor. "I hate to break up this fishing party, but that's where I draw the line! The groceries in this case, as well as the pop and juice, are some of our top sellers. We're not going to dirty it up with buckets of worms." She looked to Melinda for support.

Melinda wanted to give it, but she had to be careful. She tried to stay out of the strategic decisions Frank and Miriam made about the family's business. Just because she worked there full time, and Frank had been reduced to sitting at the register for only a few hours each week, didn't mean she could completely take his place. And it had been a long time since she'd seen Frank this excited about something happening at Prosper Hardware.

"Well … offering customers a comprehensive slate of products is often a smart idea."

She knew she sounded pretentious, but the diplomacy she'd relied on during her marketing career came back quickly. "However, combining two such unique inventory categories, in the same part of the store … it might be confusing for customers."

Auggie snorted. "You mean it's disgusting." Doc had just arrived, and Auggie handed him the fishing pole for a second examination.

"Well, of course it is!" Miriam topped off her mug. "Discussion's over. People can get their rods and lures and tackle here, but they're on their own when it comes to bait." She lowered her voice as she passed Melinda. "I'm going upstairs to work on the books. Let me know if they get too rowdy."

"I suppose Miriam is right," Bill sighed. "Hey Auggie, why don't you start carrying worms at the co-op? Maybe our new venture could boost your bottom line, too."

Auggie was staring at his phone, and didn't answer at first. "What's that?"

"Worms," Melinda said, "for fishing. They'd probably be a better fit for your business, seeing as they are, well, sort of gross."

Doc and Jerry sometimes checked their messages during coffee time, but when had she ever seen Auggie this distracted by his phone? He frowned and clumsily pecked at its screen, like an arthritic old hen.

"It won't work. Why can't I get this video to work?"

Being the group's youngest member by almost twenty years, Bill didn't even glance around to see if anyone else was going to help Auggie. He set the box of lures on the floor, got out of his chair, and reached for Auggie's phone.

"Are you trying to turn up the sound, or get the file to load?"

"I don't know. Both, I guess."

Melinda leaned over for a better look, then burst out laughing.

"Now I see why you're so distracted. 'Pie Baking 101' is probably very educational, but why don't you just ask Jane to show you how?"

Auggie raised his chin. "I've got to do this on my own. If I'm going to win, it's going to be on my own merit."

George whistled. "You sound pretty determined. Where's all that gusto coming from?"

"Jane." Auggie looked at the floor. "That's what Jane told me. Melinda, how do you know if the water is cold enough for the crust? And everything says not to work the dough too much or it'll get tough. How many minutes is that?"

"I wish I knew. I gave up on pie crusts long ago. I get mine at the grocery store."

"Don't worry about it," Doc said. "The contest is going to be anonymous. Only Vicki and Nancy will know what's what. The public's not going to have any idea who made which pie, not until the votes are counted and there's a winner."

"That's just it." Auggie pointed at his friend. "I want to win."

"Making a pie is like so many things," Melinda told Auggie. "It just takes lots of time. And practice."

"But I've got only a few weeks left," he moaned. "Jerry, how is yours coming along?"

Jerry, who was next to the vintage sideboard, set his cup on its metal counter and turned in his chair, as if gathering his thoughts. At the last moment, he picked his mug up again.

"You know what? I'm not going to say. This contest is every man for himself; so much is as stake."

This time, Melinda couldn't keep quiet. "This is hardly a matter of national security. What's the big deal?"

"Bragging rights are up for grabs." Jerry straightened in his chair. "This is the first men's pie bake-off ever held in this town. There's sixteen guys already signed up, and registration's got another week to go. The competition is going to be tough."

George took a sip from his mug. "I'm taking the easy way out; no pressure for me."

"That's for sure," Jerry snorted. "All you have to do is sit there and eat."

"Well, I'm really good at that."

"Jerry's right, I think this is going to become an annual event." Auggie leaned forward in anticipation. "Besides, all the local dignitaries are going to take part."

"Dignitaries?" Melinda raised her eyebrows. "I thought it was open to any guy who wanted to sign up for it. And they don't even have to live in the city limits."

"All I know is, Prosper's finest will participate." Auggie started to hunt for another video. "Along with myself, there's Jerry, and Father Perkins from the Catholic Church, and Jake Newcastle from the city council. It's practically a who's-who of this town."

Uncle Frank, who also served on the city's board and had no interest in the pie contest, hid his smirk behind his coffee mug.

Bill glanced out the store's plate-glass windows, to where the heat was already building. "I can't believe Vicki hopes to hold this event at the city park. Even with a tent up, it'll be roasting out there."

"We're going to talk about that tomorrow night, at the next committee meeting," Melinda said. "There's got to be a better location. Maybe the school gym. It's air-conditioned."

"I don't know if there's room," Jerry said doubtfully. "The PTA has it booked for their craft show. Unless we move it to one of the churches, I don't know where else to have it other than the council chambers."

"And no one will want to eat pie there." George turned up his nose. "Not with Karen and Doctor Vogel doing cat-snip surgeries there every month. I know they scrub everything down, but ... well, it's not very appetizing."

"It'd better not move to the Catholic Church," Auggie warned Melinda. "That'd be like giving Father Perkins a home-field advantage."

* * *

Melinda tried to keep her eyes off the clock, and a steady stream of customers helped most of the morning pass quickly. As did the arrival of Esther Denner, Frank and Miriam's neighbor.

Esther was retired from the elementary school's kitchen, and had rushed to Prosper Hardware the day of Frank's heart attack to take over the register. She soon became the store's only part-time employee and relished her new role, especially when it was time to decorate the store for every holiday that came along. The job got her out of the house, and it also gave her a front-row seat to Prosper's comings and goings.

"I see you're fixing up the display window," Esther told Melinda as she came in the front door, the little bell chiming her arrival. "It looks good from the street. I bet Frank will make a nice penny on that fishing gear. Of course, my husband says the fish bite best when it rains. And there's been precious little of that lately."

"Auggie says our best chance is later this week, so we'll see what happens." Melinda arranged three fishing poles, teepee style, against the antique dresser that was her biggest all-season prop in the window. An open tackle box fit nicely on the dresser's surface. A few of the most-colorful lures, tied to bits of fishing line, dangled from one drawer's handles. There was already a cooler on display, but she repositioned it near the fishing supplies and tossed a Prosper Hardware cap on top.

"There, that should do it." The clock's hands stood only at eleven; she had thirty more minutes to burn. "Well, I guess I'll move on to the fasteners aisle. Just let me know if you get swamped and I'll come up to the register."

"I'm glad you know so much about nail and screw sizes." Esther shuddered as she reached for a small pile of returns. "All those teeny-tiny sacks and cubbyholes drive me nuts."

Melinda didn't answer. Sorting misplaced hardware supplies wasn't her favorite task, either, but it would keep her hands busy until she could get across the street to the library.

Finally, it was time. She hustled behind the counter and grabbed her purse.

"Aren't you hungry?" Esther asked. "I know you wanted to go to the library, but can't it wait?"

"I won't be gone long." Melinda waved over her shoulder, already halfway to the door. "I'll be back in a bit."

Four cars were parked in front of the library, which meant it was busier than usual. Her hands trembled with excitement when she reached for the metal handle on the library's heavy oak door.

"Get a grip," she muttered to herself. "Calm down! No matter what I find, I can't let on to Nancy or anyone else."

The library was refreshingly cool and a bit dim after the blinding brightness outside. Like city hall, this building was narrow but long. Generous front windows brightened the area by the circulation desk, but the ceiling lights were always on in the back of the space.

"Hey there!" Nancy was at the counter, helping a little boy check out a book. "I hear it's getting hot."

"You heard right." Melinda carefully wiped her shoes on the mat, even though their soles weren't dirty, in a bid to keep herself from sprinting down the closest aisle.

Nancy pointed to a stack of hardcovers on the counter. Their bright-white pages held the promise of fresh reading.

"The latest batch is all cataloged." She gestured with the pen in her hand. "You can have first dibs. When I finish helping this little guy, I'll be back across the way. Just let me know when you've found one you want."

"I'll go through them before I leave." Melinda returned her friend's smile. But not even new books could deter her today. "I'll just look around a bit first."

The library's media center, which consisted of three computers, wasn't the answer. "Maggie" was so common, and a nickname for so many female first names, that the online genealogy databases were off-limits for now. She needed a last name, at least.

As soon as she disappeared down the first row of shelves, Melinda picked up the pace. A woman and four kids were in the children's area, and an older man was browsing the magazine rack. As long as Melinda kept quiet, no one should pay her any mind. Her pulse was pounding in her ears by the time she reached the local history titles.

There weren't as many as she'd hoped. With no surname to work with, the land records in the plat books were of no use. Nor the county history books, which looked fascinating but would have to wait for another time. But there was a substantial collection of Prosper High School yearbooks. The newest was from a decade ago, right before the merger with Swanton left only elementary students at Prosper's brick building, and went back to the early 1900s. All she had to do was scan the names under the girls' portraits, and compare any possible matches with the snap of the old photo on her phone.

The 1947 yearbook was in surprisingly good condition. A musty smell met her nose as she flipped the volume open and carefully thumbed through its pages. The book wasn't very thick, but it held an impressive number of both posed and candid shots of the high school's sports teams, organizations and activities. She found the senior portraits and, holding her breath, scanned the first page.

No Maggie there. Or on page two, but on page three ...

Melinda gasped, but then frowned. "That can't be her."

This girl's name was Margaret; but she was blond, and Horace's girl was a brunette. Melinda pulled out her phone, just to be sure. Not a match. Hair color could be changed, of course, but their faces were too different.

The senior photos went on for a few more pages, the class being larger than Melinda would have guessed. But teens from all around this part of the county used to attend high school in Prosper, and families were bigger back in the day.

Her shoulders slumped with defeat when the rest of the seniors' photos turned up no leads. Was Maggie left out of the yearbook for some reason? What if she hadn't been able to afford a senior photo? But the portraits all had the same bland backdrop, nothing like the elaborate photo sessions seniors now expected. The yearbook headshots may have been free, and the students only had to pay for prints for their family and friends.

Melinda was very certain about the dates, but decided to check the volumes from surrounding years, just in case. No 1946 juniors, or any girls in any grade, were likely candidates. The 1945 yearbook, which held Horace's senior class, wasn't even on the shelf. Other volumes from the World War II era were missing, too, and the 1948 yearbook held no clues.

Melinda pocketed her phone and shuffled to the stack of new books on the circulation desk. Even the latest title from one of her favorite authors couldn't raise her spirits. She was at a dead end in her search for Maggie. The only way to move forward would be to tell Horace about the letters, admit they'd been keeping him in the dark, and hope he was willing to help them find her.

If only Horace had burned the letters long ago, or hid them somewhere else, or Joe and Al hadn't been so nosy ... none of this would have started in the first place. And Melinda had no idea how it would all end.

"Busy day at the store?" Nancy called from beyond the archway into city hall, where she was tapping at her computer. "You look beat."

"Oh, I think it's just the heat."

Nancy came into the library, reached for the book in Melinda's hand, and went behind the counter. Melinda soon saw she wasn't the only one with a heavy heart. Every hair of Nancy's blunt-cut dark bob was in place, and its streaks of gray were, as always, more fashionable than frowsy. But behind her angle-rimmed glasses, Nancy's eyes looked tired.

"What's going on with you?" Melinda asked her friend.

Nancy leaned back in her librarian's chair, the walnut one with the heavy spindles, and stared out the window. "Oh, I don't know. This is a strange time of year. School's out, but we're not fully into the summer groove yet. Of course, given the nasty winter we had, it's a wonder the kids weren't in class even longer than they were."

"Is everything fine at home? What are Ryan and Kim doing this summer?"

In addition to her dual role for the city, Nancy was a single mom of two teenagers. She'd moved back to the area ten years ago to be closer to her parents, who lived in Hampton.

"Well, they're at their dad's the rest of the week, so they won't be home until Sunday. The house seems so empty. I know they'll be back, but they won't be around much once they are. Both have part-time jobs lined up, and Kim's playing softball. I just can't believe Ryan will be a senior in the fall."

She pressed both palms to the desk, her brown eyes filling with tears. "What I am going to do when they're gone? They're my life! I have my job, of course, but it seems like just yesterday they were so small, and needed me for everything. Ryan's already got his college choices narrowed down, and in just a few weeks it'll be time for senior pictures. And it'll be the last of everything, once school starts again."

Melinda couldn't completely relate to what Nancy was going through, but she understood how the most benign things could mark the end of one of life's chapters. A year ago, she'd started having her own "last things" in Minneapolis, but she hadn't realized it at first. Everything was such a whirlwind that by the time she understood what was happening, her life had changed completely.

"You know," she said gently, "maybe you should talk to Bev. Her kids are out of the house, have been for years. Maybe she could give you some perspective."

Nancy managed a smile. Bev Stewart was a member of the library's book club, a no-nonsense farm wife whose blunt manner concealed a kind heart and a quick wit. "I could. Of course, there's Vicki, too, but I suspect that's why she throws herself into so many projects at once. She's lonely, and trying to fill the holes as fast as she can. I don't think that's the approach I want to take."

"Have you seen her ideas for her store?" Melinda shook her head with wonder. "They're really stunning. But I just hope she can draw enough customers to get the thing off the ground. I think you're right; she's got all her hopes pinned on this business plan."

"I was so relieved when she offered to chair the Fourth of July festival; it gives the rest of us a break. And I love her idea to start a farmers market, but it's going to take a serious commitment from several vendors to make it happen."

"We'd have to keep the stall rental low," Melinda said cautiously. "The farmers market season has already started, growers may have their calendars full. And if it stays hot and dry like this, people may not have much garden surplus this year. The soil's been awfully dry lately."

Suddenly, she laughed.

"What?"

"I'm starting to sound like Auggie."

Nancy smiled. "Well, people aren't harvesting much yet, other than strawberries and rhubarb. Maybe it's not too late. I'll talk to Jerry about it."

She slid Melinda's selection across the scanner, then handed the book back with renewed energy. "It would be fun if we can make it happen. But we better get started. Time moves so fast these days I can barely keep up."

❋ 8 ❋

Annie's bellows were full-throttle now, but Melinda stood her ground.

"Nope, I won't do it." She crossed her arms and planted her chore boots firmly in the straw. "You can't go outside this morning. I won't allow it, Miss Annie."

Annie made another grumbling protest, then haughtily turned away. She stared through the open top half of the pasture door, out to where the sky was blue and the grass was short but mostly green, and stomped one front hoof. Melinda understood the sheep's nervousness and frustration. It was shearing day, and she wanted it to be over, too.

This change in routine had the ewes restless and on alert. Even the lambs were pacing, sniffing the air for any hint of what might happen. Clover bumped her nose on Melinda's jeans, seeking reassurance, and Melinda rubbed her ears.

"Don't worry, you and your little friends are too young for haircuts this year. But everyone's due for vaccinations, so Karen's coming out and we'll get it all done at once."

A lump formed in Melinda's throat as the other lambs gathered around her. Their number was one less than before, as Caesar had gone to his new home last week. John would give him a great life, and the roll of cash her neighbor pressed into her palm would put a dent in some projects around the farm, but she still missed her goofy boy.

"Today's going to be crazy, but it'll be a good day," she said to herself as much as the sheep. "And all you big girls, just think about how much cooler you'll be once you get rid of those winter coats!"

Three ancient box fans, hooked to the rafters with twisted lengths of wire, buzzed away in the dusty corners of the sheep's feeding area. Melinda had hoped to move at least one fan into the south section of the barn for the day, as that was where the shearing would take place, but the thick cobwebs wrapping the fans' metal frames stopped her short. She had arrived at some sort of truce with the tenacious brown spiders that patrolled the barn, and she wasn't about to break it. Opening the top sections of the other doors might be enough to get more air moving in the building's back half.

She pulled off her grubby canvas cap and fanned herself before settling the hat back over her braided hair. Stormy sashayed down the aisle fence's ridge and meowed at her elbow, wanting attention.

"You just wait, mister. You thought it was bad when the electricians were here, but that was nothing compared to the upheaval you'll find in your barn today. You and Sunny might want to head for the windbreak before everyone arrives."

Joe's crew had thoroughly cleaned up after themselves, leaving Melinda with only some plaster patches needing a touch-up of paint. All the chaos had been worth it. She sometimes found herself smiling when she flipped a light switch or powered on an appliance, knowing the lines that hummed in her walls were at last up to modern standards. New wires also stretched from the house to the yard's light pole, and across to the barn and the machine shed. Another fresh line served the chicken coop.

As she started back toward the house, Melinda could see the hens scuttling in their run, the eight rapidly growing chicks right in the mix as the older half of the flock scratched for bugs and grubs. The nearby windbreak provided their screened run with some shade, but Melinda knew they'd move inside by midday to miss the worst of the heat.

Even Hobo seemed to be taking it easy. It was barely eight in the morning, and he was already stretched out in the cool dirt under the picnic table. He could go inside, of course, and snooze with Hazel and Grace in air-conditioned comfort, but Melinda suspected he was secretly on watch. Something was going to happen, and soon, and he didn't want to miss a thing.

This shearing crew had clipped Horace's ewes for almost a decade. She had yet to meet them, as last year's visit had taken place before she'd arrived in early June. They also tended to John Olson's much-larger flock, and John would only ever hire the best. There was nothing to worry about, and Horace had told her the very same thing, yet she cringed as she recalled the excruciating conversation she had with him two nights ago.

Horace had cheerfully updated her on the comings and goings at Scenic Vista, unaware of how she was hunched over in her reading chair, awash in guilt. She'd tried to satisfy his "what's new at the farm?" queries by telling him how the young chicks were thriving, and about the crickets Grace and Hazel were catching in the basement. But the electrical upgrades were at the top of his mind, and he wanted a hole-by-hole recap of everything Joe and his crew discovered.

"I bet they found their share of cobwebs and mice droppings," he'd laughed. "You never know what's back in those walls!"

Melinda was exhausted by the time she managed to get off the phone. She'd always looked forward to Horace's calls, and had never hesitated to dial his room at the nursing home to get a question answered or just to chat. But everything was different now. How was she going to keep silent, and how long would she have to dodge her friend? Thank goodness she'd visited Horace and Wilbur just a few days before the letters were discovered. Because for now, it would be best if she stayed away. Lying to his face would be even worse.

The dead-end search at Prosper's library had only fueled Kevin's demands to turn the letters over to Horace. But Ada wanted to hold off as long as possible, and suggested they confide in Mabel and ask her to make discreet inquiries among her family. Kevin put his foot down, saying he trusted Mabel but this was the sort of story most people couldn't resist blabbing around, and the idea was dropped.

Melinda understood why Kevin was so cagey; it was getting harder and harder for her to keep this secret, too. Yesterday was Father's Day, and she had spent most of it at her parents' in Swanton. She'd almost blurted everything out to her mom when they were alone in the kitchen, but caught herself just in time.

Her dad had insisted on helping shear the sheep, but at least there would be plenty of distractions today to keep her from sharing her emotional burden. At least there was somebody Melinda could talk to about this.

"Hobo, I'm glad you're such a good listener." She reached under the picnic table and gave him a gentle pat on the head.

"You'll keep the secret, as will your kitty friends. But sometime, we'll have to 'fess up. I just hope that when we do, we've got good news for Horace. That's the only way we might be able to make amends."

Ed was coming over, too, and had heartily agreed to accept a rhubarb crisp as payment. He was the first to arrive, his battered farm pickup letting out a few belches as it chugged up the lane. An empty burlap bag slumped inside the truck's bed.

"Had to make a delivery on the way over." Ed's voice was laced with secrecy, even though there was no one around but Hobo. "It's been a few days since I've found something good enough for our new neighbors."

Melinda wasn't sure which Ed was enjoying more: having a family of bald eagles nesting nearby, or sneaking around to supplement their diet.

"Poor raccoon never knew what hit him. But my guess is one of the milk trucks, given how things turned out. Heavy axles, a full load ... anyway, it'll make a good feast for the little ones."

"I saw some flapping in the trees down the waterway the other evening. But the canopy's so full, I couldn't make out how many there were."

"I think there's two, and then Mom and Dad. Eagles don't raise large broods, like a songbird. They'll start venturing out more pretty soon, going further from the nest. Isn't this fun?" Ed chuckled. "People would be really shocked if they knew!"

Melinda didn't know whether to laugh or groan. The eagles' arrival was nothing compared to the other secret she was keeping under her hat. Ed would be flabbergasted; he'd known Horace for fifty years ...

"Yeah, we've gotta keep this quiet as long as she can," she finally said. "But I'm sure it'll get out, sooner or later."

"Oh, I know," Ed said ominously. "Things always do."

"It's just as well I didn't find a good way to let my chickens free range this summer. Sixteen's too many to chase in and out of the run twice a day, and I never wanted them roaming at night. None of that would be safe now, not with eagles around."

Ed nodded in agreement. "Your hens have a good-sized run, and that wire mesh over the top will keep the winged predators away. How are they handling the heat? Have you made them any corn-sicles yet?"

Since Melinda had moved to the country, the online homesteading community had become a useful source of inspiration as well as a huge waste of time.

It was too easy to search for a new project or the answer to a problem, then spend hours salivating over everyone else's ideas. One called for freezing corn kernels and water in small containers, then setting the blocks out as a refreshing treat for chickens.

"They love those things," she told Ed. "I put another batch in the freezer last night. Those small margarine tubs are just the right size."

Roger soon turned up the lane. He was still too far away for Melinda to see the grin on his face, but she knew it was there. You can take the boy out of the country ...

"Glad your dad could make it today," Ed said. "I haven't seen him in a while. Just make sure he doesn't eat all my rhubarb crisp, OK?"

"Don't worry, I made a second one for him to share with Mom."

Karen soon arrived, her usual blonde ponytail wrapped into a messy bun that barely fit under her wide-brimmed straw hat.

She was so petite that no one would assume she spent a good chunk of her waking hours slogging through muddy pastures and wrangling obstinate livestock. But the farm critters around Prosper had learned to show Karen respect, and the farmers who'd raised their eyebrows at Doc's choice of a business partner eventually had, too.

Ed was once in that group, but now he was eager to shake Karen's hand. She'd quickly made friends with Sammy, Ed and Mabel's dog, during Sammy's annual checkup, and came through for Ed when one of his beef cattle took sick and Doc was already out on a call.

Karen chatted with Ed and Roger for a few minutes, then she and Melinda started for the barn.

"I told the shearing crew to come at nine." Melinda opened the main door and stepped aside to let Karen pass through with one of her large metal totes. "I've got all the extra fence panels ready to go. I'll let you decide how you want to set things up in the back."

Karen set her medical box on the floor and took a second to say hello to Sunny. Both barn cats loved Karen, as long as they weren't on the clinic's exam table and under her thumb.

"Let's put that wraparound aisle to use. We can make a chute on the left side of the lambing pens to do the meds. When we let them out, they'll go on to the shearing crew, then we'll pen them up on the right when they're done."

"Sounds easy enough. I hope it actually is."

"Oh, it'll be fine. Once that's done, we'll vaccinate the lambs. But it might be a good idea to separate out the youngsters before we get started." Karen pointed across the main aisle to the barn's other large feeding area, which was last used when the lambs were weaned. "Let's shoo them into there."

Hobo was smart, for sure, but he was no herding dog, and sheep were usually easy to lead if treats were offered. So the women filled several small buckets with corn and set them on the haymow stairs' bottom step. Once the bribes were ready, they fastened fence panels in strategic locations in the back half of the barn to meet Karen's specifications.

A rumble of conversation soon filtered in from beyond the barn's entrance, then Roger and Ed appeared with the shearing crew in tow. Carter was its leader, and he was as stocky and grizzled as Melinda expected him to be. One of the younger men looked like he might be Carter's son, but the other was so thin Melinda wondered how he was able to wrangle sheep. But even the smallest guy was muscular, and they were all in surprisingly cheerful moods considering the task ahead of them.

If they weren't worried, Melinda decided, she shouldn't be, either.

"You must be Melinda." Carter offered a beefy hand and squeezed hers so tight she nearly gasped with pain. Bits of wool fluff stuck to his gray tee shirt, which was already dirty with sweat.

"Always liked coming out to do Horace's group, they're pretty easy to deal with. Guys," he called over his shoulder, "these ewes will be a tea party compared to that first bunch this morning."

Roger and Ed fastened fence panels across the main aisle, and started to lead the lambs out of the way while Melinda helped Karen organize the dewormers and vaccines.

"Those clippers are huge," she whispered to Karen as the shearing crew unpacked their gear. "I don't want my girls getting all nicked up."

"Don't worry. Those electric shears are far safer than the old-school kind. And so much faster. Most of these guys can get the fleece off in just a few minutes. And in one piece."

"I like your setup," Carter called to Melinda over the roar of the fans and the "baaaas" that echoed across the stuffy barn. "They won't be able to get away from us. But there's still lots of room to throw 'em, you know?"

Melinda nearly dropped the bottle of dewormer in her hand.

"*Throw* them?" she hissed to Karen. "No one is throwing my girls around! I thought this wasn't going to hurt?"

"It won't," Karen said soothingly. "Shearers like to get a sheep on the floor, do one side and flip them over to do the other. That's all he means. Once they're off their feet, the sheep just give up. And before they know what's happening, it's done."

She handed Melinda an empty plunger and gestured for her to fill it. "You'll be too busy helping me to watch. Honestly, having goo pushed into their mouths and being poked with needles will bother the ewes far more than being sheared."

"The lambs are all moved," Roger told Melinda. "How about I help Karen hand out the meds? The sheep know you best, they're more likely to follow you around the bend than me. Ed will shoo them along to the shearing station."

Once everyone was in place, Melinda released the gate latch with one hand and held out the corn bucket with the other. One of the easygoing ewes soon came forward. Melinda shut the gate behind the first patient, and drew her around the corner.

"That's the way." Ed gave his approval. "Nice and gentle. Now, open that panel and hand the corn to Karen, see if our girl will head on through."

She did. Roger wrapped his arms gently but firmly around the ewe while Karen, in a burst of efficiency and speed, administered the vaccine with one hand and reached for the dewormer with the other. While the ewe was still trying to process the quick stick of the needle, Karen pushed the plunger into the side of her mouth. Ed opened the next makeshift gate, and the bewildered ewe took off around the bend. The younger shearers had her off her feet quick as a wink, and Carter set to work.

"Easy-peasy." Roger grinned at Melinda. "One down, eleven to go. We'll be done in no time. Bring us another."

The next few sheep were also accommodating. But as more ewes left the feeding area, the rest grew suspicious. Who were these strangers, hollering back and forth? And why were their friends over there, not where they belonged? They looked different, too. The buzz of the shears didn't help, nor did the distressed bleats of the lambs pacing across the aisle.

Melinda soon had no idea what to expect when she opened the gate. Either no one wanted to come through, or two or three ewes would try to charge past her.

Karen came to help when two sheep got out at once. "I think we got the calm, easy ones at the start. Whoever comes around the bend first, goes first. Just let the other one wait in the aisle; she's so nervous, we'll never get her back in." Even Roger couldn't hold the second ewe on his own. Melinda crowded into the makeshift chute, too, and her palms soon turned slick from the lanolin in the sheep's deep fleece.

None of the ewes that were left seemed to care much for the corn snacks. Roger watched the main gate while Melinda went into the feeding area to see which ones she might coax forward. Two of the five sheep started to move her way, but the rest paced behind them, panting from the heat and their nerves.

"Come on," she cooed, rattling the grain bucket. "There's treats, and haircuts just around the bend. Annie, how about you? Doesn't anyone want to ..."

"Melinda!" Roger shouted. "On your left! Look out!"

One of the larger ewes, the one who'd given birth to a sturdy set of triplets last winter, suddenly bolted for the gate. She had her head down, and was so scared she may not have noticed Melinda, standing there with the bucket, urging her to stop.

The corn went flying when the ewe rammed Melinda's side. Her boots slipped out from under her and the cobwebbed ceiling suddenly came into view. The thick straw on the concrete floor thankfully cushioned her fall, but something squishy and stinky was soon plastered to the rear of her jeans.

And then, the barn broke out into a bedlam of bleats and snorts and shouts. Melinda felt a hefty weight on her chest and wool rubbing against her shirt. A flash of pain shot up her left arm, but she pulled it across her face and tried to curl into a ball. Hooves seemed to be everywhere. She yelped as one hit her knee and another shoved her in the stomach.

"I got these cornered!" The shout came from far away, maybe from Carter. "Did they trample her?"

"She's hurt, I don't know how bad." That was Karen. "Roger, get the first-aid kit out of my box. Melinda, don't move!"

"I don't think I can. Hurts too much." She was gasping for air and from the pain. "They got away from me. I tried to stop them and …"

"Hold still." Karen pressed along Melinda's leg and finally sighed with relief. "Good, nothing's broken. Thank God that straw's as thick as it is. You landed at a bad angle, though. Here, we'll get you up."

Roger and Karen helped her to her feet. But her left leg was too painful to put much weight on, and she only made it as far as the wooden crate in the aisle.

"She … she sucker-punched me! Plowed right over me … like I wasn't even there."

"She just missed your head, as did her friends." Karen pulled out some antiseptic and began to dab at a nasty scrape on Melinda's forearm. "Can you move your wrist, and your hand?"

"Yes," Melinda managed to say through gritted teeth.

"It's already swelling up." Roger shook his head. "Between that, and your leg … honey, we better get you over to the clinic in Swanton. Have it all checked out, just in case."

"You'll have some nasty bruises." Karen ripped open a large bandage and reached for the adhesive tape. "But as long as this cut doesn't get infected, you'll pull through in a few days. You're very, very lucky."

"I think we're going to need these." Ed appeared with Horace's three rope halters draped over his arm. "They're too spooked to follow a bucket of corn."

"Give me a minute and I can watch the gate, at least." Melinda struggled to her feet.

"Don't worry about it." Carter handed Melinda her trampled hat. She felt as torn and rumpled as it looked. "We'll take it from here. Before you go ... what did you want to do with the fleece? I can take it off your hands if you like, give you a fair price for it."

Melinda knew the fleece wouldn't bring much, especially since she only had a dozen adult sheep. Besides, she had a special project in mind, if she could pull it off. "Just bag it up and set it there by the stairs, thanks."

"Are you sure?" Ed asked gently. "You'll have to haul it over to the Eagle River auction barn to sell it. Auggie doesn't take fleece at the co-op."

Roger started to laugh. "Diane and Melinda have a plan. See, Diane loves to knit, and they want to find someone to clean the wool and spin it, and Diane will recycle it into scarves and throws and such."

Carter grinned. "Actually, I might know someone who'd help you with that." He nodded at the surprise on Roger and Ed's faces. "It's a going thing these days, processing wool by hand. And I hear knitting is very relaxing. Might give it a go myself, this winter. My wife swears by it."

While everyone tried to picture this hulk of a man rocking by the fire with a skein of yarn in his lap, he shook Melinda's good hand. But this time, he offered a more-gentle grip.

"Thanks for an interesting morning. We'll take the fleece up to the haymow for you, if you'd like. If you're as banged-up as you look, you'll have a hard enough time getting yourself up the stairs for a few days."

* 9 *

The woman Melinda saw in the mirror the next morning looked like she'd been on the wrong end of a fist fight, which wasn't too far off the mark. Adult ewes could easily reach one-hundred-and-eighty pounds, which meant Melinda's foe had out-classed her in weight and maybe also adrenaline.

Hobo stuck to her side when she hobbled out to do chores, forgoing his usual race around the yard to keep Melinda in his sights. It seemed like she'd never make it to the barn. When she did, she leaned against its weathered boards for a moment, and tried to focus her feelings before opening the door.

She couldn't be afraid of her sheep. If she let that happen, she might as well haul them off to the Eagle River auction barn. It had been a simple accident, brought on by all the commotion and strangers' voices and maybe even the heat. Her physical pains would eventually heal. But if she didn't get them in check, the emotional scars could become permanent.

Her right side wasn't so bad, but her left was a mess. That arm was too sore and bruised to be very useful today. The dressing that protected the deep gash was covered by her long-sleeve tee shirt, which was uncomfortably close on such a humid morning. Sweats stood in for her still-filthy chore jeans, as the heavy denim was too restrictive on her battered-and-bruised left leg.

The squeak of the barn door's hinges brought a chorus of "baaaas" from the sheep, and her sore stomach flipped over once, then twice, as their hooves pounded toward the aisle fence. But she couldn't dwell on those thoughts for long, as it was going to take a serious one-handed effort to pry the lids off the grain barrels.

For the sheep, it was as if yesterday had never happened. Their pasture access had been reopened once the shearing was done. The barn was quiet again, and their meals were arriving on schedule. She saw nothing but trust and expectation in their dark eyes as they gathered at the troughs. And they were so much more comfortable without those heavy fleeces.

"You all look so easy-breezy! But now, I can really see how many of you girls have been hitting the snacks a little hard."

Annie put her front hooves on the feed bunk and leaned over the wooden fence for a pet. Melinda rubbed the ewe's forehead, and her heartbeat began to slow. "I'm sorry about yesterday," she whispered. "All those people, Annie, trying to tell you what to do. But they're gone, so hopefully you all can relax."

Melinda wanted to get in with the sheep again, and prove to herself she could walk among them without fear. But that wouldn't happen today. She could hardly limp around, and would probably lose her footing in the thick straw before any ewe had a chance to knock her over.

It took a long series of halting movements to break off enough slabs from the hay bale waiting in the aisle, but she finally got it done. Thanks to Horace and Wilbur's old automatic waterer, she didn't have to haul buckets from the hydrant.

Sunny and Stormy were now at her feet, rubbing against her sweatpants and wanting their breakfast, too. She longed to sit down, hold them in her lap for a few minutes, but she had to keep moving. At this slower speed, she would probably be late for work even though she'd forced herself to rise earlier than usual. The chickens still needed to be looked after, and then she had to get herself presentable enough for Prosper Hardware.

The coffee guys' conversation died away when they noticed Melinda's wavy brown hair was down around her ears, rather than in its usual low ponytail. She'd also applied a full face of makeup to balance the layers of concealer and foundation spread over those scratches and bruises.

Auggie, as usual, was the first to comment. "You got a lunch date or something? You're all spiffed up."

"Oh, I doubt that." Jerry shook his head. "Not if she's wearing those baggy old jog pants." His brow furrowed. "Kinda hot for long sleeves, don't you think?"

"Good morning to all of you as well." She thumped her purse on the counter and leaned against the oak cabinet for a moment to lift some of the pressure off her left leg. Prosper Hardware had never seemed so big; she was almost sweating from the effort it took to drag herself in from the back lot. She should have parked out front.

"I had a run-in with one of the ewes yesterday, when the shearing crew was there. Or actually, a run-in with several of them. One jumped me, and then her friends joined in."

Doc whistled. "Where'd they get you?

"My stomach, my left arm and knee, my face." She gently tapped her cheek, hoping the generous layer of powder would stay put for most of the day. "But I think the facial bruising came when I hit the floor."

Uncle Frank disappeared into one aisle and returned with a stack of towels from the store's modest selection of housewares. "Here, use these for pillows in my fancy behind-the-counter chair, and stay off your feet. There's crates in the back, Bill can make you a footrest."

"Thanks. Can you take my lunch up to the fridge and grab the ice packs? I forgot mine at home."

George hurried over with a cup of coffee and the entire cannister of creamer. "Here, take as much as you like."

Jerry went for the watering can, which was tucked into a corner next to the ladder needed to reach the light poles out front. "I'll do the flower baskets. Looks like they could use a drink. How is your garden doing?"

Melinda's shoulders dropped. "Probably dying as we speak. I should have asked Dad to run around with the hose before he went home yesterday. But by the time we got back from the clinic and he got me settled on the couch, I'd forgotten all about my poor plants. And I won't be able to water things for a few days."

"Might get a shower tonight." Auggie sounded surprisingly hopeful. "Anything else you need?"

"Well, since you asked ... I promised Angie I'd hand-deliver some invites to the women's luncheon at our neighborhood church. It's coming up in three weeks, so it can't wait. What are you doing the next few nights?"

"Oh, sorry, I'm booked." Auggie's horrified expression made her laugh for the first time since yesterday.

"Could Angie take them around herself?" Frank came back with the ice packs. "I'm sure she wouldn't mind."

"Angie's about to pop," Auggie said quickly. "That baby boy's going to be here in just a few weeks. And she's been really miserable in this heat."

All the men stared at him. Melinda was also in awe. Auggie's grasp of gossip reached further than she thought.

"What?" He crossed his arms. "Nathan came into the co-op yesterday. Got it right from the source."

Melinda's aches and pains were much improved by late afternoon, helped along by ibuprofen, ice and get-better-fast wishes from customers. But she needed to take it easy that night, a sudden shift in gears that was going to be hard for someone so accustomed to handling things on her own.

Her parents came by to water the garden, and brought a takeout pizza for supper. Diane ignored her daughter's protests and insisted on doing a load of laundry, as the washer and dryer were down in the basement. Roger caught up the dishes and made a pass through the strawberry patch. He was going to put the ripe fruits in the freezer, but Melinda insisted her parents take most of them home as payment.

Chase had texted several times since yesterday, worrying about her and wondering how she was doing, but Melinda had gently dismissed his offers to come down and "take care of things." It was nearly an hour's drive, she reminded him, and her parents were already picking up the slack. She'd be mostly back to normal by the weekend, and promised to see him then.

The next evening, with her mobility and spirits slowly improving, she stared into her closet. What should she wear to deliver these invitations?

The wedding-themed luncheon would be a surprisingly elegant affair, based on the stack of sleek envelopes Angie dropped off last weekend, and Melinda's usual farm clothes didn't seem the right fit for this errand. Besides, her knee was still swollen and, while her bruises were less hurtful, they were more colorful. Thank goodness the scratches didn't extend all the way down her calves. She finally reached for a floral skirt that landed just below the knee, and a lightweight cream-colored blouse with long sleeves. She couldn't easily reach down to paint her toenails, but a pair of flats would cover her rough, dry feet.

Melinda was a bit nervous as she redid her makeup and tried to smooth her hair. This wasn't just about helping Angie with the luncheon. It was a chance to meet more of this rural neighborhood's residents. Her path was carefully planned, the invites shuffled so she could cover the stops to the north tonight, then head south tomorrow evening.

Sunny and Stormy were lounging on the picnic table when she started for the car, her best purse over one arm and a thick stack of envelopes in her other hand. Eyes wide with surprise, the cats sniffed her elegant clothes when she paused to say hello.

"Don't recognize me? I hardly do, either. But boys, remember this: you don't make social calls in chore gear."

Melinda had washed her car over the weekend in advance of this errand, even though it was impossible to keep vehicles spotless on these gravel roads. The dust build-up wasn't too thick yet, at least, and she took it easy as she made her way down the drive and turned to the north. She caught a glimpse of the young eagles as they winged from one treetop to another along the creek. They were still small enough, and their feathers were such a drab brown, that they could be easily mistaken for hawks at a distance.

She turned west at the crossroads, instead of east toward Angie and Nathan's, and felt like she was setting off on an adventure.

"I really need to get out more. Haven't I been saying for the past year that I want to meet more of my neighbors? I don't think I've ever been down this road, and it's barely a mile from home."

Brambles filled with wild roses, Iowa's state flower, dotted the roadside. They were accompanied by clusters of coneflowers, whose electric-purple petals were easy to spot in the thick grasses and weeds. Goldfinches and sparrows flitted about, their evening perches occasionally overtaken by bossy blue jays and red-winged blackbirds in an endless round of musical chairs. Clumps of orange lilies lined one field drive, a hint of the homestead that once stood there. Even when houses and their outbuildings were abandoned, and the lawns plowed under and planted to crops, these hardy perennials often continued to flourish along the lanes.

Melinda's first stop, unfortunately, didn't hold much promise for meeting anyone new. No vehicles were in the yard, and her knock at the home's front entrance went unanswered. Except for a band of mosquitos that followed her everywhere, no one was around. She dropped the invite between the storm door and the front door, and moved on.

At the next farm, a kind-faced older woman came out of the barn. Her brown eyes glowed with excitement when she saw the invitation. "Oh, it's that time of year again! I love this luncheon, and the program is always so interesting. I don't get many chances to dress up, you know."

She stared at Melinda's elegant blouse and wrinkled her brow. "So ... you say you live around here?"

"I do, just through the mile." Melinda felt as foolish as she probably looked. Her neighbor was wearing a faded blue tee shirt, cut-off shorts and dusty sneakers.

A black-and-white dog ambled over to them and barked, then nosed Melinda's cream-colored flats.

"Reggie, stop that! This lady's dressed so nice." There was a note of suppressed humor in the woman's voice. "She doesn't want your muddy snout sniffing all over."

"Oh, don't worry. I have a dog; I know how they can be. And I'm not normally dressed like this. I bought Horace and Wilbur Schermann's place, just southeast of here."

"So you're the one that came down from the city? Glad to have you in the neighborhood." Her smile broadened.

"You know, I don't recall Horace and Wilbur having any cats." She pointed to a trio of orange-tabby youngsters sizing up their visitor from the edge of the concrete patio. "If you're an animal lover, maybe you'd like to have a kitten, or even two, or ..."

"Oh, I'm all set." Melinda held up a hand as if she were full. "But thanks for asking."

"I think Reggie just made a deposit there along the drive," the woman called after Melinda as she started toward the car. "Watch out! I'd hate for those pretty shoes to get ruined."

Melinda shuffled away as fast as her sore knee would allow, because Reggie and the kittens were determined to see her off and the woman was trying to corral them with her arms. Once she was back to the road, Melinda memorized the name on the mailbox. This woman needed to be made aware of Karen's monthly spay clinic, and fast.

Invitations were dropped behind three more screen doors, and Melinda started to wish the envelopes had just gone out through the mail. How could she meet more of her neighbors if nobody was home?

One farm looked promising, with a light on in the house and a truck parked by the garage, but the size and apparent strength of the family's overly protective dog kept her in the car. She was in no shape to start a foot race with an angry canine. That envelope would have to get a stamp. But then she met two more friendly women, and one man who promised he'd pass the invite to his wife. And at one house down the road from Angie and Nathan's, Melinda discovered someone yearning for adult conversation.

Four shrieking children and two boisterous dogs darted back and forth across the yard. The young mom looked like she might cry with joy when Melinda handed her the envelope.

"Oh, I would love to come! We just moved in, everything's been so crazy. If I can get away, I'll be there for sure. Do I need to bring anything?"

"Oh, no, everything's provided. It's just a way for women in the township to get together. All you have to do is show up."

"I don't know what I'd wear." The younger woman glanced at Melinda's skirt and self-consciously brushed her hands over her paint-splattered tank top.

"Don't worry about it. Just come if you can." Melinda pointed over her shoulder. "Angie Hensley, one of the organizers, lives right around the corner. She has two young girls, and a boy on the way." The woman's face lit up. "Her number's inside there, for the reservations. We'd love to have you!"

Melinda's skirt was now wrinkled from too many trips in and out of the car, but she didn't care. If anything, her slightly rumpled appearance might make her more approachable. Besides, she only had one more stop to make. Tomorrow night, she'd do things differently.

The light was starting to dim, as sunset was coming on and a line of heavy clouds was advancing from the west. When she neared the driveway, she stopped on the gravel shoulder and checked the invitation again.

"Is this really right? I guess so; there's the last name on the box. Someone must actually live here."

The rusty mailbox listed to the side, as if it had never recovered from a run-in with the county snow plow. The lawn was rough and shaggy, and forgotten lumps of machinery crouched under several of the trees.

This had to be the oldest house she'd ever seen, with a second story that hinted at a dangerously steep stairwell and not enough headroom. The windows were narrow and unfriendly, even though they glowed with light, and the chipped clapboard siding was the color of mud. A rusted-out truck leaned against what was left of an oak tree. A vicious gash sliced through the ancient wood, the kind left by a long-ago lightning strike.

Melinda rolled to a stop at what felt like a safe distance from the house, then anxiously scanned the yard for the snarling dog she assumed would live at a place like this. When nothing emerged from the gathering shadows, she finally found the courage to get out of the car.

Clutching her purse close, a defensive habit from years of walking in downtown Minneapolis at night, she shuffled up the cracked sidewalk. She flinched when a faded plastic whirly-gig, jammed into a weed-choked former flowerbed, screeched to life in a sudden gust of humid air.

"Whaddya want?"

A stooped-over old man, too thin and with watery blue eyes, shoved open the rusted screen door. His sudden snarl almost caused the cigarette to fall from his mouth.

"I'm ... I'm here to see ..." Melinda glanced at the invitation, trying to get her bearings. How did he get to the door so fast? He must have been watching her the entire time.

"Marjorie? Yes, Marjorie. Is ... is she home?"

"Hah." A snake tattoo glared over the neck of his dingy shirt when he turned his back. "Marge! Some girl here to see you." The way he said "girl" made Melinda step back. "And I just bet she's selling something."

"I'm not ..."

"What's all this fuss about?"

Marge was as stooped and shriveled as her husband, although much heavier. Her faded top was frayed at the hem. "What's that thing?" She narrowed her eyes at the envelope.

Melinda squared her shoulders. The sooner she got this over with, the sooner she could leave.

"Marge, hello, I'm Melinda, I live north of you, on the old Schermann place."

"The what?" She squinted and turned her head, as if hard of hearing.

"The Schermann farm." Melinda spoke slower and louder. "Horace and Wilbur? I'm the new ..."

"She's that city woman. Up by the creek." The old man made a disgusted face. "Dammit Marge, don't you remember nothin'? You went to school with the Schermanns, for God's sake!"

Marge's confused expression didn't change, but a sudden chill ran down Melinda's spine.

No, it couldn't be.

Not right here, less than two miles from Horace's home. Melinda looked again at Marge, at her brown eyes and white hair. Surely, she was too young to be Maggie. But Marge was so beaten by life and, Melinda hated to think of it, maybe by the man hovering over her, that it was impossible to tell how old she might be.

Melinda shoved the invitation into Marge's hand, desperate to escape. "There's a women's luncheon at the church, two weeks from Sunday. There's going to be a fashion show of wedding gowns and ..."

It all seemed so ridiculous now, she couldn't get the rest of the words out.

"Got no use for church," Marge muttered. "I know the one you mean, south of here. Won't set foot in there. Mama used to make me go. And wedding dresses are a damn waste of money. I borrowed mine from my sister."

She finally noticed Melinda's blouse and skirt, and her lip curled into a sneer. "You wear *that* to milk the cows?"

"She don't have no damn cows!"

The way this man scowled at his wife made the bruises on Melinda's arm throb. "Just those sheep. Horace and Wilbur ain't milked for years, don't you remember?"

Melinda shuffled her feet, nearly tripping on the warped sidewalk as she started to back away. "Well, we understand if people have ... conflicts that keep them from attending. Nice to meet you."

She didn't breathe again until she was back to the road. A sharp gust smacked the car's bumper as she turned east, and the ditch grasses bent away from the wind. At the crossroads she shifted into park, then sat there for several minutes in the gathering darkness, trying to collect her thoughts as her hands trembled against the steering wheel and the sweat dripped down her neck.

Marjorie, Marge, Maggie ... The name might fit, but Maggie would be ninety by now. Marge may have attended school with the Schermanns, but she had to be closer in age to Ada, or at least Edith. So if Marge wasn't Maggie, why did it matter?

Melinda had assumed that Maggie, if she were still alive, would simply be an older version of the laughing, carefree girl in the photo. A gentle great-grandmother, an educated woman who'd enjoyed a meaningful teaching career and a happy marriage to someone who just happened to not be Horace.

But what if she wasn't? What if she was a bitter, hard-hearted woman whose life had been filled with sorrow and disappointment?

That woman back there hadn't always been so rough and haggard. She'd surely been a hopeful girl once, too. But then life dealt her a tough hand, and she'd folded under it.

Something had happened to Maggie, too, something so shameful that Anna had sent her away. Whatever it was, it could have changed the course of Maggie's life forever. Maggie may not have become the woman Melinda hoped her to be.

Maybe Horace wouldn't want anything to do with her. Or worse, maybe she would hurt him all over again.

* * *

This was the first time, and surely the last time, that Melinda would take fashion advice from the guys at Prosper Hardware. She started out the following evening in a worn green tee shirt, a messy ponytail and a makeup-free face. Her left knee still wasn't quite ready for jeans, so a pair of old knit shorts would have to do.

The men had quietly listened to her rundown of the previous night's escapades, which carefully excluded any mention of Horace. But the moment she was through, they were quick with advice.

"There's your street cred, right there." Auggie had pointed at her arm as the other guys nodded. The bruises were finally starting to fade. "Or should I say, your 'gravel cred.'"

"Nothing will cement your place in the neighborhood faster than a run-in with livestock." Doc had raised his mug in salute. "You just show off those scars and laugh about them, and you'll be in for sure. And leave your little hatchback at home. Take that beater truck out for a spin instead." Horace had given Melinda his old pickup and, after a few lessons from Ed and a decision to name the truck Lizzie, she indeed felt like a real farmer when she was behind the wheel.

A quick consultation with Mabel confirmed everything the men suggested. And she also answered Melinda's carefully worded questions about the strange elderly couple in the rundown house.

The Wildwoods were only in their early eighties. Marge's rudeness mostly came from her memory problems, but Bart had always been difficult and liked the bottle too much. Their children had tried for years to get them into a nursing home, or at least into town. But they stubbornly refused all offers of assistance or support, including several efforts made by the women's group at the neighborhood church.

Taking Lizzie out on this errand was the right approach, Melinda had to admit as she pulled on the machine shed's rolling door. Its screeches of protest were a reminder she needed to get on a ladder and oil the metal track's bearings before they turned so dry the door wouldn't open at all.

"Thank goodness I can count on you." Melinda gave Lizzie's worn dashboard a pat when the engine grumbled to life. "Let's get these envelopes delivered, huh?"

The air conditioning barely worked, and the radio dial hardly turned. But as Melinda rolled down the gravel, she felt more like her real self than she had last night.

When had that changed? In Minneapolis, she'd never left for work or a night out with friends without carefully applying her makeup and selecting just the right outfit. She'd loved to shop, and felt that thrill when she found the perfect handbag or a pair of must-have shoes. But while she loved fashion, she loved a bargain just as much. And during her downtime, she'd always stayed in knits and sweats.

Maybe she hadn't really changed much in the past year. Instead, she had just allowed herself to be who she really was.

Lizzie chugged south toward the church, which was the northern boundary for tonight's deliveries. It was a fine evening for a drive. But as Melinda slowed for the crossroads leading to the Wildwoods' place, a weight settled in her stomach. She had to call Ada; it couldn't wait. And not just to ask about including Anna's wedding dress in the fashion show. She had to warn Ada about Marge.

Not who Marge might be, thank goodness, but the possibility she represented. Of course, it was an outcome Ada may have already considered, one of the reasons she was so cautious about how and when they told Horace what was going on behind his back.

Melinda had been so excited when the letters were discovered. How thrilling it would be to reunite Horace with his lost love! But now, she was only discouraged and sad.

And it wasn't just the dead-ends she'd met in her search, but the sense that somehow, Horace had let someone special slip through his hands. It would be different if he had later fallen in love with someone else and started a family. Then, it would be easy to say Maggie was just a stop along the way, and it wasn't meant to be. But that hadn't happened, and she wasn't sure why.

Instead, Horace went on alone. Wilbur had done the same, though his story was a little different.

Ada said one girlfriend jilted him while he was overseas in World War II, and was married to another man by the time he came home. Edith had hinted Wilbur found plenty of female companionship in his younger days, but none of those dalliances ever materialized into matrimony. Why?

Melinda suspected neither Horace nor Wilbur made some dramatic decision to never marry. More likely, a week went by, and then a month, and a year ...

"And then one day, you look up and wonder where the time has gone." She shook her head as she passed the church, where generations of Schermanns rested in the cemetery. "Change is hard. It's too easy to stick with what you know."

Melinda thought about that for a moment. The older she became, the faster time seemed to fly. "I like my life, but maybe I won't always prefer to be single. I have to find the courage to take that chance."

She was very attracted to Chase, and enjoyed spending time with him. The thought of seeing him tomorrow night made her smile, a simpering grin she tried to wipe away, but couldn't. But a part of her was so independent, so hesitant to really open her heart again.

Between a broken engagement a few years ago and her demanding career in Minneapolis, Melinda had found it easier to date casually or not at all. And then, she'd spent the past year rebuilding her life from the bottom up. Now that she'd adjusted to so many significant changes, Melinda was faced with the daunting task of figuring out what she really wanted her life to be like.

She was forty now, and life had brought so many hard lessons along with its joys. Motherhood might never happen for her, but that didn't mean she had to be alone. But if she were going to be alone, it had to be by choice, not because she was too afraid to try.

At the very least, she needed to keep an open mind about who, and what, might come her way.

It was kind of like navigating this maze of gravel roads, she decided as she turned west toward her first stop. She had a vague idea where she was going, but didn't exactly know what she'd find when she got there.

"Wow, this looks interesting." She checked the nameplate on the forest-green mailbox, which stood tall and proud on a weather-proof post and was surrounded by cheerful purple petunias. "That has to be the fanciest farmhouse I've ever seen."

The home was smothered in scrollwork brackets and countless windows, and scalloped wooden siding highlighted its peaks. The design was a combination of Victorian and Queen Anne, and its proud builder had clearly taken only the best elements of both. Signs of renovation were everywhere, from the fresh lavender paint on the front of the house to the sparkle of the second floor's new windows. Even the attic level was impressive. The sharply angled roof was frosted with dormers, and a grand turret pointed skyward from one corner.

A middle-aged man looked up from a makeshift work bench, which was two sawhorses balanced by a sheet of plywood. Lengths of lumber were stacked at his feet. He gave a friendly wave in Melinda's direction, then called to the woman pulling weeds along a weathered picket garden fence.

Melinda returned his wave and smiled as she cut the engine. "At least tonight, I'm dressed for the occasion."

Two chocolate labs, one considerably older than the other, darted around the corner of the barn and began to bark. Melinda had considered bringing Hobo along, as he loved to ride in Lizzie and would have made a wonderful icebreaker, but so many people had dogs of their own. These two looked friendly, but she'd been smart not to risk trouble.

"Hello there!" The woman brushed her gray bangs out of her eyes. A long braid hung down her back. "Can we help you with something? Are you lost?"

Given the storm of emotions she'd experienced on the drive over, Melinda had to laugh.

"Well, I hope not. I'm Melinda Foster, I bought the Schermann place a while back. I'm here about the women's luncheon at First Lutheran. It's coming up in a few weeks, and I hope you can join us."

"Oh, I'm so glad they're having that again this year!" The woman's green eyes lit up with excitement. "It's a great way for everyone to get together."

"And she does mean *everyone*." The man rubbed his short gray beard and reached for another length of lumber. "The Lutherans, the Methodists, even us Catholics ..."

The woman swatted her husband with the pair of worn work gloves in her hand. "Don't mind him, he's full of it. Oh dear, what happened to your arm? That's a nasty bruise you've got there."

Melinda explained and, just as the coffee group guys had promised, the man and woman burst into knowing laughter.

"That's why we don't have anything around here bigger than a goat," he said. "When I played football in high school, getting tackled was nothing. But that was over twenty years ago."

"Closer to forty." The woman cut her eyes at her husband.

"Well, she doesn't know me. Figured it was worth a shot." The man pushed back his sawdust-coated cap and offered his hand. "You've taken our title from us, then. Until you came along, we were the crazy city slickers trying to find bliss in the country."

"Sorry we haven't been by to say hello," the woman chimed in. "But as you can see, we've got too many irons in the fire."

Adelaide and Mason Beaufort met in Madison, Wisconsin during their college days, and remained in the area until they took early-retirement buyouts a few years ago. Mason had grown up west of Swanton, and they'd decided to retreat to a fixer-upper somewhere in northern Iowa. When this once-grand house came on the market, they snatched it up.

"Our kids and friends thought we were nuts." Adelaide pocketed the invitation. "They were probably right."

"We love it, though." Mason beamed as he gestured around the yard. "Just look at that house. The craftsmanship! Renovations have taken longer than we thought, of course. But we've got a little of everything out here: a garden, our dogs and cats, a few chickens, some bees and ..."

"Hey, goats!" Adelaide suddenly shouted. "Get off that truck!"

Melinda turned to find two brown-and-white goats tap-dancing across Lizzie's hood, their thick hooves making a terrible racket. Apparently she'd parked too close to a wide tree stump, which was all the boost the critters needed.

Instead of meekly obeying Adelaide, the smaller goat let out a stubborn bellow.

"Oh, those goats." Mason sighed. "I think they need to stay in the pasture with the pig. They're into everything, the minute she lets them roam. And they don't know the difference between weeds and flowers, of course."

"So ... you said you have a pig?" Melinda reached for conversation as they watched Adelaide return with two rope halters. It was clear she'd handled such a situation before.

"Well, yeah, sort of." Mason swatted away a lightning bug. "I mean, he's the potbellied kind. A rescue pig. The goats are, too. Our neighbor had these goats, but they're so poorly mannered that they were going to end up at the sale barn. Adelaide insisted we take them."

Melinda took in the patch of native plants and flowers just beyond the garden, and the line of beehives along the back fence. A cheerful orange rain barrel sat proudly on its platform by one corner of the majestic house. This place was a homesteader's dream! And the chickens ... not only were their feathers awash in unusual patterns and colors, but their coop was unique, too.

"What is that ... that framed thing your chickens are in?"

"It's a chicken tractor," Mason said proudly, eager to explain the contraption to a new pair of ears.

"Built it myself. We only use it in good weather, they've got a regular coop over there by the barn. See, we roll this thing around, let the birds forage in a new space every day. There's that covered part, at the front of the A-frame, where they can get out of the weather. The mesh is small enough to keep out all the predators lurking around these days."

Mason was suddenly silent, as if considering something. "You know, um ... owls and such."

He looked away quickly, and Melinda understood. Maybe Ed's secret wasn't as secret as he thought.

"Oh, yes, those owls."

She nodded in sympathy. "They're everywhere this year. Gotta keep an eye out for those."

Melinda visited with the Beauforts for a solid half hour, mesmerized by their wide-ranging projects and plans to improve their acreage.

Adelaide was making cheese from the goats' milk, and the couple hoped to add solar panels to the roof of their barn. The house was too historical for such an idea, but they were excited to harness the sun's power and shrink their carbon footprint.

Even better, Adelaide was involved with a knitting group in Swanton, and encouraged Melinda to pass their meetings' details on to Diane.

The rest of the route passed smoothly and quickly. Not everyone was home, but Melinda dropped envelopes behind screen doors and greeted new faces with a rising spirit and a grateful heart.

Her trips around the township proved that no two farms were alike, and the same could be said for its residents. But the people who lived in this area were all connected, to the land and to each other. She cranked the radio as she rounded the last mile section, and soon reached the road that would lead her home.

Just as she rolled through the last crossroads, she spotted a motionless lump on the gravel's shoulder. It might be a raccoon, or even a possum, but it was clearly a recent casualty. If it had been there even a few hours ago, she would have remembered it for sure.

Far ahead, past her lane, the creek bridge's metal rails gleamed in the glow from the setting sun. Shadows were already gathering under the trees lining the waterway.

Melinda glanced in her rearview mirror. How clean was the truck's bed? It wasn't, not at all. Maybe she should ...

Then she shook her head and stepped on the gas. "I may be a country girl these days, but I'm not *that* tough. I'll call Ed when I get home."

* 10 *

Jerry burst through Prosper Hardware's front door, layers of fabric draped over one arm. "OK, everybody, I need your honest opinion."

"You've come to the right place, then." Auggie took one peanut-butter cookie off the tray Doc handed him and then, with barely any hesitation, grabbed another.

The coffee-group treats rotation had never taken hold, but snacks still appeared a few mornings each week. Cookies, like the ones George's wife baked last night, were commonplace, as were muffins and an occasional quick bread. Melinda had expected to find a test pie here and there, as the competition was coming up in just a few days, but none ever appeared. Jerry and Auggie had become strangely secretive, a sure sign a serious grudge match was brewing.

"So, I have two Prosper polos to my name." Jerry carefully draped both shirts over the counter's edge, pushing aside the metal basket of pens to make room. "One white, one purple. You all know that TV crew will be here to shoot our parade on the Fourth, and I gotta look ... well, like the person in charge."

"Isn't that Nancy?" Auggie snickered. Doc joined in.

Jerry crossed his arms. "I'm serious. This is important."

He suddenly brightened and turned to Melinda. "Hey, there's an idea! Why don't we let Nancy go on camera, do the, well, that on-the-corner thing?"

"The spot interview? Nope, sorry, you're our top elected official. It has to be you."

"Fine, then, I'll do it."

Melinda raised her eyebrows. They'd worked this out weeks ago; it was no longer up for debate.

She was proud of her efforts to get the Mason City station locked down for not only parade footage, but a brief conversation with Jerry to highlight Prosper's business district and community spirit. Writing Jerry's talking points had been easy; getting him comfortable enough to deliver them in a conversational tone was proving to be a challenge.

Jerry picked up the white polo and held it over his faded tee shirt. "All the more reason why I have to look the part. Now, this white one is really summery, cool and fresh."

"Until you spill on it," Doc reminded him. "The parade's at ten, but I know you love to hit the pancake breakfast first thing in the morning. Syrup and greasy sausage and a white shirt? A bad combination."

Jerry's shoulders sagged. "Well, what about the purple, then?"

"Much better." George pointed at him with a half-eaten cookie. "Dark colors are more slimming."

"And your hair's getting grayer all the time," Auggie said. "That white will just wash you out."

Uncle Frank arrived as Jerry was holding up the purple polo. "Still trying to decide, huh? What hat are you going to wear?"

"A city one, of course!" Doc said quickly.

"No hat!" Melinda jumped in. "Too casual."

"What about a school cap?" Auggie leaned forward. "It'd be good branding to have one apparel item for each."

Jerry tossed the purple polo on the counter. "I'd rather be weeding my peppers and beans than trying to sort this out." He was a Master Gardener, and his yard was his escape from the dramas of small-town public service.

"And it's not just what I'm going to wear. I have to figure out what to put on the signs for my car." Jerry's brother had a vintage convertible that was the perfect ride for the Fourth of July parade.

George shrugged. "Won't last year's work? Nothing's changed."

"But it's about to." Frank shook his head as he filled his coffee mug. "Word is, Jake's made up his mind to take a run at the mayor post. It's not just talk anymore. He's going to be in the parade, too, and launch his campaign during the festival."

"So what?" George swatted it all away. "Jake's a jerk, he doesn't have the diplomacy to run this town. And it's still four months until the election. Jerry, don't worry about Jake. Why stir up a hornets' nest until you absolutely have to?"

"Because the hornet is getting ready to sting." Auggie's brown eyes narrowed. "Jerry, you need to get ready. Pick the purple shirt, and work on your platform."

Jake Newcastle was in his thirties but already in his second term on the council. He was also the physical education instructor at the local high school, over in Swanton, and well known in Prosper, but not always for the best reasons. Jake loved to stir up controversy, and his antics were often the unintended highlight of little Prosper's council meetings. Jerry tolerated Jake's obnoxious behavior as a bit of local theater, but now saw that bluster in a different light. This was Jerry's first term as mayor and, as the only person on the ballot, it had been an easy race. The coming election was shaping up to be much different.

"My platform," he sighed. "And what is that going to be?"

"I'd help you out," Frank told his friend, "but I didn't have one, either."

Uncle Frank joined the council last November, filling a vacancy created when a member passed away. No one requested to be on the ballot and, with his role reduced at Prosper Hardware and Miriam begging him to find something to do, Frank had thrown his hat in the ring.

"Keep your signs," Melinda suggested to Jerry. "You've only got a few days until the festival, anyway. If anyone asks you about Jake, just steer the conversation toward the great things you've done for the community, or your willingness to bring people together. The rest can wait. Is this really much of a fight, anyway? I mean, this town respects you. I don't think most would say the same about Jake."

Doc, who used to serve on the council, seemed more concerned.

"Some people like Jake's attitude, they say he's refreshing. It's how he weaseled his way on to the council in the first place. And now he's got a massive ego; he thinks he's got all the answers and can run the show. Don't let him. Play fair, and you'll come out on top."

"OK." Jerry finally nodded. "I'll let things slide. For now." He looked hopefully at Melinda. "But when the election gets closer, will you help me figure this campaign stuff out?"

"Absolutely. One thing at a time."

With Vicki chairing this year's festival committee and the final details wrapped up yesterday, Melinda could now focus on prepping Prosper Hardware for the holiday. The Fourth of July was one of the store's busiest days of the year, as the tiny community's slate of activities drew thousands of visitors from around the region.

The store would stay open later than usual on the Fourth, not closing until just before the fireworks display. Even with Diane and Roger's help, Melinda would be on the run from the moment she arrived that morning. But she'd promised Vicki and Nancy to duck out long enough to help with the pie contest, which the Methodist church had thankfully offered to host in their air-conditioned community room.

Miriam had increased the store's shipments of several necessities to make sure Prosper Hardware was ready for the swell of holiday shoppers. Extra bottled water, pop, snacks, sunscreen and bug spray waited in the storage room. Last year's handheld flags, with the store's logo etched on their wooden sticks, were such a hit that Melinda had doubled her order. Extra boxes of Prosper Hardware caps and tee shirts waited in the upstairs office.

But while the shelves were mostly stocked for the celebration, the store itself needed work. The hardwood floors should be polished, and the aisles' end-cap displays rearranged. If there was time, Melinda wanted to wash the two plate-glass windows and hang patriotic streamers from their corners. Esther would be in that afternoon to help, but there was still so much to get done in just a few days.

Uncle Frank spoke at just the right time.

"Melinda, I know I can't rework the displays, but I can sit there behind the register for a few hours. That is, if you need the help." His eager tone said he hoped she did. "My project across the street is winding down, and Bill's already got the parade signs dug out for my truck. My favorite lawn chair's clean and ready to go, so I'm all set."

Frank had taken on a volunteer position with the city last winter, sorting the papers and documents stuffed in city hall's upstairs storage space. Important records were being converted to digital files, and several boxes of unique finds had already been donated to the library and the county historical society.

"That would be wonderful!" Melinda downed the rest of her coffee in a quick gulp. "It's time to get to work. I'm going to move the Prosper Hardware merchandise display up here by the register and put the caps on sale."

* * *

Melinda started for town earlier than usual the morning of the Fourth. Jerry wasn't the only one eager to enjoy the pancake breakfast, which was held at the Methodist Church, and Diane and Roger were already there, saving her a seat.

As she neared the creek's bridge, Melinda saw a magnificent sight: Both adult eagles soared above the treeline along the creek, their majestic wings lifting and swooping in the warm, humid air.

"This is the perfect day to see them in action! I'm going to take this as a sign the festival is going to run smoothly. As for tonight, well ... we'll have to see what happens."

Chase had to attend a cookout for his family's business that afternoon in Meadville, but promised to get away in time to spend the evening with Melinda. Food vendors were setting up in Prosper's small city park, and a classic-rock cover band would take over the temporary stage at eight. Watching the fireworks together would be romantic, but that probably wouldn't be the end of their evening. Chase had a light workload tomorrow, as he'd mentioned more than once, and wouldn't be expected at the office until late morning. Nothing more needed to be said.

Melinda wasn't one to constantly seek advice on how to run her life, but was grateful for Karen's support as she navigated this new relationship. Karen was kind and honest, as Melinda knew she would be, and told her to go for it.

"If nothing else, it's a summer fling," Karen had said with a wink. "Enjoy it while it lasts. But it sounds like you and Chase might have something special. Who knows where it might lead?"

Susan and Cassie, Melinda's best friends from Minneapolis, were also eager for news about Chase. That made Melinda happy, but also a little wistful. This situation was one more reminder of how her world had changed, and that her old friends were no longer such a large part of her life. They had visited the farm several times in the past year, but their last trip ended with strained goodbyes and hurt feelings. Cassie had cornered Melinda about not giving Chase a chance, and Susan indirectly took Melinda's side with her assertion that the newly divorced Cassie partied too much.

The rift between Melinda and Cassie had blown over ... mostly. Cassie shrugged it all off later, saying she'd been tired and stressed, and that her ex's threats to seek custody of their children now had her spending more nights at home.

Of course, Melinda's announcement that she was dating Chase made Cassie shriek with happiness. But Melinda wasn't sure if Cassie had really let go of her resentment, or merely felt vindicated for her cutting comments about Melinda's personal life. Melinda was still close to Susan, but the thought of running up to the Twin Cities for Cassie's August birthday bash had her searching for excuses to stay home. That made her feel guilty, and ...

She took a deep breath as she reached the county highway and turned toward Prosper. That was a worry for another day.

Chase wasn't exactly something to worry about; she couldn't wait to see him. But everything was moving fast, maybe too fast. Maybe she'd be sorry later. Or maybe ... her heart wasn't all-in enough yet to get hurt if things went wrong.

"Who am I kidding?" Melinda shook her head and smiled as the co-op came into view. "I know exactly where this is going."

* * *

A county sheriff's deputy was already directing traffic, diverting cars away from the parade route and toward Prosper's side streets. Melinda took First, then threaded her way through the congestion over to Oak Street, and reached the back of the store by turning up Third. It wasn't yet seven, but the gravel space behind this block of Main was nearly full of vehicles.

Her parents had been some of the first people through the line at the pancake breakfast. "The lawn chairs are in the car if we get desperate," Roger said as he waved his fork at Melinda. "But the best spot to see the parade is standing under the awning in front of the store."

Diane got up to give her daughter a hug. "Today's one of the biggest days of the year in this little town. We couldn't get down Main, of course, but from what I could see, the flowers are holding up pretty well in this heat."

"Between Jerry and Miriam, they've brow-beaten everyone into keeping their baskets looking lush for the holiday. But if it stays dry, I don't know what's going to happen the rest of the summer."

Miriam and Frank were already at the store when Melinda and her parents arrived. There was a huge rush when the door opened at eight, and Roger sacked purchases so Frank could run the register.

The television crew arrived, and Nancy and Melinda helped them set up on the corner, right in front of the post office. Jerry made it through his interview with only minutes to spare and then, grinning with relief, hopped on a golf cart and zipped over to the elementary school to get in place for the parade.

The hubbub in Prosper Hardware died down as the clock ticked closer to ten, and the store was nearly empty by the time the local veteran's group marched down Main Street to start the procession. As soon as the end of the parade passed by, the store's aisles were once again crowded with shoppers.

Esther arrived just before one, wearing a patriotic tee shirt and sporting red-and-blue earrings. "There's a line already forming in front of the Methodist Church," she told Melinda. "Looks like that pie bake-off is going to be a hit."

"Thanks for coming in a little early. I need to get over there and help Vicki. Dad's keeping the shelves stocked and Mom's at the register. Could you grab some more caps and toss them on the display? They're selling like crazy. I'll be back as soon as I can."

The sun was bright, and the air was stifling. Melinda was sweating by the time she zigzagged through the crowds to reach the church. Just as Esther had said, dozens of people were waiting for the main entrance to open.

Melinda hurried through the side door and found the judges in the kitchen, awaiting their marching orders. The panel included the home economics teacher at the local high school, and the woman who owned the bakery on Swanton's town square. A man Melinda didn't recognize and one woman from the Prosper Library Board were also serving as judges. The last official taste-tester arrived a few minutes later.

"Well, I'm here and hungry," Doc told Melinda as he patted his stomach. "Only had one brat for lunch, but it's for a good cause." The bake-off's proceeds were going toward new computers for the library.

"Vicki says she's cutting the pies into sixteen thin slices each," the home ec teacher said. "Three bucks for one sample, five dollars for two. Do you think people will pay that much?"

"Who knows?" Melinda shrugged. "There's plenty of people out there already, and this doesn't start for twenty minutes yet."

Vicki had the long serving tables covered with patriotic fabric, and numbered cards noted where each pie would be displayed. A cash box waited on another table just inside the door, and a voting station with pads of paper, pens and ballot boxes was ready by the refreshments table. The winner would be announced at the bandstand at four o'clock.

"We've got twenty-one pies!" Vicki rubbed her hands together. "I'd say this is already a success. I'm so glad Jerry talked the church deacons into hosting; I don't know how we would have managed this outside today, in this awful heat. Even so, we'll leave the pies in the refrigerator until the last possible moment."

She patted her purse. "Just so you know, I've got the master list of competitors right here. If I keel over from excitement, you'll know where to find it."

Melinda had enjoyed a pork tenderloin sandwich and part of a funnel cake for lunch, but couldn't take her eyes off the pies that soon marched down the tables. There were pumpkin and apple varieties, of course, but also several variations on berry desserts. A few of the men had gone the extra mile, delivering meringue-crowned rounds that looked blue ribbon-worthy.

The steep price didn't seem to keep anyone away, and the community room's tables were soon filled with eager eaters. Melinda stayed busy at the admission station, where she kept her back to the array of mouthwatering desserts and made change. She saw many people she knew ... and someone who shouldn't be there.

"What are you doing?" she hissed at Auggie. "You promised to stay away! All this drama about keeping the contest on the level, and here you are."

"Gotta see what the competition's up to. Besides, I love pie." He handed her a twenty. "I don't need any change, thanks."

Melinda felt like she was taking a bribe. But then, Auggie wasn't the first person to donate more than the price. "Fine. But you'll have to leave if you can't keep your mouth shut."

He rolled his eyes and reached for a plate. "That's what the pie is for."

* * *

Melinda slipped away from Prosper Hardware again to hear the winners of the pie contest. This time, her mom was able to come along. Main Street's sidewalks were still crowded, but most of the activity was now clustered at the park, where local musicians were taking turns on the stage and a face-painting station was entertaining the children. The softball tournament was still going on at the fields behind the elementary school.

Prosper Hardware wasn't the only business benefiting from the crush of visitors. The Watering Hole, the town's only restaurant, was also packed, and the aroma of French fries drifted out as three more people went inside.

"You have to hand it to little Prosper." Diane shook her head with admiration. "Only two hundred people in this town, yet they continue to host one of the best Fourth of July festivals around. Swanton has a parade and everything, but so many people said they were coming over here instead, at least for part of the day."

"Didn't Grandma and Grandpa Shrader help get this event off the ground?"

"They sure did. There had always been an informal celebration, of course. But my mom and dad were in that group of business owners here in the late forties, after the war. Many of them had young children, so they decided to launch an organized event, including a parade."

Diane pointed as they approached the stage. "There's the guys. Guess they'll get through the suspense together."

Jerry and Auggie stood side by side, hands in pockets, looking uneasy. George was there, too, in a show of support.

Auggie was studying the other men lingering nearby. "I'm just wondering who else was in on it," he told Melinda. "Oh, sure, this is for a good cause and all. But at the end of the day, it's every man for himself."

"There's plenty of prizes to go around," she reminded him.

Vicki had decided early on that while the top two vote-getters would be announced, the actual tally would never be made public. Judges had been secured to not only break a tie, but to choose winners for a few special awards, allowing more of the contestants to take a turn in the spotlight. Vicki might be bursting with big ideas and new to this community, but she knew how to manage people's expectations. Maybe her new business would be a success after all.

She soon came to the microphone, and the buzz of the crowd died away.

"Good afternoon, everyone, thanks for coming out! Isn't this a great day to be in Prosper?" People clapped and whistled in response.

"It's a hot one, but it looks like the rain's going to hold off for tonight. Be sure to stay around for the street dance! And don't forget, there'll be fireworks at dusk. And now, let's find out the winners of our first annual men's pie contest."

Nancy walked across the stage and passed Vicki a large white envelope.

Jerry elbowed Auggie. "May the best baker man win."

"Biggest loser brings doughnuts to the store every day next week."

"Deal."

Before Melinda could ask the guys how such a dishonor would be determined, Nancy took the microphone.

"All the proceeds from this event will benefit technology upgrades for our public library. We raised almost a thousand dollars this afternoon!" More cheers and clapping echoed across the park.

Vicki opened the envelope. "And now, the moment we've been waiting for! First, the judges have a few special honors to hand out. The crust can be the best part of the pie, and the hardest to get right. So, the best crust award goes to ... Oscar Pembleton for his pumpkin entry!"

A white-haired man approached the stage, grinning from ear to ear.

"I had some of that, it was fabulous," Auggie said, more graciously than Melinda expected. "I wonder if he used lard, or how cold the water was."

"Well, just keep trying," Jerry said in a patronizing tone. "We're always up for samples down at the store."

"And our other special award, for best overall presentation, goes to ... Auggie Kleinsbach and his coconut cream pie!"

Auggie raised his hands in triumph and bounded up the stage's steps. The roar from the crowd was even louder than before. Melinda noticed a surprising number of men hooting and hollering, and it was clear Auggie had made sure his regular customers knew he was in the contest.

"Look at him." Diane shook her head, but she was grinning. "You'll never hear the end of it."

"I saw that pie," Melinda said. "The meringue was sky-high and perfectly browned, and it was topped with toasted coconut, too. He must have worked hard to get it right."

"And finally, we'll announce the top two vote-getters." Vicki motioned for the crowd to quiet down. "This was decided by popular ballot only. Second place goes to Fred Hartsinger, and his apple-cranberry pie!" More clapping and cheers.

"OK, here we go." Jerry put his hands on his hips.

Vicki held up a green apron with the words "Prosper's Best Baker" emblazoned across its chest. "And the winning entry, which earns this cool apron along with bragging rights for the next year, is ... Bill Larsen's raspberry-crumb pie!"

The park went crazy with cheers, but Auggie and Jerry were shocked into silence. Bill pushed through the crowd, accepting high-fives and pats on the back from friends and strangers alike.

"When did he enter this thing?" Auggie gasped.

"Hey, you," Jerry said as Bill strolled past. "What's with all the secrecy?"

Bill gave an easy shrug. "Those who can bake a little, work hard to get better. Those who can't, well, I guess they don't stand a chance."

Auggie's mouth fell open.

"OK, change in rules," Jerry grumbled. "The *winner* brings the doughnuts."

While the guys were trying to fathom how Bill had snatched the prize out from under their rolling pins, Melinda was pleasantly distracted by a text. It was from Chase.

I can be there around 6. Should we meet in town or at the farm?

The question made her catch her breath, as it wasn't about how their night would start, but how it was likely to end. He was making this so easy.

In less than a heartbeat, she had her answer.

The farm. No need to take 2 cars. Can't wait to see you!

∗11∗

Melinda opened her eyes and for a moment, something seemed strange. Then a smile spread across her face when she remembered why she was sleeping on one side of the bed, rather than in the middle. She rolled over and reached out, and the second pillow was still warm. The room was brighter than usual at this early hour, but then, she and Chase had been too distracted to pull the shades.

She rubbed her face, glad she'd had the foresight to wash her makeup off before they'd fallen asleep. The bedroom door was open, and she could hear faint clinks and rattles coming from the kitchen, and smell pancakes and frying eggs and bacon. She couldn't make out what Chase was saying, but Hobo answered him with a happy bark.

Everything had changed, and yet so much was the same. Melinda had no idea how this next chapter would end, but she might as well get up and see how it was going to start. Besides, there were chores to do, and she had to be at the store by seven.

As she pulled on her summer chore clothes and shuffled down the stairs, she decided it was time to spread the word about Chase among the rest of her friends.

If they were going to be seeing each other regularly, and like this, the time for secrets was long past. And really, did she have a choice? They had bumped into Auggie and his wife by the food stands last night, and she had also introduced Chase to Nancy and Vicki.

The living room was slightly askew and Grace, lounging on the top of the sofa, was clearly annoyed.

"What? Don't judge me, Princess Grace." The kitten narrowed her green eyes and flicked her fluffy calico tail. "I'll put things back where they belong, right this minute."

Melinda located all the couch's throw pillows and arranged them back in its corners, then picked up the empty wine glasses still waiting on the mantel. "Chase is very nice, you'll see," she whispered to Grace. "I take it your sister is hiding this morning. But Hobo's already made friends."

Chase was at the stove, showered and dressed in khakis and a polo, so he could head straight to the office. "Good morning, milady. How about a kiss for the cook?"

Melinda was only too happy to oblige, and with more than one. Chase pulled her close and for a moment, the pancakes were forgotten.

"Careful, they're about to burn," she finally said. "This old stove is temperamental, especially that main burner. Barely warm one minute, blazing hot the next."

"Well, that sounds familiar." Chase kissed her neck and they both laughed. "I know you have chores to do, but breakfast will be in about five. I already fed Hobo and the kittens. Just the food there on the back porch, right?"

Melinda blinked, trying to get her bearings. A hot breakfast was on the way, and a few of her morning tasks were already completed. There were other benefits to having a man around, if only once in a while. "Thanks for doing that, it'll save me some time. I'll set the table."

She soon realized she was starving, and filled her plate. She hadn't felt like finishing her cheeseburger last night, between the heat and her nerves. But all those worries had been for nothing. She looked up to find Chase grinning at her.

"What?" She returned his smile and reached down to pet Hobo, who was resting at her feet, so she didn't have to meet Chase's gaze.

"Oh, I was just thinking about what a good time I had last night." He looked up and around.

"But that's not all of it. This is some house! The built-in buffet in the dining room? That's some serious craftsmanship. My grandpa was a carpenter, so I notice those things."

Melinda gave him a knowing look. "I'll overlook your comments about the woodwork, since you've never been inside this house before. But, come on! The very first time you drove into my yard, I recall some seriously fawning praise about this farm. It was such a fabulous place, and the prettiest acreage your company had ever photographed."

Chase reddened, then busied himself mopping syrup with his last forkful of pancake.

"Actually, I said it was the prettiest we'd shot that *day*. It's a standard line. Although," he pointed his fork in protest, "it's always like that. Sales pitches are worked out before we make the rounds, based on the condition of the property."

Melinda broke off a scrap of bacon and passed it to Hobo. "Oh, I've got to hear this. I bet it's good."

He leaned back in his chair. "Well, if it's like your place, I say basically what I told you. Stuff up on a hill? I try to work 'majestic' in there, or something like that. Valley farms are 'cozy' and 'inviting.'"

"And if it's a dump?" She put her chin in her hand, her eyes dancing. "What do you say then?

Chase laughed. "Well, depends on what I see in the yard when I pull in. If there's signs of renovation, for example, I'll comment on how it's an 'exciting work in progress.'"

"And if the porch is pulling away from the house, and the barn's fallen over?"

"Now those ... those are 'a farm steeped in history,' or maybe 'a diamond in the rough.'"

"Hmm. there's a predetermined answer for everything."

Chase put down his fork and reached across the table. He covered her hand with his, but there was a beat or two before she squeezed it back. He noticed.

"Yes, when it comes to selling photos. But only then."

She looked down at the table. "And so ... all of this? Us?" The word seemed strange to her ears and it hung in the air between them, new and fragile.

"This is real. I'm not working from any script here. I hope you aren't, either."

"No. Definitely not." She hesitated for a moment, trying to gather her thoughts. "In fact, it's been a while, and I'm not even sure what that script would be. Busy woman looking for a distraction from her over-scheduled life? Lonely farm lady needing a man to make her happy, and make breakfast sometimes? Neither of those really fit. Although I have to say, these from-scratch pancakes are amazing."

Chase let go of her hand. "You can take care of yourself, that's clear." His voice was gentle. "I don't want to be in the way. Just keep being you, and I'll see where I fit in, OK? And I can write down that recipe, if you like."

She softened. "I didn't mean to sound defensive. I just ... normally I have things planned out, you know? Even if the pieces don't fall into place, I like to have a plan."

"Well, how about you plan to see me next week? Let's start there."

* * *

Chase left right after breakfast, and Melinda was almost glad to see him go. A little romance was fine, but the world went on as usual. And she'd have to hurry to catch up.

The sheep were lined up at their troughs, waiting, when she burst into the barn.

"Sorry, sorry!" She passed out grain and hay with so much speed that a few of the timid ewes took a quick step back. "I'm all of, what, twenty minutes late? Here you go. Promise me you'll spend the afternoon inside, and not out in the pasture. It's going to be hot again today."

Sunny and Stormy circled their dishes in the grain room, meowing their impatience. At least the chickens' feathers weren't so ruffled. They bobbed and clucked around her feet, in no real hurry to start their day. Melinda liked to think the canvas tied over part of their run, which gave them some shade on these high-summer days, was part of the reason.

"What do you think of your patio umbrella?" she asked Pansy, who was the most fractious of Horace's original flock. But the hen was too busy shoving two younger birds out of the way to answer.

At least she wasn't pecking them anymore. When Melinda first brought the young chicks out from their basement brooder pen, Pansy had been furious and territorial, so much so that Ed suggested it might be time for the stew pot. But Pansy was one of the flock's best layers, and Melinda admired her pluck.

She made a quick scan of the brooder boxes while the hens focused on their breakfast, and settled the fresh eggs into the bucket on her arm. There wasn't time to wash them and sort them into cartons; she'd just have to take a bigger batch of eggs to Prosper Hardware tomorrow.

Aunt Miriam had agreed to let Melinda sell some of the flock's offerings at the store, due to the speed at which the shipped-in cartons disappeared from the refrigerator case and the growing demand for farm-fresh everything. Prosper would be sleepier than usual on this holiday weekend, as some residents would be camping or visiting family and friends, but Melinda knew whatever eggs she took would still be snatched up fast.

If only her garden could be as productive as her chickens. She studied the plot as she filled the hens' bucket at the hydrant, shaking her head at the too-pale leaves on the tomato plants and the cracks spreading in the dirt between the rows. Even if she had five minutes to spare, which plants would she take pity on?

She'd have to come out after supper, mosquito repellant and sunscreen in place, and drag the hose up and down the rows. The dry grass snapped and rustled under her chore boots as she hurried back to the house. It was only the first week of July, and brown patches were already spreading across her lawn. If it stayed this dry, she wouldn't have to mow as often. But she'd happily trade hours of yardwork to have her grass lush and green like it was last summer.

But there was one bright spot this already-hot morning. Inspired by Adelaide and Mason's efforts, she'd ordered a rain barrel for her own garden and, if the shipment hadn't been delayed by the holiday, it should arrive that afternoon. But then, what use was a rain barrel if it didn't rain?

* * *

Prosper Hardware felt different that morning. And while most of the guys were already gathered around the coffee pot when she ran in at seven-fifteen, her greetings were answered with barely a mumbled "hello" or "hey."

Then she saw why. Bill sat next to the sideboard, a cup in his hand and a smirk on his face, with his "Prosper's Best Baker" apron tied over his tee shirt and cargo shorts.

"Bill, really." She dumped her purse and lunch tote on the counter.

"Why not?" He shrugged, clearly enjoying the way Jerry gave him the stink eye, and Auggie wouldn't look at him at all. "This is my victory lap, my chance to just soak it all in."

"Rub it in, more like it," Auggie muttered.

"I brought treats, didn't I?" Bill pointed at the paper plates and the remnants of a white cake layered with raspberries and blueberries waiting on the sideboard.

"Party leftovers don't count." Jerry pointed at him. "We said doughnuts. Besides, I bet Emily made that."

"Of course she did." Bill snorted. "She's the real baker in the family. And I wasn't in on your wager in the first place. Besides, I'd have to drive into Swanton to get doughnuts, and that's like a twenty-mile round trip." He pocketed his phone and, with a generous slice of cake in one hand and his coffee cup in the other, started for the wood shop.

"I sure like this apron," he said as he strolled down the main aisle. "Two deep pockets! Might just keep it here at the store, wear it every day."

The metal door closed behind him with a screech of triumph. Doc was trying to keep a straight face, but Frank and George couldn't hold back their laughter.

With those dark-rimmed glasses perched on his nose, Auggie glared after Bill like a mad owl.

"I never liked that kid," he finally said. "And the worst of it is, he cheated! I spent hours working on my crust, trying to get it just right. He just smashed some graham crackers and melted a little butter, and *ta-da!* First place."

"No one said the crust had to be the flour kind," George reminded him.

Jerry sighed. "Come on, Auggie, you like Bill just fine. Good for him if he's in such a great mood. I haven't been this tired since, well, probably last year's Fourth of July celebration. Just look at all that trash!" He gestured out the front windows to where crumpled napkins and orphaned plastic cups shuffled down Main Street in the breeze. "The Swanton Jaycees will be here soon to clean it all up, and I'll have to pitch in."

"You're still in the club?" Melinda was surprised. "I thought you were going to bow out, ease your schedule a bit."

"He keeps saying he's going to quit," Frank explained when Jerry didn't respond. "But when they call him about another community-service project, he always says yes."

Doc plated a piece of cake and passed it to Jerry. "I have to say, you handled yourself well last night, there at the park. Jake tried to draw you into a spontaneous debate about property taxes, and you made him look like a crazy hothead."

"Thank God the council doesn't meet for two weeks yet." Jerry tucked into his slice. "He'll either forget all about it, or he'll spend the coming days deciding how he's going to challenge me right there at the meeting."

"There's protocol to follow," Uncle Frank reminded his friend. "He can't do that, not when the council's in session."

Auggie's mood seemed to moderate as he enjoyed his cake. "So, Melinda," he suddenly said, "are we going to hear all about this new man in your life?"

"I hoped it wouldn't come up."

"Not a chance. His family's the one with the aerial company, right?"

"The one up in Meadville?" Doc was all ears. "Karen's still out of town, and I have to get going, but ... when did this happen?"

"Wait a minute." Uncle Frank leaned in. "Who's this? Miriam hasn't said a thing."

"That's because I asked her not to."

George sat up straighter. "When do we get to meet him?"

"Not sure. Look, I'll fill you all in, but then I need to start restocking these shelves."

She reached for a mug and then, even though she'd had a hearty breakfast, cut herself a generous square of cake. Jerry wasn't the only one with a holiday hangover. She was already yawning; it was going to be a long day.

* 12 *

Sure enough, a cardboard carton over three feet tall was waiting on the front porch when Melinda got home that evening. And there was a scrap of white paper taped to its top, a note penned in a now-familiar script.

> *You should have seen the cats' faces when I unloaded this thing! Great idea, have one myself. Now all we need is a real rain!*

A brown delivery truck turned up this lane on a regular basis, since Melinda was quick to hop online to find whatever she couldn't purchase locally. It was a thrill to come home and find a box waiting on the front porch, and she looked forward to the notes that sometimes accompanied the deliveries. The observations included how fast the lambs were growing, and how beautiful the peonies along the drive had been that spring. She had yet to be home when a package was dropped off, but one day, Melinda hoped to have a two-way conversation with this sort-of friend.

Sunny and Stormy were nowhere to be found. But Hobo's excited barks as she lugged the shipping container to the back side of the house soon brought both cats out of hiding. With Melinda nearby, Sunny was confident enough to sniff the carton's corners with wide eyes.

But when she ripped the cardboard flaps and the fifty-gallon orange cylinder emerged, he scurried away to join Stormy in the safe space under the picnic table.

"What is that big thing, huh? Don't worry, it won't attack you. See, Hobo's not afraid." Neither cat seemed comforted by her words. "Wait until Mom and Dad come over tomorrow night, then we'll really have some excitement." Roger had volunteered to build the rain barrel's wooden stand, and help Melinda reconfigure the downspout on the northwest corner of the house.

The barrel was surprisingly light for its size, so it would need to be tucked away until it could be installed. Even though she was exhausted, Melinda was grinning with excitement as she rolled the garage door over her latest project. The Beauforts had inspired her to make her little homestead more self-sufficient. While the idea of fresh honey was appealing, hundreds of bees buzzing in her yard was not. And she didn't see any solar panels in her future. But a rain barrel? That was something she could handle.

Karen was the farm's next visitor, and she wasn't alone. Her collie, Pumpkin, sat proudly in the passenger seat as Karen's truck hummed up the lane early Sunday morning. Karen and Melinda had struck a bargain: Melinda would sew custom curtains for Karen's oversized living-room window, and Karen would help her freshen up the farmhouse's front porch by painting its ceiling and furniture.

Hobo was excited to see his furry friend, and the dogs quickly ran behind the house, eager to explore. Karen held the front porch door so Melinda could carry out the rattan chairs, which were two consignment-store scores coated in a dull, brown stain.

"I'm excited to see how these turn out," Karen said as they arranged the frames on a sheet of weighted plastic on the lawn. "When they're painted white, they'll look like new."

"It's too bad I haven't had time to recover the cushions yet, so we could see the full effect. But at least we can give the porch swing a fresh coat to match."

Karen held the wooden bench steady while Melinda unhooked its chains, and they balanced it on two buckets under the maple tree.

"So, are we going to have any helpers this morning?" Karen peeked under the picnic table as they fetched the painting supplies from the back porch. "Where are Sunny and Stormy?"

Melinda grinned, and pointed to the stand of ferns on the back side of the garage. One gray ear and a single green eye were barely visible in the foliage. "I think we'll be allowed to paint in peace. That's the perfect spot for them to keep tabs on Hobo and Pumpkin, but I bet they run off to the barn sooner rather than later."

Karen pointed to the patch of old-fashioned flowers on the west side of the house. "Those look better than mine, they're struggling in this heat. Only the native grasses in my butterfly garden seem to be holding their own."

"Ada says those phlox and coneflowers have been here for decades, and they're tough. And the sunflowers I planted on the far end of the garden are hanging in there. But if we don't get a soaking rain soon, I'll have to give up on the rest of the flowers and just keep the garden going."

"Well, it's the perfect day to paint. I guess this dry weather is good for something." Karen vigorously shook the first pressurized can of white paint, and the rattles brought irritated squawks from the blue jays supervising in the maple tree. "You got such a steal on these chairs! It took us a few wrong turns before we found that second-hand store out in the middle of nowhere. But it was worth it, snagging all those bargains."

"And meeting those sweet cats." Melinda stirred the gallon of white at her feet. "Queenie and her tribe."

"Queenie's crew sparked our plans for the first spay-and-neuter clinic. And now look at us, our third one's coming up next week. Forty kitties on the list! I'm so glad Josh wants to keep helping out. This program is already bigger than anything I could have imagined."

"Maybe it's time to start applying for those grants. When you have enough data to prove how well the clinics are working, let me know."

Melinda started on the back of the bench, and her brush slid across the boards with ease. She'd already cleaned the slats and sanded them down, and hoped the bench would look like new with only a coat or two. So many Schermanns had sat in this swing over the years. She could imagine Anna, with a large bowl in her lap, snapping a batch of string beans. Or Henry and Wilbur, enjoying a glass of sun-brewed tea after a long day in the fields. Had Horace and Maggie ever sat here, side by side, planning their future?

A bark-filled duet started up somewhere behind the house. "Sounds like the pups are having a good time." Karen started on the second wicker chair. "Pumpkin just loves it out here. She has her fenced yard, of course, but this is ..."

A dark shape, low to the ground, crashed through the peony bushes and darted in their direction.

"What is that?" Melinda jumped to her feet, so startled she didn't feel the wet paint oozing between her fingers as she tried to hold the porch swing steady.

"A woodchuck?" Karen took a step back, the aerosol can still in her hand. "What is ... quick, grab that bucket of paint!"

Hobo and Pumpkin rounded the house, their tongues flopping with excitement. The woodchuck was small and squat, but it picked up a surprising amount of speed as it reached the front lawn. It slipped between Melinda and Karen and raced for the safety of the windbreak's underbrush.

"Pumpkin, stop!" Karen's spray can went flying as she grasped the large collie's collar.

Melinda had only a second to set down her paint bucket and reach for her dog. "Hobo, stop barking, let it go!" He growled and tacked to the left, pulling her down into the grass, but she held on. The woodchuck slipped into the treeline and disappeared.

"They can climb trees if they're threatened," Karen panted, as Pumpkin was still straining to chase her prey. "Or maybe he'll get back to his burrow, now that these potential murderers are in custody."

"Oh, no!"

"What happened? Did they knock the paint over?"

"Nope. But I got it on my hand and ... Hobo, you've got another white patch in your fur that you didn't have five minutes ago. I guess that's your punishment for being such a naughty boy."

When the woodchuck didn't reappear, both dogs soon calmed down. Melinda tried to dab at Hobo's coat with a paper towel. "I had no idea there were any woodchucks out here. Do they normally come out during the day?"

"Oh, sure. They're very shy, though. They eat a variety of plants, but they love berries, too."

"That explains things. There's wild black raspberries behind the chicken house. They're so small, it's hard to get enough at one time for even a bowl of cereal or ice cream. I keep finding berries scattered on the ground, and I blamed the birds. I guess I'm not the only one who's picking that patch."

Hobo and Pumpkin refreshed themselves at the water bowl by the back steps and flopped under the picnic table, worn out from the chase. Once it became clear the chairs and swing didn't need to be guarded, Karen and Melinda turned their attention to the front porch's interior while they waited for the furniture's first coats to dry.

The charming beadboard ceiling had been painted the same dull, dark gray as the floorboards decades ago. Inspired by a spread in a magazine, Melinda decided to paint the porch ceiling a peaceful shade of aqua. After testing four colors on a scrap of wood, she finally had the perfect hue: a pale blue with just a hint of soft green. It played well with the farmhouse's white clapboard siding, gray window trim and speckled green-gray shingles.

Karen spread the drop cloths while Melinda set up both of her ladders. Grace and Hazel soon appeared in the dining-room window, content to watch all the commotion from a safe distance. When Melinda popped the lid on the first paint can, Karen hurried over for the reveal.

"I can't wait to see this! I know you've been agonizing over it for a few weeks. Oooh, that's beautiful! What a tranquil shade; it's perfect for this house." But then Karen lowered her chin.

"What?" Melinda furrowed her brow. "I went with high-gloss for durability. You think it's too shiny?"

"No, I would've done the same. It's the color that caught me off guard. My grandma would say that's the perfect shade of haint blue."

"Haint blue?" Melinda's jaw dropped. "You mean like ..."

"Spirits. Ghosts. It keeps them away. The ones that can't seem to move on." Karen reached for a stir stick and the paint came to life, undulating like creamy waves inside the can.

"That's the reason so many porch ceilings are this color. It's a tradition that goes back a long way, especially in the South. My great-grandma was from South Carolina. She met Great-Grandpa when he was stationed down there, during World War I. Her porch ceiling was always this color, and my grandma painted hers the same shade."

Melinda reached for one of the paint trays and motioned for Karen to pour. "Wait a minute. Say some spirit is trying to get to Heaven, and they think this color signifies the sky ... wouldn't it have the opposite effect, make them want to hang out here?"

Karen laughed. "Yeah, I always thought the same thing. But Grandma swore by it. Grandpa just shrugged and said blue was his favorite color, and who cares what the porch looks like? So they stuck with it."

Melinda started up the closest ladder. Karen filled the second tray and carried it to the other side of the porch.

"Who knows what's true, but it's a fun bit of folklore." Karen began to edge the ceiling's corner with a brush, then turned on the ladder. "Anything strange going on around here? Maybe something, or someone, who just won't stay in the past? Who knows, maybe this will help."

A knot formed in Melinda's stomach, and it wasn't because of Maggie. If anything, she wished there was a magical way to make Maggie appear on this farmhouse's doorstep one more time.

Someone else had been on her mind lately, too. With Chase now in her life, she'd found herself haunted by memories of an old love that went wrong. She picked up her brush and tried to focus on the ceiling.

"It's funny you mentioned that. I'm happy with Chase, really I am, but it's ... been harder than I thought it would be."

"Oh, I should have known. Your ex, the guy you were going to marry ... Craig, right?"

At the sound of his name, Melinda shivered despite the heat. "Yeah. There's been a few other guys since then but, well, this thing with Chase feels different. Like it has real potential. That's what so scary about it."

Karen said nothing and kept painting, giving her friend the space she needed to talk things through.

"It was wonderful with Craig, too, at first. Then things started to move so fast ... and before I knew it, there was this ring on my finger, and I was trying on dresses and we were looking at houses."

Melinda put down her brush and closed her eyes. "We signed a contract on a house. Did the papers and everything. I thought I was going to throw up when we did it. I should have ended it sooner. But the longer I waited, the messier it got. By the time I got the courage to walk away, it was ..."

She put a hand over her face. "It was awful, the hardest thing I've ever had to do."

"But it was also the right thing." Karen reached for the roller waiting in her paint tray, and more of the dark gray disappeared. "You saved yourself from even more heartbreak. And when all this came up," she waved around with her free hand, "you were able to make the leap, take that chance."

"I know. I thought I could handle things with Chase, that I was cool with jumping into things so fast. I'm not sorry," she said quickly. "But I think I really care about him."

This paint wasn't just the color of the sky, she realized as the soft blue spread across the beadboard, it was the color of water, too.

And sometimes, Melinda worried she might drown, that what she felt for Chase might cause her to fall head-first into something that may not be real, or may not last.

"What's Chase say about all this?" Karen moved her ladder toward the middle of the porch.

"He says he understands, that he's not going to push me."

"And do you trust him?"

Melinda hesitated for only a second. "Yes."

"Well, then, I'd just let things play out. Enjoy it. But just to be safe, let's plan on three coats for this ceiling, make sure this haint blue goes on nice and thick."

Melinda finally nodded in agreement. Karen was right; the last thing she wanted to do was push Chase away. Suddenly, she thought of something.

"Oh, I forgot to tell you! One morning, when I came into the store? The guys were gossiping about you and Josh. Auggie saw you together at the coffee shop in Swanton. I told them you were just planning the next spay clinic, but ..."

"What?" Karen nearly dropped her roller. "You can't be serious!"

"I told them nothing was going on. Doc did, too. I think they finally accepted it."

"Well, my love life is nowhere near as exciting as yours. There's this single teacher at the school Nancy wants to fix me up with, but I don't know. I guess it's worth a try; that app I signed up for hasn't brought me any decent matches in weeks."

"Nancy is an excellent judge of character, she wouldn't steer you wrong. Besides, isn't that how they did it back in the day? No dating sites back then."

"Very true." Karen refilled her paint tray. "Most people married someone within a few miles of where they grew up."

The sun was climbing higher in the sky, and the temperature was rising along with it. The porch turned stuffy and close, even with two fans trying to push around the hot air drifting through the screens. But they were making good progress, and Melinda hoped there'd be time to get a second coat on the furniture before lunch.

As she tried to focus on her work and block out her thoughts about Craig and Chase, her mind kept returning to Horace and Maggie.

Karen's observation was correct. Maggie might have moved far away, but her roots had to be close by. Melinda couldn't give up. But what was her next move?

First Lutheran had records, but she couldn't get access to the church's files without inventing some sort of lie to protect Horace's privacy. Where else could she go?

She was having lunch with her parents tomorrow ... maybe the Swanton library? Then she thought of the courthouse, where the county historical society's archives were tucked away on the top floor. She wasn't even sure where to start, with so little to go on, but she had to try again. It might be her last chance to find Maggie.

* 13 *

The windshield wipers screeched in protest when Melinda kicked them into high gear. She hadn't pressed them into service for at least two weeks, but the clouds had already been low and threatening when she woke that morning. By the time she left the farm, the sky was pouring buckets. She was smiling by the time she reached the county blacktop and turned west toward Swanton, envisioning how the water was already rising in the rain barrel.

Now she wouldn't have to rely so heavily on the farm's well, and the old hydrant by the garden would get a rest, too. Melinda had oiled the iron pump's pistons, following Ed's directions, but the contraption was so worn she worried it could break at any time. Replacing it would cost money, of course, but maybe it was better to change it out now, rather than risk being stuck with only the hydrant in the barn?

This was the sort of conundrum she used to take to Horace. Not just because she was still learning to manage her little acreage, but because it made Horace feel needed. But she'd been calling him less and less lately, and wondered how much longer she could sidestep him without hurting his feelings.

"I know how you feel," Ada admitted last night on the phone. "When I go see them, I can hardly look Horace in the eye. This has dragged on for far too long. Maybe we're not meant to find Maggie. I'll have some groveling to do with Horace either way. Kevin was right, we should have told him first. If you hit another dead end, I think we need to give up."

But there was one bit of good news: Ada had carefully examined her mother's wedding dress and found it was in surprisingly good condition. Being packed in a cedar chest for decades had served it well. If she reinforced a few seams, it would be sturdy enough to be worn for just a few minutes. The dress might be the star of the fashion show, if the committee could find a teenage girl tiny enough to wear it. When Ada read off the dress' dimensions, Melinda made her repeat them. Twice.

She'd emailed the measurements to the new chair of the luncheon committee just this morning. The event would go on, one way or another, even though Angie had gone into labor late last night. She was at the hospital in Swanton, and Melinda was anxiously waiting for another update from Nathan. The impending arrival also meant more volunteers were needed for the luncheon. Melinda and Mabel would craft the cream-cheese mints, and Melinda had agreed to take over one of Angie's dishes: calico beans for a hundred.

It wasn't just the welcome rain that had her smiling when she pulled into her parents' driveway. There were several perks to small-town life, but the best one was seeing her parents as often as she wanted. Roger insisted on grilling his specialty burgers for lunch, despite the rain, and Diane was soon on board to help Melinda and Mabel fulfill the church committee's request for five hundred mints before next weekend.

The courthouse, which was an imposing three-story limestone structure that looked more like a castle than a government building, anchored the east side of the town square. Melinda found a parking spot on its back side and, as it was still drizzling, clutched her tote bag close as she dashed for the entrance.

The historical society held an impressive collection for such a rural county, according to Nancy, and Melinda was glad for an excuse to see it for herself. She went through security, and then left her purse in a coin-operated locker just inside the archive's entrance.

"Just sign in here, please." An older man at the archive's main desk gestured at the guest log. "Can I help you find anything special today?"

"Oh, I'm just working on some family history." Melinda shrugged as she signed the registry. She had come up with a cover story on the way to town that morning. Blurting out "I'm trying to find my elderly friend's long-lost love" would raise eyebrows and draw too much attention.

"Well, that sounds exciting!"

Melinda almost laughed at his earnestness. If he only knew ...

"I'd suggest you start with the online databases over there." The man pointed at a bank of monitors along the far wall. "Once you have some names and dates down, we've got a little bit of everything. Microfilm's off to the left, and we've got most of the old newspapers from around the region. Census records, too. Those shelves on the right hold the county history books, and there's a good selection of titles from around Iowa in the back."

The archive's heavy oak doors opened and another patron arrived, allowing Melinda to cut short her chat with the librarian. With so little to go on, she wasn't sure where to start, but she had to hurry. It was already after one, and the library closed at four.

She drifted into the stacks, weighing her options. She'd already checked the census database for any Maggies close to the right age, but there was nothing in Prosper or anywhere in Fulton Township. She could start sifting through girls with similar names, but there would be so many variations and she would have to track down each potential candidate. It would be a great help if she could narrow the search area. But how?

From her letters, Melinda had the impression Maggie's family was rather prosperous. Along with her parents' promise to send her to college, her letters mentioned traveling to Des Moines to see an aunt and uncle in the summer of 1947, and she'd described the grandness of their home in great detail. Like most teen girls, Maggie was obsessed with her wardrobe, and her letters held references to brand-new dresses and shoes on a regular basis.

Melinda was well aware of the Schermann family's thrifty lifestyle, and suspected most, if not all, of their rural neighbors had been in the same boat. If Maggie's family had money, maybe they lived in town?

She searched the 1940 census database for Prosper residents whose first names were variations on "Maggie," and didn't find anything promising. The girl's letters were light on her family members' names, which was a problem. "My sister" and "Mother and Father" were of no use. In desperation, Melinda clicked over to the scans of the actual enumerator logs from Prosper, and began to skim the lists. But her eyes soon tired and her frustration mounted. This was a fool's errand; she just didn't have enough information to go on. She'd have to call Ada and tell her that unless some other clue surfaced, the search was over.

But she was already here, and she loved local history; she might as well browse around and see what else the collection offered. Nancy had been right about the size of the society's holdings. Some of the titles she recognized from the modest section of history books at the Prosper Public Library, but there was so much more. She reached for a Hartland County history book and dropped into a chair at a nearby table.

The publication was only ten years old, and made excellent use of modern technology's ability to scan and restore old photographs. There was an entire section on Prosper history, and her family's business was clearly visible in several historic photos of Main Street. And here was one from the city's Fourth of July parade in the 1950s! She would have to tell Mom and Aunt Miriam. If they didn't have these photos, there had to be a way to get copies.

Another chapter focused on the history of the region's school systems, and included old township maps showing which crossroads hosted one-room schools back in the day. She zeroed in on her neighborhood in Fulton Township and found the Schermanns' farm, tucked down in the southwest corner. And there was a dot on the map, just north of the creek and on the east side of her gravel road, marked "Prairie Valley School." Helen Emmerson had been right!

Melinda could imagine Horace and Wilbur walking the half-mile to class, and getting distracted by all the excitement two little boys could unearth along the creek. She was about to turn the page when something caught her eye. On Fulton Township's western border, just a mile from the Schermann farm, was a red line running north and south with the words "Prosper School District Boundary."

If everyone east of the red line had been in Prosper's district, everyone west of it was part of Swanton's system.

And in the Swanton High School yearbooks. Which Melinda had yet to examine.

She jumped out of her chair, startling a man at the other end of the table, then tried to slow her steps as she scanned the shelves. Hadn't she passed an entire section on the area's schools? This row of Prosper yearbooks was longer than the collection at the Prosper library, but the Swanton section was even more substantial. She grabbed the ones from the mid-1940s, hurried back to her seat, then powered up the old photo on her phone.

She started with 1947, and her hands trembled as she flipped the pages. The seniors were in the front, as usual. These classes were larger than the ones in little Prosper, but Melinda might be on the right track, at last. And there she was: Magdalena Kaiser. The same brown eyes, the same smile. She was even prettier in this studio portrait.

Melinda had been searching for a "Mary," or a "Margaret" or a "Marge," if not a true "Maggie." But this made so much sense. Magdalena was a common German name; one of Melinda's great-grandmothers carried it as well. She snapped a scan of Maggie's senior photo and stared at it for several minutes, pondering the implications of what she'd just found.

"Are you OK?" A woman passing by put a hand on Melinda's shoulder. "You never know what you're going to find in this place."

"I'm fine. Great, actually." Melinda let out a deep sigh. "A solid lead, at last. Now I just have to follow it."

"Genealogy is more exciting than most people give it credit for." The woman set a stack of ledgers on the table and pulled up a chair. "Why, just last week, some guy found out his great-great-grandfather was a horse thief! They hanged him, right out there in front of this courthouse. It was all over the papers. And you know the craziest part? We all had a good chuckle over it. Just goes to show ... time mends most things, doesn't it?"

Melinda hoped the woman was right. She had finally found Maggie, but was about to open another box of secrets. "Is there a water fountain?"

"Of course. Right over there, by the atlases. Is there anything else I can help you find?"

"Not just now, thanks."

Melinda took a deep drink and tried to figure out her next move. Now that she had a full name, the online databases would be her fastest way to search. In just under an hour, she confirmed the Kaiser farm was two miles west and a mile south of the Schermann place. Melinda realized she drove by it when she passed out the invitations to the women's luncheon, but a First Lutheran member lived there now, so she hadn't had a reason to stop.

Maggie married in 1950 in Cedar Falls, three years after her last letters to Horace and a year after the fateful summer day Anna turned her away. The microfilm collection took her to a wedding announcement in the Waterloo paper. It included a large photo of the bride and groom, unusual for the time, but Melinda soon saw why:

Maggie's husband was from a wealthy family, and the item focused on his mother's and father's roles in the community as well as the bride's gown and what was served at the wedding breakfast.

There was Maggie in a beautiful satin dress, clutching a spray of lilacs, on the arm of a man who looked a little older but was dignified and handsome. Maggie's smile stretched from ear to ear. If there was any hesitation, if she had any regrets, she hid them well. Melinda hoped Horace had never seen this photo, and she'd let Ada and Kevin decide whether he ever saw it now.

After snapping a scan of the wedding announcement, she started looking for an obituary. There wasn't one, and Maggie was listed as a survivor when her husband passed away five years ago.

Then, and only then, Melinda allowed herself to tap a database of current addresses and phone numbers. Maggie lived at a Cedar Falls care facility. Melinda wrote the address and phone number in her notebook, then doubled back to Maggie's husband's obituary to get the names and locations of the couple's children: two daughters, Barb and Wendy.

"So, did you have any luck?" the librarian asked as she signed out.

"Oh, a little." Another vague smile.

"Well, we're open every day but Sunday. When you get things processed and organized, come back and see what else you can find."

The doors hadn't seemed this heavy when she'd entered the archives. Melinda was suddenly drained, and felt like she wanted to shout her news to everyone she passed in the corridor and burst into tears at the same time.

She made it around a corner and ducked into a quiet nook, then slid to the floor, leaned back against the dark-varnished paneling, and closed her eyes.

A few simple pieces of information had changed everything. She had to call Ada. Right now. Because until she shared this burden with someone, Melinda wouldn't be fit to get behind the wheel.

* 14 *

Melinda glanced at the clock above the kitchen sink. The plastic barn's hands were moving closer to eight, and she had yet to load the car.

"Grace, look out! I almost stepped on you. Here, why don't you chase after Chicky?"

She snatched the kitten's favorite toy, a colorful stuffed bird, off the floor by the stove and tossed it toward the dining room. Hazel and Hobo were out of the way, under the kitchen table, but close enough Melinda could see their pleading expressions.

"I'm sorry, no more hamburger. And you," she waved her largest ladle at Hobo, "got bacon, too, so you won't starve. We won't tell the church ladies we shorted the calico beans. I can't imagine anyone's going to notice, since there's enough here to feed nine-dozen people."

Last night, she'd browned several pounds of ground beef and cooked the bacon, so all she had to do this morning was mix them with the varieties of beans and make the sauce. Easy-peasy.

But she hadn't calculated how long it would take to open all the cans and divide the finished product among every lidded serving bowl she owned. Even then, there were still leftovers; the last few cups were scooped into a dish that wouldn't make the trip to the church.

Two scrubbed-down totes would keep the beans safe in the backseat of the car, leaving room for the containers of mints to ride up front with Melinda. The petite confections were almost too beautiful to eat, but she'd enjoyed several to be sure they tasted as perfect as they looked.

The mints had actually been easier than the beans, thanks to all the extra hands. Diane and Mabel helped Melinda mix the cream-cheese dough and tint it shades of light blue and pale green, then Emma and Allison got in on the fun. Once they pulled on plastic gloves, their tiny fingers were perfect for filling the sugared molds, and having the girls over for a few hours gave Angie and Nathan a much-needed break. Little Blake was doing well, but Melinda made Angie promise to stay away from the luncheon and get some rest. Everything was going to plan. And hopefully, that wouldn't change before the day was over.

The wedding-dress fashion show would start at ten-thirty, with the lunch to follow. Ada was on her way down from Mason City with Anna's dress, as the new committee chair had found an eighth-grader slender enough to wear it. The rest of the models were high-school girls from the church's youth fellowship group. They'd all gone to Swanton this morning to get their hair and makeup done, just as they would for the homecoming dance or prom.

At least the models didn't need to figure out what to wear. Melinda finally settled on her nicest black capris, sensible flats and a pale-blue top, as she wanted to look a little festive but be ready to spend several hours setting tables, serving food and washing dishes. It would be nice to spend a few minutes on her hair for once, but a low ponytail would have to do. She snatched a stretchy band from her purse, grabbed the last containers of mints, and rushed out the back door.

Several cars were already parked in front of the small white church, and the organist pulled in just as Melinda was getting out of the car. "Here, give me something to carry." The woman stuck out her free hand. "Looks like you've got plenty to haul inside. I've only got my tote bag."

"Thanks, you got here just in time." Melinda pushed the stray hairs out of her face and reached for the first tote of calico beans. It was another humid morning, and the temperature was already climbing.

The little church had been built in the late 1880s, but at least it now had air-conditioning. Even so, the basement kitchen was stuffy and crowded with women, with rows of roasters and slow cookers warming on its two long counters. Once the calico beans were settled in one of the church's large roasters, Melinda helped spread heavy white tablecloths over the long metal tables. Lengths of light-blue polka-dot ribbon served as table runners, and canning jars filled with white candles and wrapped with faux leaves made up the centerpieces. The tables were set with the church's heavy silverware, clear glasses and white china plates.

She was adding aqua paper napkins to each place setting when Ada appeared at the foot of the stairs. Melinda was eager to open the garment bag Ada cradled in both hands, but there was something else on her mind.

"Have you heard anything?" she whispered.

"Not yet." Ada leaned in. "I just left that message for one of Maggie's daughters, so they can discuss ... well, whatever they decide to do. I swear, this waiting is worse than when we didn't know anything."

Mabel soon arrived, bringing the secretive conversation to an abrupt halt. "Oh, I can't wait to see that dress!"

Ada's blue eyes started to sparkle. "Where can I hang it?" she asked Melinda. "I don't want to set it down, for even a moment."

"One of the Sunday-school rooms is going to be the dressing area." Melinda gestured for them to follow her down a short hallway. Two ladies bustled around three roll-away racks, carefully arranging the wedding gowns so their bows weren't flattened and their poufy skirts could breathe.

"Ada!" The tallest woman squeezed her shoulder. "It's been ages. I can't wait to catch up! But, let's have a look ... this has to be the oldest dress, by far."

Another woman raced over, an empty garment bag over her arm. "The next in line is from the 1940s. But we aren't going in chronological order for the fashion show, as the line-up is based on which girls are wearing which dresses. They'll need plenty of time to change, so nothing gets damaged."

All the ladies gasped when Ada gently lifted out Anna's cream-colored dress. The satin bodice was sleeveless and the dropped waist fell into a pleated skirt, a nod to the flapper fashions just starting to take hold in the early 1920s. The entire gown was covered by a tulle overlay, edged with embroidered lace, that extended into elbow-length sleeves.

"There were just a few rips, but I mended them so they won't show." Ada beamed as she carefully adjusted the gown's padded hanger. "We found the veil, down in the cedar chest, but it's so fragile I wasn't able to repair it."

"But you still have the headband," one of the women said. "It's going to be lovely. Hey, Sandy!" she called to a middle-aged woman trying to wrestle an oversized garment bag down the narrow hallway. "I see you somehow got yours in the car."

Sandy repositioned her grip. "Can't believe it's been thirty-four years already for Steve and I. Getting this out of storage brought back so many memories. And a good laugh." As soon as she pulled on the bag's zipper, armfuls of gathered tulle tried to escape.

"It was the eighties, you know. Big hair, big skirts. Puffed sleeves. And if that wasn't enough, there's a wide-brimmed hat." Sandy jerked her chin toward the stairs. "I have to get that out of the car yet. I love my husband, I've never been sorry I married him. But I'm feeling sorry for the poor girl that has to wear this thing."

"Oh, we've got the perfect model lined up." One of the organizers reached for the garment bag. "An older girl, she's got the confidence to pull this off. Besides, who doesn't dream of being Cinderella, if only for a few minutes?"

Sandy left to fetch her hat, and Melinda took a turn at trying to get the gown out of the bag. The dress had several petticoats and a hoop skirt that didn't want to cooperate.

"What goes around, comes around," she explained to the other women through gritted teeth. "The eighties are back in style, actually. The girls will probably think this dress is really cool." She finally got the gown free, but nearly lost her footing on the final tug.

"Oh, dear," Mabel said quietly as Melinda brought the heavy dress around. She was barely visible behind the layers of lace and tulle.

"I do declare, Scarlett," Ada drawled, "that's a ... well, it's an unforgettable dress."

The noise level was rising in the kitchen. Women hurried in and out, and the dual refrigerators were soon filled with salads and side dishes. Two ladies arrived with the white-frosted sheet cakes that would serve as the main dessert. Iced lemon cookies, wrapped in cellophane and tied with aqua ribbons, would be placed on the tables as party favors.

The models began to arrive, flushed with the heat as well as their excitement. Amy Westberg, the pastor's wife and a member of Melinda's book club, popped into the kitchen long enough to say hello. Amy's task was to help the girls get ready for the runway, and she'd brought along deodorant, washcloths, and a sewing kit for fashion emergencies.

Conversation and laughter echoed down the stairwell as some of the guests started to arrive. Two committee members greeted visitors at the double doors to the sanctuary, Inside, the pews' ends were festooned with greenery and faux white flowers.

Melinda was helping Mabel distribute the mints and mixed nuts into several cut-glass bowls when someone tapped her on the arm. "Amy needs you in the dressing room."

The hallway was filled with chattering girls, some of them already in gowns and others still in shorts and tank tops. A woman with a clipboard was trying to make her way through the throng. "Where's Lauren? Has anyone seen Lauren?

"She's sick," one girl called out, her hands protecting her artfully messy bun as a wedding gown was draped over her head. "She texted me this morning."

"Did her mom call someone and let them know?"

The models were too busy polishing each other's makeup and hair to answer. The woman sighed. "Oh, well, I guess a few of the girls can get a second turn. Or a third."

Amy was in the dressing room, next to a model in a 1970s gown with an empire waist.

"Can you hold this train?" she asked Melinda. "I hate to put safety pins through this satin, but the hem's way too long. The last thing we need is an injured girl, or an injured dress."

Melinda lifted the length of fabric out of Amy's way, and flattened herself into the corner as two more girls came in and started to undress. A woman soon followed, a gown over each arm. The fashion show was about to start, and there wasn't a minute to spare.

The small space was now packed with people and nervous energy. Melinda's pulse pounded in her neck, and she bent her knees slightly to steady herself. It was an old trick from her high-school choir days, good for standing on a narrow run of risers in a heavy robe as hot lights flooded the stage.

It's just too warm in here, she told herself. *Remember to breathe, and you'll be fine.*

Two other girls flounced past, giddy in their elaborate gowns. It was all a lark to them, a chance to play dress-up and dream of a day they might walk down the aisle for real. But as the organ boomed its introductory notes above her head, Melinda was suddenly blinking back tears. The memories flooded into her mind, too fast for her to push them away.

She'd found her wedding dress in the side parlor of one of the Twin Cities' best-known bridal shops, just a few weeks after she and Craig announced their engagement. The gown was elegantly simple, all that she'd dreamed of, and thankfully on sale. There were several fittings and then, one last time on the stand in front of the mirror.

Her mom was there, as were Susan and Cassie, oohing and aahing as Melinda humored their requests for a full turn. But as she slowly shuffled her feet, the room began to spin. Then her neck was on fire, and her throat swelled up so fast she could barely beg the attendant to unfasten the gown. An angry rash spread up and over her cheeks, a sudden flush everyone assured her was just some random allergic reaction.

Melinda wanted to believe them. But that night, tossing and turning and unable to sleep, she had to admit it was panic.

She couldn't marry Craig. It was all a mistake, an honest but terrible mistake. She'd paced the floor of her apartment until dawn. And then she called him, insisted he come over, right away, and ...

"Melinda, you're free to go!" Amy called to her over the room's deafening buzz. "The hem's all fixed. Thanks!"

She hurried away, out to where she could breathe, and calmed her nerves by counting the last of the mints into the trays. Once those were spaced down the tables, she volunteered to place the cookies on the plates. Anything to stay in the main area of the basement, away from the chaos of the kitchen and the dressing room.

The fashion show was now under way, and the girls carefully navigated the main stairs as their mothers and some of the other ladies looked after trains and veils. Melinda had just distributed the last of the table favors when another woman flagged her down.

"I need your help. Hurry!"

One of the girls was in the hallway in her gown, tears running down her cheeks. "Mom, can't you get it? I have to get back up there!"

"Oh, honey, we're trying! But we can't rip the dress. Hold still, OK?"

Amy's face was pinched with worry. "The zipper is stuck," she told Melinda. "I've tried everything! It's not coming down. Amanda was supposed to be finished after this dress, but she's the only one of the girls who can wear the gown Lauren was going to model. We need her changed and upstairs in less than ten minutes!"

The zipper was stuck only inches from the top; it would be impossible for Amanda to shimmy her way out. Layers of embroidered lace covered the satin bodice and wrapped into the zipper's seams; one impatient tug, and the overlay would be damaged.

"What about wax?" Melinda suggested. "Might that work?"

"We need a candle." Amy rushed off to the storage room.

Mabel popped into the hallway. "They're trying to stall upstairs, shuffling the lineup and telling the girls to walk a little slower. But there's not much time."

Amanda's mother gave Melinda an appraising look, then reached for Sandy's gown. "Hmm, it'd be close but I think ..."

"Oh, no." Melinda jumped back, as if the elaborate dress might attack her. "I can't! I just ... I'm forty! I can't get up there with all those girls and ..."

Amy returned with a candle and started to scrape its base along the other dress' zipper. "You know, that might work. Melinda, I'm afraid you're our only hope. You can carry it off, I know you can!"

"Down the aisle and back, it's easy." Amanda's mom pulled Sandy's dress off the hanger. "Ten minutes, tops."

Mabel saw the fear in Melinda's eyes and pulled her aside. "Honey, I know why this is hard for you. But it's just a fashion show, it means nothing. What do you say?"

Melinda thought of Angie, about all the hours it took her friend to put this event together, and finally nodded.

"Amy, hand me that hideous thing," Mabel called over her shoulder.

Melinda left her capris on, afraid the skirt's hoops might get a mind of their own and fly up in her face. The heavy lace over the sweetheart neckline was itchy, but at least her bra straps were covered.

"Here, let me do your hair." Still trapped in her gown, Amanda reached for a handful of bobby pins and twisted Melinda's ponytail into a low bun. Mabel added the wide-brimmed hat and reached for the train. "At least there's no veil. Forget what you're wearing, if that's possible. Just don't look down. If you can get up the steps, you've got this beat."

Melinda expected smirks and eye rolls from the models lined up in the entryway, but they silently cheered and clapped when she appeared.

"You're on right after me," one girl whispered. "Slow steps. One-two, one-two … When we get to the front, we're doing a slow turn."

She gave a slight nod to the narrator, who smiled and checked her notes. "Up next, we have a simple, sophisticated style from the sixties … "

"You're so brave!" another girl whispered to Melinda. "I could never wear that thing. You're gonna crush this!"

The first girl made her turn at the front of the church and started back down the aisle. When she passed Melinda, who was now waiting in the doorway with trembling hands, she grinned and offered a high-five.

And somehow, under the bad memories and the mortification and the ache in her neck as she tried to keep the ridiculous hat steady, Melinda took one small step forward. At least she was wearing her comfy flats under all this tulle. Maybe she could make it down the aisle and back without falling on her face.

"And now, we have a very special guest!"

Gasps echoed around the sanctuary, followed by a few sympathetic snickers, as Melinda passed the back row of pews.

"This 1980s design is a perfect example of the era's excess," the narrator said with humor in her voice. "Sandy Hamilton was brave enough to wear it for her wedding, and our last-minute model, Melinda Foster, has graciously stepped in to help us today."

Sandy was on the end of one aisle, cheering her on. "You're doing great!"

"As you can see," the narrator continued, "this gown features a floral embroidered overlay, high neckline and long sleeves. The underdress is white satin, and Sandy tells me there's three ruffled crinolines beneath that. My goodness, it must be heavy. Melinda, does that sound about right?"

Melinda nodded, and laughter rippled across the room. As she started her slow turn, which required her to grip the skirt with both hands to keep the hoops in line, someone began to clap. The sanctuary soon erupted with applause and the ladies rose to their feet. Beaming from ear to ear, Melinda tried for a little curtsy of thanks and nearly lost her hat. The roar of approval grew louder, drowning out the music from the organ, as she found her way back down the aisle.

Mabel and Amy were waiting in the entryway.

"You're the star of the show!" Amy cheered.

Mabel tried for a hug, but the hoops got in the way. "You did a brave thing. I'm so proud of you!" Then she lowered her voice. "I have good news. Ada knows where they keep the communion wine."

* * *

The event was an incredible success. As the church women gathered in the kitchen to wash all those dishes and take down the tables and chairs, there was already discussion about how difficult it would be to top that program next year. Melinda was happy for Angie, as most of the credit was rightfully bestowed on her friend's shoulders, but she was yawning with exhaustion by the time she loaded her car and started for home.

The lingering aroma of calico beans greeted her when she finally staggered into the farmhouse's kitchen. Those leftovers and a salad of garden greens would make a quick supper. There was cake, too, as Ada had sent her home with a generous slice. Maybe she could get in a quick nap before chores. She was so tired ...

What was that, dripping down the front of the cabinet by the stove? And splattered across the linoleum?

She stepped around a gooey pile that could have caused a wipeout, and spotted the tipped-over container of calico beans by the sink. In her rush to get out the door, she'd forgotten to put it in the refrigerator. Or snap the lid on tight, apparently.

There'd been some sort of struggle on the counter, as beans and hamburger and sauce were everywhere. Melinda heard toenails clicking on the linoleum, and thought she had her culprit.

"Oh, Hobo! What have you done!"

Bits of calico beans still stuck to his fuzzy brown cheeks, and he hung his head in shame. But then he gave a little bark and wagged his tail, as if to say, *but it was so good!*

Guilty-faced Grace peeked around Hobo, her calico ruff stained with ketchup sauce. Behind her hid Hazel, who had a noticeable smear across her nose and a lima bean wedged behind one brown ear.

"So, Hobo, you had help, I see." Melinda shook her head, too tired to laugh or cry. "Now I know how some of the beans made it to the floor."

Would a wet washcloth or a wide-tooth comb get that gunk out of the kittens' coats? How dirty were their feet? And it would take several rounds of lemon juice and baking soda to lift all the stains from the laminate counter and the linoleum ... once she got the goop scooped into the trash.

"My little girls are growing so big!" She ripped off a paper towel, then grabbed the rest of the roll. "I wasn't sure you could get up on the counter yet, but I guess you can. And those beans! I'm sure you've all had more than your share. There might be trouble later on."

As if on cue, an unmistakable sound came from Hobo's rear. Melinda closed her eyes for a moment. Life was never dull around here.

"Well, I guess it's frozen pizza for dinner ... again." She shooed Hobo toward the door. "But not for you, mister. Let's get you outside and under the hydrant."

* 15 *

The rumbles next door were bad enough, but soon there came a crash so loud Auggie nearly dropped his coffee mug on the sideboard's counter. He spun on his heel, his brown eyes flashing with irritation behind his glasses, and glared at the far wall of Prosper Hardware.

"Good God! It's not even eight in the morning. I can't believe Vicki has those guys working at this hour." He gave the canister of powdered creamer another disgusted shake, then started for his usual chair by the window.

"And it's not just the noise! This is the fourth day in a row I've come down Main, expecting to have my pick of parking spots, to find three oversized, muddy trucks hogging the best spaces on the curb."

Melinda buried a smirk in her insulated drink holder. It was so warm, even this early in the day, that she'd started packing the cup with ice before pouring in Auggie's brew.

But while Auggie's frustration was heating up, George found it easy to keep his cool.

"Oh, I wouldn't worry about it." He crossed his ankles and leaned back in his chair. "It'll be nice to have another business on Main. And even if Vicki's shop is a success, I doubt we'll face any traffic jams anytime soon."

"Progress is fine and all, but I'm not looking forward to two more months of that racket." Auggie sighed and stared at the wall again. "Vicki says it'll be open in October. That space was nearly empty when she bought it. Wonder what they're doing over there that's taking so long?"

Melinda wondered if Auggie's grumbling really stemmed from the noise, or the fact he didn't have full knowledge of what was happening next door. Thick sheets of filmy plastic now blanketed the inside of the storefront's windows, as Vicki was trying to keep the mess to a minimum while letting a little light seep through. With most of the work hidden from prying eyes, her new business venture was one of the hottest topics in town.

Well played, Vicki, Melinda thought as she sipped her iced coffee. *A little mystery is the perfect way to build some buzz.*

"I'm sure the worst is nearly over," she told Auggie, who was still muttering to himself. "It's been three weeks since they started demolition."

Doc came in the front door, wearing a pair of khaki cargo pants and a white tee shirt. At this hour, he looked like he'd be more at home in a preppy fashion spread than out in some farmer's field. That would change, of course, as he'd be covered in smears and dirt before the end of the morning. But with the thermometer hitting one hundred more days than not, he'd decided it was too hot for heavy jeans and dark-colored tees.

"Just wait," he told Auggie. "They'll be done smashing things over there soon, but then it'll be time for hammers and nail guns. That's the price of progress."

"At least they're not parking around back." Uncle Frank searched for something positive to add. "A dropped nail or screw would be impossible to find in that gravel. Out front, they can sweep up at the end of the day; I've seen them doing it. And I'm glad. The last thing anyone around here needs is a flat tire."

A visible shudder rippled through the group. Punctured tires were a constant threat in rural areas and Prosper's residents were especially careful, as the closest mechanics were ten miles away in Swanton. Auggie had an industrial air compressor behind the co-op's office, and it was free to anyone needing a boost to get their vehicle to a repair shop. The only other option was to swap the tire yourself.

"Melinda, that reminds me," Auggie said, "I'm still meaning to show you how to change a flat. Anyway, I'm eager to see what Vicki's really got planned for next door."

"She brought in those fabric samples, remember?" George peered at Auggie over the top of his mug. "I'm the oldster here, but my mind must be sharper than yours. And those drawings? Blue and white, I think. Lots of flowers."

Auggie waved George's comments away. "I know. But that's not the same as seeing it for real. But, Jerry, I'm serious now ... isn't there something you can do about the racket? Doesn't the city have a noise ordinance?"

"It sure does. But the code says construction is permitted between sunrise and sunset. As long as they aren't working at night, they're fine. Besides, I wish more people would fix up their buildings. We've got quite a few empties along Main."

He gestured out to where the sun was already beating down on the asphalt. The city's tiny business district was looking rather dull these days, and not just because of the vacant storefronts.

The hanging flower baskets began to disappear after the Fourth of July, as some of the property owners grew tired of scaling ladders every day just to give their plants a drink. But Prosper Hardware's impatiens were hanging on, thanks to Miriam and Jerry's stubborn determination, as were the baskets across the way at City Hall and the library.

"And if you want to push back against the noise ordinance," Jerry pointed a warning finger at Auggie, "I can tell you right now what causes most of the complaints: your co-op. When you run those grain dryers in the fall, the emails roll in and the phone starts to ring."

"Well, we gotta go all day and all night, to keep up with the loads coming in." Auggie raised his chin. "Harvest's our busiest time of year."

Doc shook his head. "If we don't get some serious rain soon, I'm wondering if you'll have much of a rush this year. I can't believe what I'm seeing in the fields. Or, should I say, what I'm not seeing. The corn's way behind, and the beans are terrible. Saw the worst ones yet just yesterday, east of town. Wondered if they'll amount to anything by fall."

"I'm hearing the same." Auggie stared intently out the plate-glass windows, as if he could manifest a soaking rain by force of will alone. "We're nearing record highs, day after day ... and the nights aren't bringing much relief. Worse yet, the long-range forecast is bleak."

The group turned reflective and silent, which was especially strange since they were already on their second cups of coffee.

"Hold on," George finally said. "Could be a bumpy landing this year."

Melinda started to buff the oak showcase's counter. Even with the air conditioner rumbling away, the vintage piece's varnish was a bit tacky from the humidity that crept in every time the front door opened. "How soon will the farmers know if they're going to turn a profit?"

Grandpa and Grandma Foster had been farmers, and Roger still couldn't pass a soybean or cornfield without commenting on its condition. Melinda was no expert, but even she had noticed the fields were a paler shade of green than last year, and their crops seemed short in stature for late July.

"No one knows," Auggie sighed. "The next few weeks are going to make or break most fields. And the futures markets are down, which is surprising given everyone thinks there's going to be a shortage."

"Shouldn't they be rising, then? Supply and demand ..."

"Well, you'd think so." George crossed his arms. "But it's more complicated than that. So many things are out of the farmers' control, and the weather's just one of them."

"But it's been years, I mean decades, since it's been really bad, right? Are people that worried?"

When no one answered, she looked up. Doc stared at the floor, his jaw tight. Auggie rubbed his chin and looked at Frank, who shook his head and shrugged. Finally, Jerry tried to answer.

"No one knows what might happen. But this could get bad. Really bad. For Prosper, and for everyone, not just the farmers." One by one, the other men nodded in defeated agreement. "And it's not just the crop futures. The markets around the world affect the overall economy, even here, in our little town."

"Especially in our little town." Frank reached for the coffee pot. "If things get hard, and people can't turn a profit or even make back their expenses, then they don't have the cash for things they need. One bad year, and things might bounce back ..."

"But last year wasn't so great, either." Auggie shook his head. "Tiny profit margins. Lots of guys just breaking even. If they don't get big wins this year, there's going to be trouble."

He thought for a moment, then turned toward Melinda. "How much hay do you have out at the farm?"

Melinda had to think: When was she in the haymow last? Had to be at least a few weeks ago, when she dropped a few bales through the trap door in the loft's floor. The sheep mainly lived off the pasture this time of year, and ownership of the loft had been mostly transferred to Sunny and Stormy, as well as the barn swallows and sparrows that called it home.

"I ... I don't know," she finally said. "Last year, I don't think Kevin had me put out much hay until, oh, maybe October?"

Doc leaned forward. "You'll need to start sooner this year. And if we don't get a good rain this week, you'll have to watch the sheep closely, make sure they're getting enough to eat."

The pasture was adequate for just twelve ewes, but the six lambs were gaining every day. Even though her sheep were quick to find the fresh grass the minute it appeared, their meadow desperately needed a soaking rain if it was going to bounce back.

"I've been giving them extra oats and corn, just to keep them happy," she admitted. "It seems to be enough, for now."

"Feed's going up, too," Auggie said ominously. "You won't be able to rely on that alone. John Olson supplies your hay, if I remember right. Take a good count of what you've got, and have John bring you a load. Don't wait."

"You look really tired." George studied Melinda closely. "Feeling okay?"

"Oh, I didn't sleep well last night, that's all." She turned her back and put the dust cloth away. "Look at the time! I better straighten up before we open." She buzzed into the grocery aisle, where she was out of the guys' line of sight, and their conversation took off in another direction.

It was only a partial lie to say she hadn't slept well. It had been easy to collapse into a deep sleep when she got home from Chase's ... but by then, it was almost one in the morning.

Yesterday, she'd hurried home after work to do chores and spend a few minutes with Hobo and the kittens before hopping in the shower and starting the hour-long drive to Chase's house in Meadville. He grilled steaks, they split a bottle of wine, and then ...

Melinda smirked as she lined up the cereal boxes. Everything was going great, and they had a wonderful time last night ... until the grandfather clock in Chase's living room struck midnight. He laughed at first when she rolled out of bed and pulled on her clothes, then called her Cinderella and asked if her hatchback was going to turn into a pumpkin.

"Stay," he'd said. She could still feel how tightly he'd gripped her hand, and see that look in his eyes that she found so hard to resist.

But she'd insisted it was time to go. She hated driving long distances at night, out on dark country roads, but it made no sense to wait until sunrise. She had to be in the barn at daybreak to make it to Prosper Hardware by seven. And she hated the thought of Hobo and the kittens listening for her key in the back door, staring out at the road, wondering when she would come home.

and his family's business was based in a rural community, but
he now lived in a modest bungalow with just one short row of
vegetables planted along a patio wall. His dog passed away
last year, and he'd yet to find another one. Chase came home
from work, checked the mailbox, maybe turned on the lawn's
sprinkler system, and kicked his feet up for the evening. He
liked to go for a run in the morning, but didn't go to work
until nine. It was a life more like the one Melinda used to
know, with fewer responsibilities.

She turned into the seasonal housewares aisle, and stifled
another yawn as she straightened the shelves and checked the
clearance tags were in the correct places.

Aunt Miriam had discounted their small selection of
coolers and fold-down canvas chairs a few days ago. Several
of the fishing rods had sold, which thrilled Frank and Bill, but
Miriam gently declined to order more as fall merchandise
would start to arrive in early August, which was just two
weeks away.

"Hey, Melinda, I forgot to ask," Jerry called in her
direction. "Got any new neighbors out your way?"

She poked her head out the end of the aisle. "Not that I
know of. I'm sure I would have heard about it."

"Oh, we're talking about the feathered kind." Auggie
wasn't going to let her off the hook. "Someone came into the
co-op yesterday and said they saw a pair of bald eagles
swooping over the pastures along the blacktop, just a few
miles from your place."

"Such majestic birds." George shook his head in awe.
"Used to be thick in this area, when I was a kid. I'd love to see
their numbers pick up again."

The guys were still waiting for her to say something.
Melinda looked at her friends' hopeful faces, and almost told
them the truth. But she was full of secrets these days.

"Sorry, I haven't seen any." She turned away. "Doesn't
mean they aren't around, though."

"They're making a comeback," Doc said. "There's a few nests to the east, along the river bottom. It'd be great if a few more of them set up house around here." He drained his cup and set in on the sideboard. "Well, best get after it. I want my farm rounds out of the way before noon, so I can get back to the clinic where it's cool."

The guys' concerns stayed with Melinda long after they left the store. As soon as the early-morning rush was over, she texted John about getting another load of hay. He could get some to her within a few days, but that wasn't all. He offered to stop by that evening to evaluate her pasture.

Prices are going up right now, he wrote. *I'd hate for you to buy more than you really need.*

Melinda let out a sigh of relief as she texted her thanks. This wasn't the first time she'd been grateful to count an experienced sheep farmer among her friends and neighbors. John was in his barn right then, and his response included a quick snap of Caesar, posing proudly by a gate.

He's getting huge! Thinks he owns the place.

* * *

John's truck was already angled by her garage when she drove up the lane. She'd hoped to get home a few minutes' earlier, but Vicki had stopped in just before four to share her updated plans for the community's first farmers market.

Vicki was determined to give it a whirl, despite the drought, and had set the date for the first Thursday in August. Melinda's only official role was to write the press release, but Vicki's enthusiasm was so contagious, she promised to bring some tomatoes from her garden.

But the sight of her struggling plants as she pulled up to the garage made her heart sink. Would there be anything ready to eat in just a few weeks? The plot was still green, but wouldn't stay that way much longer if reliable rains didn't arrive.

Her bean plants sagged against their fence, baking in the sun, and the slow-turning tomatoes hiding under their leaf canopies were fewer and smaller than last year. The rain barrel was a wise purchase, and had collected a surprising amount of roof runoff the few times there'd been a passing shower. But it didn't generate enough pressure to run a hose to the garden, so she still had to bucket everything over. Keeping the garden going, much less growing, was becoming a part-time job.

John was out of his truck, leaning against the side that was in the shade of the oak tree. Sunny and Hobo were at his feet, but the pasture across the drive was empty. "Looks like your sheep are staying inside today. They're smarter than some people give them credit for."

"I told them to. I like to think they listen to me, at least sometimes. Annie doesn't, of course. But it's shady in there, and I've got some fans running."

They all started for the barn, and Stormy suddenly appeared out of the ferns to join the procession. The sheep hurried toward their troughs when Melinda appeared in the aisle, just in case supper would be served early, but they froze when they saw John.

"Don't worry, nothing's going on," she told the ewes as she handed out a few nose rubs. "We're going upstairs, that's all. Nope, Hobo, I won't open that gate. You'll have to be content with sniffing the lambs from this side."

The fort of hay bales seemed smaller than Melinda remembered. John put one hand to his chin as he ran calculations in his mind.

"Let's see, you've got eighteen head ... six of those half-grown, of course, but still ... Well, if we get some rain, you might be able to hold off on a full load for another month. But if we don't ..." He shook his head. "What's left might last only a few weeks. Especially if the pasture's in rough shape."

"But if prices are going up, shouldn't I get more right away?"

He nodded slowly, still thinking. "Maybe. There's always the chance prices will fall back a bit, especially as more of this summer's hay crop comes on the market. Everything's a gamble these days. One thing's for sure, it's going to be a lean year. No guarantee things will get better anytime soon."

"That's what the guys told me this morning at the store," Melinda said as they started down the stairs.

"You were right to jump on this, for sure. We farmers always need to be looking ahead." That made her smile. "Let's see how the pasture's doing."

Melinda had assumed they would lean over the fence and give the grass a quick evaluation. But John unlatched the front gate, and they started a slow march to the east.

Once they left the shadow of the barn, there was nothing between them and the blistering sun. Melinda flipped her sunglasses down, but soon wished she was wearing a cap. Within minutes she could feel the heat stinging her scalp. The ground must feel the same, day after day. It was amazing the grass survived at all in these conditions.

"This part here doesn't look so bad." John tried to sound positive as they reached the road and started toward the south boundary. Much of this grass was still green, but yellowed strands were visible. Conditions deteriorated, however, as they neared the back half of the pasture. And the farther west they walked, the worse it became.

The grass here was fading fast, and there was soon an unnerving crunch under their boots. John stopped before they reached the far fence, and Melinda also came to a halt.

When he said nothing, she knew.

"It's bad, isn't it? I can see that, this last third is terrible."

John sighed. "Yeah. But no worse than ours. You're lucky the pasture's as good as it is, and you don't have more mouths to feed. But we need some serious rain. If we don't get it ..."

Melinda's face burned hotter, and it wasn't from the unrelenting sun. She tried to keep the tears away. "What's it going to take? I'll do it. I don't want them to go hungry, I won't skimp on their food just to save a buck or two."

"No one's suggesting that," John said gently. "We feel the same about our flock. That's not the way to handle that, anyway. You just sell off some, if you must ..."

John saw the look on her face. "Don't worry, that's not needed, either." He paused, and Melinda sensed the words he refused to say: *not yet.*

There was nothing to fear; or at least, nothing she could see. The sky was eerily blank, an endless stretch of blazing blue devoid of even the smallest clouds. But it was that emptiness that made Melinda suddenly feel cold, despite the blazing heat.

They walked in silence for a few more minutes, following the fence back to the farmyard. Hobo was waiting for them, stretched out in the shade on the north side of the barn. He got to his feet and wagged his tail when they climbed over the back pasture's wide gate. Melinda crouched down and wrapped her arms around him, needing his reassurance, as John stared out across the struggling pasture.

"OK, here's what I think," he finally said. "Keep doing what you're doing. If we get a good rain this week, that'll make a big difference. Otherwise, you'll want to put out even more hay. And remember, sheep love greens and veggie scraps and stuff like that. It all adds up."

"I wish my garden was doing better. I'd share more of it with them, if I could." When Melinda made a salad, the sheep got one, too. So did the chickens. Only the bad, rotten stuff went into the compost pile. But where could she get more? And then, she remembered the Watering Hole had a salad bar. Jessie might be throwing out odds and ends she could use. She'd stop in sometime soon, and try to strike a deal.

"You know, I think we're better to be safe than sorry," John said as they rounded the garage. When he opened the door of his truck, Melinda reached for Hobo's collar.

"How about I bring over a half load this weekend? There's a hay sale Saturday at Eagle River, and I need to stockpile for us, too. Wish I had more to sell out of my own stash, I could give you a better deal."

"No, no, I understand. I'm just glad you can get it for me. Between that, and the boys unloading it ... well, you're spoiling me."

John laughed as he started the truck. "Oh, it's good for them. The more work they have to do, the less likely they are to get into trouble."

* * *

Only one line of thunderstorms rolled over Melinda's farm the rest of the week, but the half inch it left in her rain gauge was better than nothing.

She was able to water most of the garden before the rain barrel was empty. And things got even better when John's sons, Tyler and Dylan, arrived Saturday evening with that half load of hay.

None of this was exactly a sign of plenty, but Melinda was grateful for whatever she could get. That included the totes of leftover veggies Jessie Kirkpatrick promised to have ready, free of charge, every morning Melinda came to town.

Jessie thought it was a great idea. So great, in fact, that she cautioned Melinda to keep their little agreement on the down-low. A few other farmers in the area had sheep; and several people, even right in Prosper, raised chickens. If word got out, Jessie would have to either split the goodies or turn others away.

That meant Melinda had to store the greens somewhere discreet, and Prosper Hardware's office refrigerator wasn't an option. Frank and Miriam could probably be sworn to secrecy, but Esther loved to gossip and Auggie, who worked there during high school, still made himself at home at the store.

More than once, Melinda had found some of his coffee-group treats stashed in that fridge.

Bill, she decided, was the one most likely to keep his mouth shut. He had a half-size refrigerator in the woodshop that was usually empty, except for a few cans of soda, and was willing to share.

So Melinda came to town a few minutes earlier than usual, then turned the opposite way off Third Street to reach the back door of the Watering Hole.

She looked left and right and, when she was satisfied no one was around, rapped her knuckles on the heavy steel door. In seconds, it flew open and Jessie's dark curls popped out.

"Hey," she whispered, "come on in." Jessie pulled the door closed behind them. "I've got a good-sized bin ready." The plastic container was crammed with carrot tops, potato and cucumber ends, and mounds of barely fresh lettuce.

"They're going to love this! I keep offering to pay, but you keep saying no. Let me give you something. How much?"

Jessie shrugged. "Don't worry about it. This is better than tossing it in the Dumpster. We've got a compost pile for our garden at home, but there's only so much it can handle in a day's time. This is a much-faster method of disposal."

"My sheep and chickens say thanks. M wallet does, too."

Jessie snapped the tote's lid on tight. "Prices are going up everywhere, I hear. The farmers that come in? That's all they talk about. If feed prices skyrocket, the cost of meat will go up, too."

"Oh, no. I hadn't thought of that. That'd be terrible for you and Doug."

"It's a good thing we get all our beef, pork and chicken locally. We can't control the markets, but there's something to be said for knowing your suppliers. When you're bound to run into someone at the store, or see them across the gas pump, you have to play fair. Those personal relationships can make all the difference."

Melinda nodded, thinking of John Olson's kindness. The per-bale cost of her most-recent batch of hay was higher than the last, as expected, but from what Auggie said about the markets, she still got a very good deal.

And she knew John would brush off any offer of extra payment, even if she tried to disguise it as a tip for quick delivery.

Where would she be without the support of her neighbors? Back in the Twin Cities, probably.

"You just let me know when you need a favor," she told Jessie. "In the meantime, I'll keep coming by first thing in the morning for the latest stash. It works out perfectly that you don't open until eleven."

Jessie laughed. "We could come up with a secret knock, I suppose."

"Maybe we'll get by without one. But I promise, only Bill knows about this."

"Bill's a nice guy." Jessie got the door, as Melinda's arms were as full as her heart. "He plays on Doug's rec-league softball team. I trust him to stay quiet. I'm so glad your critters can eat some of this stuff for us. But just to be safe, I'll leave out the onion tops and peels."

* 16 *

The overstuffed floral-chintz chair left Melinda room to sit back and relax, but she couldn't. Ada and Jen perched on the matching sofa, also on edge. Through the arched opening into the kitchen, they could hear Wendy, Maggie's oldest daughter, preparing a tray of coffee and cookies they were all too nervous to enjoy.

A muffled knock at the front door, then faraway voices. That would be Barb, Wendy's sister, arriving for what promised to be a tense tea party. Ada flinched and Jen reached for her hand, a gesture that was as much a request for comfort as a show of support. Even the new engagement ring sparkling on Jen's finger wasn't enough to keep a smile on her face.

Maggie wasn't coming today. Wendy had made that clear when she'd finally called Ada back just a few days ago. But the rest of them were going to "talk this whole thing through," according to Ada's report. What that meant was anyone's guess. Kevin had begged off on this trip to Cedar Falls, reminding his mom that classes at the community college started in less than two weeks and he had lesson plans to finalize. It was probably true, but the tension between Kevin and Ada still lingered.

All those weeks of searching, and waiting ... Melinda tightened her grip on the faded cigar box, even though it sat squarely on her lap. She didn't want to drop it, didn't want all of its secrets to spill out at once. But if they shared them with Maggie's daughters, one by one, maybe they could get enough answers that the emotional fractures in the Schermann family could finally begin to heal.

Wendy and Barb were having a low-level conversation in the kitchen, the maddening kind where a listener knows they're being discussed but can't make out the words. Melinda tried to focus on something else, anything else, to pass the agonizing minutes until this awkward meeting would finally begin.

Prosper's farmers market was no longer just one of Vicki's big ideas. The first event would be held Thursday evening, with a whole five vendors on the roster. That number was a great improvement over last week, when there had been only two. But really, they couldn't expect better than that this late in the summer.

The next test would be whether Prosper-area residents would support the new market. Early reaction from the community had been positive, but Melinda hoped people were keeping their expectations in check. With this drought, it might be a blessing if only a few people showed up; there might be enough produce to go around. Her own garden was only a sad shadow of last summer's glory, and she'd be lucky to rustle up a few pint boxes of tomatoes to sell.

Wendy finally appeared in the living room's arched opening with a tray in her hands and a nervous smile stretched tight across her face.

"Ladies, this is my sister, Barb."

Barb only nodded at their guests, and gripped the lemonade pitcher so tightly that Melinda was afraid its glass handle might snap off. Both women had brown eyes, just like Maggie, but their lined faces contained only faint glimpses of the girl in the photo.

Wendy set the tray on the coffee table, then passed the oatmeal cookies to Melinda. She took one out of politeness and handed the plate to Jen as strained introductions were made. Jen's ring flashed in the light; Barb saw a safe topic of conversation and latched on quick.

"That's such a lovely ring! When's the big day?"

"Oh, thank you!" Jen's infectious smile lowered the tension in the room. "We'd been talking about this for a while but, well, it was still a surprise. We'll probably get married in the spring, but, oh, I'd love a fall wedding. But they take so long to plan ..."

"I know what you mean." Wendy motioned toward the coffee and lemonade and began to pour her guests' requests. "My Amanda spent over a year planning her wedding. It's so much work! The church, the flowers, and of course, the dress!"

"And the dinner!" Barb jumped in. "That was an ordeal. How many caterers did Amanda interview?"

"Too many. But she finally found the one she liked. They did the cake, too, which was wonderful. Vanilla with strawberry filling."

"I live in Hampton," Jen explained, "so there's not many options close to home, but I'd be willing to travel for an amazing cake. Before we go, I'd love to get the name of that caterer."

"Sure thing!" Wendy smiled. "You won't be sorry."

The ice was finally broken, but Melinda and Ada and Jen hadn't driven down here to find Jen a caterer. Who would speak first? Suddenly, Melinda had to choke back a laugh. Here they were, discussing weddings, when a wedding that never happened was the reason they were meeting in the first place.

The sisters sat on one side of the coffee table, on chairs pulled from the dining room, while Jen and Ada were on the other. Melinda was on the end, stuck in the middle, and maybe that was where she belonged. She wasn't a member of either family, but her renovations had started this mess.

Ada seemed hesitant to speak, and Jen had done her part by getting the conversation flowing. It was Melinda's turn. She sat up straighter and lifted the cigar box from her lap.

The chatter died away as everyone stared at it and, before she could say anything, Ada found her voice.

"Thank you, both of you, for meeting with us today. This has been quite an emotional roller coaster, for all of us. I can't imagine what it's been like for the two of you."

Wendy's shoulders dropped as she let her guard down. "Yes, that's an understatement. I'm glad you reached out, Ada. And I'm sorry, I should have called you sooner. It's just … well, we've … it's been a lot to process. Barb didn't want to meet you, at first, and …"

"Wendy, please!" Barb's face began to turn red.

"Well, you said that …"

Melinda broke in before a sisterly squabble could erupt. "I can see how hard this would be for you, us barging into your life like this. There's been days I wished we'd never found this box. But I think …" She looked at Ada, who nodded for her to continue. "I think it would be wonderful to fill in some of the blanks, if we can."

She opened the cigar box and reached for the old photograph. The letters could come later, but it was the snapshot Wendy and Barb were anxious to see. Wendy took it with trembling fingers, and was overcome with emotion as she leaned toward her sister.

Tears pooled in Barb's eyes. "Oh, my God! That's Mom for sure! She was so beautiful. And she couldn't be more than, what, eighteen or nineteen here?"

Wendy pressed her free hand to her heart. "We would love a copy of this, if you can make us one. We don't have any photos of Mom that go back this far. Everything we've ever seen started with when she met Dad."

That seemed a little strange. Jen gave Melinda a doubtful look, but stayed quiet.

Melinda reached into her purse. "We already had some made. Thought you might want them."

Wendy studied the picture again, then smiled. "So, this is Horace."

"She's talked about him?" Ada leaned forward.

"Oh, no." Wendy shook her head. "Never. Mom's mind is still sharp, but I'd never heard his name until you called."

"I wonder why that is." Jen twisted her ring around her finger. "I mean, I could understand why it wasn't a big topic of conversation, seeing as she eventually married someone else. But those letters make it clear Maggie and Horace were very special to each other. You'd think, even once ..."

"Well, not everyone's life is an open book," Ada said quickly, offering Wendy and Barb an understanding smile. "And it was all so many years ago. People change, and move on. It happens all the time."

Barb suddenly seemed nervous again, and Wendy stared at the floor.

Melinda gripped the arm of her overstuffed chair. Under all the pleasant chatter and the lemonade and the cookies, something wasn't right. These women were hiding something. But what?

She thought of what Edith had said, how Anna had turned Maggie away. Anna believed Maggie had done something shameful, and Maggie hadn't denied it. Instead, she'd burst into tears, hurried to the car, and never came back. Horace was never mentioned, so the Schermanns finally concluded that whatever had happened, it didn't involve him.

Of course, there was always the possibility that it did.

Ada had turned pale; and Melinda knew she was thinking it, too. The awkward silence was back, in spades.

"Your mother wrote such great letters!" Melinda passed the cigar box to Wendy, as if making a peace offering. "And they're not all about Horace, of course. She gave wonderful descriptions of her family, her high-school friends, her plans for college ..."

The hungry look on Barb's face nearly broke Melinda's heart. Had Maggie never told her daughters about her early years? It was starting to seem like this woman had more secrets than just her teenage love for Horace.

"Oh, she's always loved to write." Wendy managed to grab the top letter before Barb eagerly snatched the box away. "She became a teacher, you see. Taught elementary grades at first, at a country school just outside of town here. Then later, English at the high school."

Wendy started to read silently. She was smiling, but there was a strange tension in the hand holding the letter and she scanned it quickly, like she was searching for something. Barb was doing the same with the next note.

"Oh, this is very sweet," Wendy finally said, her voice far more relaxed than her posture.

"This is from 1946, I see. These letters ... how far out do they go?"

"Summer of 1947," Ada answered. "We've been through the pile, several times. The last one is dated August 1947."

Wendy's shoulders slumped. Barb's letter landed in her lap. The sisters looked at each other, clearly disappointed.

"So ... it sounds like Maggie did go to college." Jen spoke carefully, trying to keep the answers coming. "Was that in the fall of 1947, like she'd planned? Uncle Horace stayed behind; it sounded like he was going to attend Iowa State with Maggie, but never did. And ... then she moved here when she got her first teaching job?"

"Our mother started college at Iowa State, yes." Barb's voice faltered. "But she ... she switched schools after her first year. Came to what is now the University of Northern Iowa, right here in town, a first-rate teachers' college, you know."

"Not that there's anything wrong with Iowa State," Wendy cut in quickly.

"Horace stayed home to help with the farm," Ada explained. "Our oldest brother, Wilbur, was back from the war by then, and Horace could have gone to college, but ... I guess he changed his mind."

Wendy seemed to consider something. "Did he ... travel much? I mean, visit friends in Ames, or anything like that?"

The oddness of the question brought Ada up short. "Horace? Oh, goodness no."

She chuckled softly. "He's quite the homebody, always has been. Even if any of his boyhood friends went off to college, which I'm not sure they did, he would have been content to see them whenever they were back in Prosper."

Wendy raised an eyebrow at her sister.

"Don't!" Barb shook her head.

"We have to find out."

"No, we don't! It's not likely, anyway, and ..."

Ada set her cup on the coffee table and crossed her arms. Melinda could see her friend was running out of patience. The letters had been found almost two months ago. It took weeks to track Maggie down, and then Wendy waited so long to return Ada's call. And now, there was some sort of deception going on here. Ada had had enough.

"Ladies, please. Out with it, for all our sakes. If there's something you want to know, that you need to ask, just do. All of this happened so long ago, it's water under the bridge. Maggie sounds like she was ... she is ... a special lady. She and my brother parted ways, but she obviously went on to have a good life. There's no need for secrets."

Jen widened her eyes at Melinda. The truth was, Barb and Wendy weren't the only ones holding something back. On the ride down, they'd decided not to share what Edith witnessed that long-ago afternoon.

Anna had insulted Maggie, and the whole incident carried more questions than answers.

Jen reached for the cookies, took one, and passed them to Barb. "These are wonderful. Anyone want another?"

Barb accepted the plate but didn't say a word. Wendy took a deep breath, then spoke so quickly that it took Melinda a moment to comprehend what she was saying.

"Our mother had a baby. She had a baby," Wendy said again, as if still trying to process it herself. "In November of 1948. A little boy."

She then recited a list of events she must have rehearsed for this meeting.

"Mom gave him up for adoption. We don't know who the father was. She won't tell us. We've looked everywhere. We can't find him."

"We even did that DNA thing, the one where you spit in the tube." Barb shook her head in frustration. "Got in the database. No matches. Oh, why are we even talking about this? It makes Mom sound so ... so ..."

"Why not? They don't even know Mom." The secret was out, and Wendy was visibly relieved. "I doubt this lowers their opinion of her any."

Wendy turned back to their guests. "We're sorry to spring this on you. But I don't know where else to look, what else to do. Mom had a falling out with her parents over this, and most of her siblings, too. Or at least, her brothers and sisters were afraid to take her side. If there's no chance Horace was the father, we're wondering if it was someone else from around Prosper, someone else she knew from home?"

"Mom said she met him at college." Barb was defensive.

"But what if she's lying? She could be lying to protect ..."

Barb was on her feet. "She wouldn't lie to us! Ever! I wish you'd drop it! Always playing detective, snooping around ..."

"Fine! Maybe she's not lying. But she is hiding something from us. Don't you want to know? I know you do. None of us are getting any younger. We have a brother out there!"

"Half-brother! Mom doesn't want to talk about it, she only did that one time, right after Dad died. I don't think ..."

Jen stood up, and Melinda did, too. Ada was still on the couch, stunned, trying to take it all in.

"We shouldn't have come." Melinda reached for the box of tissues she'd spied on a side table and passed it to Barb. "We had no idea that ... that this would be so upsetting for you."

Jen came back from the kitchen with two glasses of ice water and handed one to each sister.

"Here, let's all sit down. Tell us what you know. Maybe we can't help you find your brother, but at least we can help you talk this through. Sounds like you need to." Wendy and Barb finally sat.

Ada looked at Melinda, and then Jen. "I think we'd better tell them," she said sadly.

Wendy turned pale. "Oh, God. Yes, whatever it is ..."

"I am very certain Horace was not the father of Maggie's baby." Ada took a moment to gather her thoughts. This meeting wasn't exactly following the agenda they'd drafted.

"I'm the youngest of eight, so I was just a toddler when all of this was going on. But one of my sisters witnessed something in the summer of 1949 that I think you should know about."

Ada recounted the exchange between Anna and Maggie, her face burning with regret when she told the sisters what Anna said to their mother.

Wendy's eyes filled with tears, and she reached for her sister's hand.

"It must really be true, then. What else could that refer to? And I don't mean to pass judgement on your mother," she quickly told Ada. "A child out of wedlock was quite the scandal then, there was so much shame. We think it's the real reason she switched colleges. She didn't tell us this, I had to piece it together from college records, but she missed the 1948 fall semester."

"She would have been showing by then," Barb added. "And then the baby came ..."

"We think she went to a home for unwed mothers," Wendy continued. "She gave the baby up for adoption, enrolled for the spring 1949 semester at a different school, and never looked back."

"Except that summer, she tried to go see Horace." Barb wiped away tears. "She must have really loved him. Maybe that's why she ... dated this other guy. She was so devastated when they broke up."

"A rebound, as the kids call it today." Wendy threw up her hands. "Whoever he was, Mom must have decided he wasn't marriage material. Or, he threw her over when he found out she was pregnant."

"But some of it worked out, right?" Jen asked, filled with the all-encompassing hope of the newly engaged. Melinda remembered what that felt like. "She met and married your father, and they were happy ..."

Wendy rubbed her eyes. "Mom and Dad cared for each other, but something always seemed a bit off between them. Dad was a good man. But very quiet, very reserved."

"Did he know about the baby?" Melinda asked.

Barb shook her head. "We don't know. He's been gone for several years now. And there isn't any one left to ask."

"Except Mom." Wendy looked at her sister. "We have to try again, to try and find our brother. And we need to tell her about Horace."

Ada clasped her hands together. "Do you think she'll want to meet him?"

"I hope so." Wendy looked to Barb for support, and Barb finally nodded. Wendy took a deep breath and let it out.

"Knowing what we know now, and what we suspect, I think she would. This is going to be hard, but we have to tell her everything we know. And show her this photo."

She took one print from the coffee table and held it up. "You know, I don't think I've ever seen Mom smile like that," she said wistfully, "like she's got the whole world on a string."

"She was so young then," Ada said. "The young always think the world's their oyster. That they can do anything, be anything. But things don't always go according to plan."

Barb turned to Ada. "What about Horace? Do you think he wants to see Mom?"

"I simply don't know. He and Wilbur share a room at the nursing home, and Wilbur's dementia is getting worse. Horace has been down about that and I ... I didn't want to disappoint him. We wanted to reach out to you first."

Wendy gathered up the spoons and cups with efficient speed. Now that she had more answers, she was a woman on a mission.

"We'll talk to Mom again. It might take a while to bring her around, but I'm not about to give up. What you told us has been a great help. Maybe it's the information we need to get Mom to tell us the truth."

✳ 17 ✳

"This is the only day this week I haven't wished for rain." Vicki shuffled the cardboard tomato cartons on the folding table, wanting them to look their best. A large patio umbrella tried to keep the blistering sun at bay. Unfortunately, it also blocked most of the breeze. "I wish I had more to bring, but our patch is looking pretty bad. Melinda, what've you got?"

Melinda sheepishly added two pint boxes of tomatoes and three stunted cucumbers to the display. All of it had easily fit inside one canvas bag.

"I'm watering like crazy, but my garden's still a wreck. Even the herbs, which are hard to kill, are about done. I felt lucky last night to have one full-grown tomato and a little lettuce ready at the same time so I could finally make a BLT."

"Those heritage ones look pretty good, though." Vicki pointed to Melinda's lone carton of German Pinks. "I want to try some next year. I know some of the newer hybrids are less susceptible to blight and such, but the old-school varieties are supposed to hold up well in tough conditions."

Melinda felt like a proud parent as she smiled at her heritage tomatoes. After all, she'd worked hard to get them this far this summer.

"I guess they had to be hardy, to come all that way across the ocean decades ago, and then adapt to the soil here in North America."

She angled a vacant lawn chair to make the most out of the umbrella's shade before she sat down. "I got them from Bev, as starter plants. I'm sure she'd be happy to hook you up." Bev was another member of the library's book club. "I hope she comes tonight. I saw her in Swanton the other day, and she seemed interested in the market."

Nancy strolled over, barely recognizable under her floppy straw hat and wrap-around sunglasses, and took the last empty chair. While she had dark hair, her complexion was very fair and prone to sunburn. "We started planning this market months ago, and here we are. Where has the summer gone?"

Melinda lifted her ponytail and fanned her neck. "I think it's blown away in one big puff of hot air."

Vicki studied the five other tables set up on the north side of the small city park. The initial plan was for vendors to line up just off Main Street's curb, but that was wisely altered to put everyone in the sort-of-shade of the water tower, and the trees that hugged its base.

"I'd love to see Bev tonight." Vicki leaned on the table and rested her chin in one hand. "Lots of other people, too."

Four cars were parked along the curb. Just over a dozen hardy residents roamed from table to table, many of them with canvas bags slung over their shoulders. Three of the five vendors had produce, and some of it went beyond tomatoes and corn. The one offering seasonal fruit, including raspberries and cantaloupe, seemed to have the most business, as there were almost enough customers to form a line. The last table was the one Melinda was the most excited about: Adelaide and Mason Beaufort were trying to get their honey business off the ground, and brought some homemade lotions and soaps as well as small jars of the sweet stuff.

"It's like that saying." Vicki shook her head as she studied the scene. "'Which came first? The chicken or the egg?' Only here it's, 'the vendors or the customers?'"

Nancy adjusted her hat. "I don't think moving the tables back from the curb is keeping people away. It's just too darn hot for anyone to want to be outside for very long. Attendance has been down at Swanton's market, too, I guess."

"Did you hear about the record?" Melinda asked her friends. "The one we broke yesterday?"

Nancy groaned. "Of course! Auggie called city hall about five seconds after it happened. Jerry didn't pick up his cell fast enough, I guess, and Auggie hoped he was there. Which is silly, because there's not that much paperwork for the mayor of a town this small. I suspect Auggie just couldn't wait to tell someone, and he knew I was around."

"Let me guess." Vicki reached into the cooler at her feet for a bottle of water, then passed more to Melinda and Nancy. "It was hot yesterday. Am I right?"

"One. Hundred. And. Three. Degrees!" Melinda raised an arm in triumph. "Just after two p.m. Hottest August day ever on record in Prosper."

"I'd believe it." Vicki pressed her cold water bottle to her neck. "How long had the previous record stood?"

"I'm not sure," Melinda answered. "Maybe since the nineteen-thirties? Auggie called me after he called you, Nancy, and he was so excited, I couldn't make out the exact year."

A woman with a cranky toddler in tow stopped at their booth. After an impressive amount of reflection, given the scorching heat and the slim pickings on the table, she finally decided on a cucumber and two of Vicki's tomatoes. Once she got the woman her change, Vicki settled back in her chair and turned to Melinda.

"So, let's hear about this family reunion you had last weekend."

"It was fun, I saw so many people I rarely get to see. And as you know, my brother was back from Texas, and my sister's family was here from Milwaukee. My nephews pitched a tent in my yard, and they and Hobo had a little camping party." The canvas had lit up with two flashlight beams until after ten both nights, with the boys too busy reading comic books and telling ghost stories to bother with getting to sleep.

"I think their favorite thing, though, was chasing lightning bugs. And my watermelons are far from ripe, but we got some at the grocery store and ..."

Vicki motioned for her to stop. "Now, now, that's not what I meant, although I'm glad everyone had a blast out at the farm. How did Chase do? Did he win your family over, or what?"

"What's there to prove?" Nancy shrugged. "I only met him once, on the Fourth, but he seems like a good guy. He's rather handsome, I'd say, and certainly has a way with people, being in sales like he is."

Vicki laughed. "Oooh, sorry to break it to you, Nancy, but I think he's spoken for."

Melinda held up a hand.

"Now, just a minute! I don't know if 'spoken for' is the right way to put it. We've only been dating for two months. We're just ... well, we'll just see what happens. But he did play catch with my nephews at the picnic, and Dad and Uncle Frank both seemed impressed by his stories about crop-dusting and farm aerials."

Melinda was glad Chase was such a hit with her family. But in hindsight, the Foster reunion maybe hadn't been the best way to bring him into the fold. Roger eagerly walked Chase around for handshakes and hellos, introduced him to every second cousin and great uncle. Her dad was just trying to be welcoming, but all that exposure set a dangerous precedent for holiday gatherings, and next summer's picnic ...

"Well, I'm glad to hear he stuck it out," Nancy was saying. "I'm sure there were lots of questions and stares and such. Meeting the family is always a little awkward."

Vicki raised an eyebrow. "Hmmm. Nancy, do you have something to tell us?"

Nancy snorted. "You've got to be kidding! I've got two high-schoolers at home, plenty of work and activities going on, and I'm past fifty. Nope, I'm single from here on out."

Melinda was sure Vicki was waiting for her to say more.

So she did. She changed the subject entirely.

"But the most interesting thing was my brother. Mark's unhappy in Austin. His day job's boring and his music career isn't really taking off. And, he broke up with the latest girlfriend just a few weeks ago. He's actually considering moving back."

Vicki adjusted the patio umbrella's angle, as the sun was on the move. "Would that be starting over, or running away?"

"I asked him that very question. I think it's really the second. I told him that's a poor reason to pull up stakes, and he said I had no room to talk, then. He was rather grumpy with me the rest of the day, but he'll get over it."

Mark had always been a bit moody, so Melinda didn't think he'd hold a grudge for long. Besides, it was a message he needed to hear. No matter what kind of day job Mark had (and there had been many over the years) he'd be miserable without his music. Where would he play guitar around here? There were a few bars and restaurants in Swanton that occasionally hosted bands, but that was it. And the new Prosper farmers market certainly wasn't going to be adding live music anytime soon.

"Hey, here comes the city's official delegation." Nancy pointed out Jerry and Frank, who were climbing out of Jerry's SUV. The park was only three blocks from City Hall and Prosper Hardware, but Melinda was glad her uncle hadn't attempted to walk that far on a day like this. If the heat hadn't done him in, Miriam surely would have.

Vicki perked up when Jerry waved in the ladies' direction. "I think I can count them as attendees. There's no ribbon cutting for something like this, but it's wonderful to see our esteemed mayor and his sidekick show up."

Melinda reached into Vicki's cooler and pulled out two more bottles of water.

"Don't mind if I do." Frank guzzled a third of his bottle in short order. "Man, it's like an oven."

"Maybe I should've asked another council member to come," Jerry said. "Last thing we need is you keeling over."

"No, no, I'm fine."

Nancy insisted Frank take her chair, and he dropped into the shade with a grateful sigh. "This is exciting, a new venture. I wanted to check it out. And I would've brought some things, too, if we had anything worth sharing."

"That's the story of the whole evening." Vicki crossed her arms. "We'll have to see if this thing takes off, or not. If this is any indication ..."

"It'll just take time," Nancy said gently. "And it's not just the heat. This is something new. People have to get in the habit of showing up, and they will. Besides, even with the drought, there'll be more produce ready in the coming weeks. And just think how wonderful it'll be in the fall, with apples, pumpkins ..."

"We need a fall festival!" Vicki rubbed her hands together. "Prosper's got a Fourth of July event, and the holiday open house, but nothing big to celebrate autumn and Halloween. Nancy, that's a great idea!"

"So ..." Jerry said in a too-casual voice, his gaze sweeping over the park. "Any sign of Jake?"

"Nope." Nancy waved away a bug. "Mayor Simmons, you have the campaign trail to yourself tonight. Just wander around, be yourself. No one to compete with here."

Jerry reached into the back pocket of his cargo shorts for his phone. "That's not the half of it. I just got an email from the county; we're supposed to be rationing water, effective immediately. No watering of lawns allowed."

Nancy sighed and reached for her device. "That's going to go over really well, I'm sure. I'll get it on the website and send out a text alert."

"What about gardens?" Vicki sat up, worry on her face. "What does it say?"

"Well ..." Jerry scrolled down his screen. "Says here: 'Residents are urged to conserve water, particularly by lowering their usage between the hours of eight a.m. and eight p.m.' No specific language about gardens. But it also says we're supposed to ticket anyone caught running a lawn sprinkler."

"Who's going to do that?" Frank grumbled. "Our imaginary police force? I doubt the sheriff will send over one of his stretched-thin deputies to scold some old woman trying to save her yard."

"Excellent question." Jerry smirked. "People are just going to be on the honor system, like usual, I guess. Oh, and by the way," he added sarcastically, "the press release also reminds everyone that rain barrels are for sale at the county's maintenance office for forty-five bucks."

"A lot of good those do when there's no rain in sight," Frank said, then turned to Melinda. "You're on a well out at the farm, right? So you're good. Nobody's looking over your shoulder."

"For now. But I'm being careful. Ada said something once about the well nearly drying up during the Dust Bowl days in the thirties. I don't really know how deep it goes, or anything about the aquifers that supply it. I'm already conserving water, just in case."

"Oh, you'll be fine. It's dry, but it's not that dry." Jerry noticed the German Pinks. "Hey, my grandma used to raise those. Are they as good as they look? I'll take three."

* 18 *

Melinda adjusted the brim of her battered straw hat, squinted at her suffering garden, and sighed with a mix of acceptance and defeat. The end of the growing season was still two months' away, but she was seriously considering a last-ditch plan to harvest early, choose a handful of the hardiest plants to receive all her water and attention, and let the rest go.

"Thank goodness for the grocery store," she told the crow studying her with steely eyes from the ridge of the green beans' fence.

"I'd starve long before Christmas if I had to live off what's out here. How did Anna do it, all those years ago? Eight kids, and herself and Henry; ten people to feed from this patch. They must have all been out here, day after day, just to keep the plants alive. To keep themselves fed."

The last week had been worse than the one before. Not a drop of rain, not even an overcast day to bring a few hours of relief. The relentless heat was compounded by scorching winds that blasted out of the southwest from sunrise until after nightfall.

It was only the middle of the month, and the shiny-new record temperature for August had been matched four times already. Even Auggie had thrown his hands up in defeat.

Melinda imagined him hunched over the battered wooden desk in his weather station, carefully adding the triple-digit numbers to his ledger with a grim expression and a heavy heart.

Except for the crow, Melinda was alone. Hobo was inside with the kittens, and Sunny and Stormy preferred to ride out these grim hours of late-afternoon heat somewhere in the shade. The plastic bucket she carried was still empty, as she had yet to find anything edible enough to put in it.

She crouched along the green beans' fence and continued her search. The ground was so hard, so dry and cracked, she could feel it pressing on her knees through her old jeans.

No new beans. But there were some stunted pods that gave her reason to hope. A few stubborn watermelons and pumpkins had taken hold on the far side of the garden, and some ears of sweet corn were still trying to grow. The pepper vines were wind-whipped and shorter than they should be, but she found an almost-ready youngster hiding on the back of one plant.

Even though a surprising number of cucumbers still clung to their maze of leaves, they were so small that Melinda feared none of them would amount to much before frost. She moved on to the lettuce, and found only a few leaves so wilted with defeat that they were only fit for chicken snacks.

Melinda trudged across the lawn, where the brown patches now far outweighed the green, with her head down and her spirits low. Her lot was better than many others in this community, and she knew it. She had a job that offered health insurance and a steady salary. She was careful with her cash, and still had a bit of savings not tied up in retirement accounts.

But country life came at a cost. There was always some unexpected expense needing her money as well as her attention. Contract assignments from Susan's marketing firm had bridged more than one gap in the past year, but that once-steady stream of work was drying up amid growing fears the economy was headed south.

Worst of all, the stack of new hay bales was shrinking with alarming speed. Week by week, the sheep's diet had shifted until it was now rooted in hay, and merely supplemented by random blades of pasture grass and the greens Melinda brought home from town. No matter how many times she counted the bales, or refigured how much her flock needed every day, the answer was always the same: This batch of hay could be gone by the end of the month.

She didn't want to call John. He and his family were still at the state fair in Des Moines, as Tyler and Dylan were showing their prize lambs. But that wasn't all: Nathan was doing the Olsons' chores, and he'd mentioned how worried John was about his own hay supply.

Melinda now saw that small loads, here and there, weren't going to be enough as long as this drought dragged on. This time, she needed to stock up for the long haul, far into fall and even winter if she could. And that was going to be very expensive.

The scraps of wilted lettuce went inside the back porch door, where they would wait for chore time, and Melinda picked up the small scoop of corn she'd already brought in from the barn. Her hens loved their corn-sicles, and the current batch was nearly gone. This, at least, was one problem with a cheap-and-easy fix.

The concrete-block basement was refreshingly dim and cool. Melinda reached for the recycled plastic butter containers waiting on the counter by the utility sink, shook in the kernels, and added water nearly to the rims. She took the bowls into the canning room, settled them in the chest freezer, then gazed at the rows of still-empty glass jars.

So far, she'd only preserved a few rounds of strawberries and some rhubarb-berry jam, way back in June when the season still held so much promise. She'd dialed her hopes back since then; several times, actually. If she could manage a small batch of salsa, and some jars of the corn relish Horace loved so much, she might be willing to let the rest of her canning plans slide this year.

It wasn't just the corn relish that was in doubt. The chances for a Horace-Maggie reunion also looked dim.

Maggie's eyes had brightened when Wendy and Barb told her they'd found Horace. But she'd turned sullen and defensive when they tried to ask more questions about her past. Wendy had taken the old photo along, but later told Ada Maggie became so upset she didn't have the courage to pull it from her purse.

The visit ended with everyone in tears. Wendy promised to try again in a few weeks, once Maggie had some time to absorb the possibility of seeing Horace again.

How different Horace's life might have been if his mother hadn't turned Maggie away that hot summer afternoon! But then, there was always the possibility that something else, or even someone else, had caused the young lovers to go their separate ways. And while time may heal many wounds, some scars never fade. What if seventy years hadn't been long enough to erase whatever hard feelings had caused Maggie and Horace to part?

Melinda finally started up the basement stairs, her footfalls echoing on their wooden treads. "Life is full of tough choices. Who knows what's going to happen, to any of us?"

She wandered into the dining room, her mind still swirling with questions, and the nearly vacant buffet caught her eye. The few stacks of books she'd put behind its glass doors made it look less empty, but she still missed the lovely rainbow of china that once greeted her each time she entered the room. Most of it was sold at the auction, but the sentimental pieces had been carefully divided among the women in the Schermann family.

Except, of course, for Anna's wedding china. She'd let it go during the Great Depression, insisted Henry trade it for the feed their livestock desperately needed. Horace had been only a toddler at the time. But that day, and his mother's selfless decision, had made a great impression on him. With tears running down her cheeks but her chin raised high, Anna had packed her beautiful china in newspaper and told her two little boys that while it was a blessing to have nice things, the necessities of life must always come first.

And now Melinda stood here, in what used to be Anna's home, worrying about the future and wondering how she was going to make ends meet.

"If only I had a set of fancy china to sell," she told Hazel, who appeared around the corner with sleepy eyes. Her long, brown-tabby fur was cool to the touch when Melinda held her close.

"Napping on the floor register again? It's the place to be on a hot day like today."

She turned into the living room, Hazel still in her arms. "We'll just have to do like Anna did, won't we? Be frugal. Industrious. 'Where there's a will, there's a way,' and all that."

Hobo and Grace dozed on the bed in the next room, stretched out on Anna's faded crazy quilt. Melinda tried to keep a modern fleece throw over the patchwork, to protect it from so many small feet as well as the sun streaming in the bedroom's west window, but often found the cover pawed to the side.

"What is it about that quilt that you love so much?" Melinda asked Hobo, who yawned and thumped his tail in greeting. Grace barely opened an eye.

"Does it remind you of Horace? Maybe it's all the patterns, and the little yarn ties, because the girls seem to prefer it, too."

All of the sudden, Melinda had her answer.

She deposited Hazel next to Grace, then ran her hands over the antique iron frame's turned posts and finials. What had Horace said about this bed, the day the Schermanns carted away most of what he'd left behind?

It comes with the house.

This was her house now. Her bed. And according to the housing inspector, who'd claimed to be well-versed in such things, it was a valuable piece any Americana collector would love to acquire. He'd even mentioned an antiques dealer, someone in Clear Lake ...

Hobo would be disappointed, of course, to lose his oversized throne. But she'd get him one of those pet beds with the bolstered sides, make sure it was generous enough that he could share it with Grace and Hazel, like always. The iron bed was beautiful, for sure; but to Melinda, all the sentimental value was in Anna's quilt. She'd tuck it away somewhere safe or, even better, insist Ada take it home.

As she studied the antique bedstead, her mind running ahead to how much it might be worth, Melinda saw so much more than the farm's history. She saw a part of its future ... the money she desperately needed.

* * *

Hobo was a bit confused at first, and the kittens had to sniff their fluffy new bed from corner to corner before they finally settled in. But the change in routine was a small price to pay for the stack of crisp hundred-dollar bills the antiques dealer pressed into Melinda's hand.

"You can sleep well, my dear, knowing your sheep are provided for. Glad I could help out." The woman stared after the bedframe with adoring eyes as her two helpers carted its sections out to the truck. They just happened to be on their way to Swanton with a delivery, which had saved Melinda and Lizzie a trip to Clear Lake.

"I can't wait to get this in the shop! I already made a few calls, but it's going to attract some interest, that's for sure."

Maybe Melinda should have held out for more money, but it was too late. She'd researched the bed online, based on its motif and condition, and her jaw had dropped at the retail prices people paid for such things.

But she'd gotten a fair price, at least. She pocketed the wad of cash, and found herself returning the shop owner's ecstatic grin.

'You have such a lovely home," the woman said sweetly as she laid a hand on Melinda's arm and glanced around the farmhouse. "So charming, so much character. The same family lived here for over a hundred years, you say? You get in a bind and need a little extra to get yourself through, you just give me a call."

"Thanks, I'll do that." Melinda walked the woman out, wondering if this was how people felt when they completed a drug deal. She was elated, a little nervous, and already thinking of what else she might be willing to part with. Anna's quilt? Never. But if times stayed tough, and feed prices continued to climb ...

After the truck rumbled away in a cloud of gravel dust, she went back into the downstairs bedroom and reached for the broom waiting in the corner. She'd sweep the floorboards, give the whole room a good cleaning. It needed a rug, and a chair or desk, something to fill it up again.

"I'm glad you all seem to like your new bed," she told Hobo and the kittens. "I'm really glad I paid the extra shipping to get your package here yesterday, so you could get used to the new bed before the old one was hauled away."

Grace just stared at her, those green eyes flashing with something akin to contempt.

"I know, I'm so sorry." Melinda set the broom aside and crouched on the floor. "But I had to sell it. It's just this awful drought, I had to get more hay. You wouldn't want the sheep to go hungry, would you?"

Grace stretched out a paw and touched Melinda's hand.

"Good, we're square. There's some leftover chicken in the fridge. I think you all need a special treat tonight for being so understanding. I'm going to call Karen, and tell her we're on for Saturday."

Melinda had already taken that day off to drive to Minneapolis for Cassie's birthday weekend, and Ed and Mabel were willing do chores while she was gone.

But there was a hay sale Saturday at the Eagle River auction barn, and she was determined to be there. She just didn't want to go alone. Chase was at a business conference out of state. She couldn't ask her parents, as Roger would insist on helping unload the hay and she didn't want him to overdo it in this heat. But Karen, who was always up for an adventure or two, had jumped at the chance to go along. She'd grown up on a farm, and attended many auctions with her dad over the years. Doc suggested they borrow the veterinary clinic's small stock trailer to haul their load. It was better than driving two pickups and, as Melinda had already decided, one truck bed's worth wasn't going to be enough.

Smoothing things over with Cassie hadn't been quite so easy. Melinda promised her a girls' weekend sometime in the fall, whether there or here or somewhere in between. Susan had taken a practical approach to the situation. "You go to that sale, and get the best hay you can get. That's far more important. I bet even Annie is going to be grateful, and that's saying something."

Melinda was now comfortable behind Lizzie's wheel, but had never pulled anything with her truck. Karen, of course, was a pro, and already had the trailer hitched to her pickup when Melinda met her behind the veterinary clinic early Saturday morning.

The auction barn's vast parking lot was mostly full by the time they arrived. Melinda hadn't known what to expect, maybe a loose gathering of farmers laughing and chatting as they sipped coffee from the concession stand, but this looked to be serious business.

"Look at these crowds!" She gawked as Karen joined the line of vehicles turning off the highway. "Is every farmer within thirty miles here? I'm glad you're driving; I don't know how I'd navigate this mess with a trailer on the back."

"Oh, this is nothing. You should see me drive a combine." Karen grinned as she navigated a tight turn. "Hey, there's a good spot! It's too bad you had to give up that vintage bed, but you're doing the right thing. It's all anyone talks about, anymore, when I'm out on calls. Hay prices are still rising."

Melinda pulled her phone and wallet from her purse, and stashed them in her jeans' pockets before hiding her bag behind the seat. They'd dressed in old chore clothes and boots, and wore battered canvas caps that would not only block the relentless sun in the yard's back lot, but make them blend in with the other bidders. Karen had been right; there were very few women in the crowd.

"We'll want to keep our heads down," Karen said as she cut the engine. "No laughing or smiling. Things are getting serious around here, and everyone's out for themselves. I heard that the other day, at a hay sale over north of Fort Dodge, a fight nearly broke out over the last wagon-load. Someone was sure their competition was buddies with the auctioneer, and they were trying to rig the deal."

Melinda swallowed hard. "I just need some hay. The last thing I want is any trouble."

This scene was a far cry from a charity auction she'd attended with Susan and Cassie in Minneapolis. Everyone had been dressed to the nines, and smiled graciously at the auctioneer as they held up their gleaming silver paddles. Melinda missed out on a lovely platinum bracelet, but they'd simply adjourned to one of their favorite restaurants, split a bottle of wine, and enjoyed a nice dinner.

The bauble had been quickly forgotten, until now. This time, there was so much more at stake. "What if I raise my hand at the wrong time? Or worse, what if I can't get anything?"

"Tell you what," Karen said as they got in line for the clerk's table. "My dad's really good at this, and I learned a lot over the years. I'll do the bidding."

Melinda got a number and, as the auction didn't start for almost forty minutes, they joined the sea of farmers wandering from one flat-bed trailer to the next, evaluating the lots that would soon be up for grabs.

They walked behind the first load of hay, and Karen pulled a stem from one bale. "See, this stuff's not very good," she said in a low voice. "You can tell by the color. They cut it at the wrong time."

Several men were studying the wares on the next trailer, too engrossed in their own critiques to notice Karen and Melinda. The third batch of hay was better, and the fourth quickly earned Karen's approval.

"But that's going to go high, like crazy-high," she whispered as they moved on. "Let's see, what else ... here's an option. It's good stuff but a smaller lot, it won't be so attractive to the big-league farmers. They want a huge quantity, they'll take an entire flat and then cut a deal for more from the same supplier. If you can get this load, or most of it, then we'll piece out a few more bales here and there. Take the leftovers, if you will."

Karen lowered her cap's brim as two men, fretting about the markets, came around the side of the trailer.

"You know them?" Melinda asked after they passed by, suddenly worried. "Maybe you should let me bid. I don't want you to get on the outs with someone professionally."

"It'll be fine. I've only seen a few familiar faces. We don't want to be in the first row, but we'll keep to the front of the group. If you're in the back, the guys can turn around and see who they're bidding against." Karen pointed at the main building. "Let's hit the restroom and get some coffee."

Melinda's nerves were tingling by the time the sale began. The auctioneer welcomed everyone, exclaimed over the excellent turnout, then joked that at least they didn't have to worry about getting rained out.

Only a few of the bidders managed a laugh, and a wave of tension rolled through the crowd. Melinda stared down the row of trailers, a knot in her stomach, and tightened her grip on her foam coffee cup. The sooner they got what they needed and got out of here, the better.

The bidding was fast and furious. Melinda and Karen quietly decided how much they would pay per bale off each load, and then Melinda stayed silent while Karen jumped into the fray. She offered only a curt nod now and then, and was so stoic it sometimes wasn't clear if she was still bidding. But then the auctioneer's assistant would point their way, and they were once again in the lead.

This was far harder than Melinda expected. Karen wasn't the only one who knew which flatbeds had the best hay, and many of the bidders were determined to not go home empty-handed. Melinda was able to pick some extra bales off two of the better loads, after the large-scale farmers had cut their deals, and was feeling a little better. But she had a number in mind, and they weren't there yet.

The mass of people shifted down the line as the bidding went on, and the heat ratcheted up as the morning waned. Anticipation rippled through the crowd when the next stop was the premium load Karen pointed out earlier. But the auctioneer merely waved everyone on, saying they'd save it for last because the lot was so large.

"Folks, I've got an idea," he drawled and offered his best salesman's smile. "Let's let the little guys get what they need and head on out. There's plenty for the rest of us."

"Liar," Karen whispered to Melinda. "It's actually the opposite. He wants to make everyone stay and fight over those bales because they're so good."

The auctioneer's sidestep was met with snickers and jeers. One of the guys next to Melinda swore. Boos spread through the crowd.

"Crook!" somebody finally shouted.

"Hey, Joe, you got a hand in this? You dirty son of a ..."

"Quilt stalling and start the bids! We're paying through the nose already. I've got a hundred head to feed!"

"I wonder if this is the same auctioneer," Karen said. "The one that tried to throw the other sale."

"I don't know, but something's up. Look."

Two grim-faced men marched out of the sale barn and started toward the lot. One was on his phone. They held a short, tense conversation with the auctioneer, who finally gave a nervous laugh and took a small step back.

"OK, OK, folks, let's not get all riled up. Just trying to give everyone what they want." He adjusted his cowboy hat, glanced toward the lot's entrance, and plastered on another smile. An Eagle River police car was turning off the highway.

"It's sure getting hot out here, huh? Let's get back at it! Now, here's the load you've all been waiting for, it's a fine batch, I'd say ..."

The women didn't even try to get in on that one. Melinda couldn't believe the numbers she was hearing, and the bidding was intensifying, not slowing. When the lot finally sold, one man took every last bale.

"How can he afford that?" she whispered to Karen.

"He probably can't. Most of these guys are already in the hole for the year, he's gambling on credit. So, this next load looks pretty bad, I'd pass on it."

After that came the one Melinda really wanted. She whispered a number to Karen, more than she would have liked to pay but something she could live with, and they were off and running again.

The auctioneer's assistant knew where they stood. They were the only women toward the front of the pack, and bidding on the middle-of-the-road lots. As soon as the first bid was placed, he pointed at Karen. *You in?*

She tipped her chin. *Yes.*

Three more bidders jumped into the fray. Melinda felt cold despite the sweat trickling down her back. She needed that hay, but she was going to have to fight for it. The rest of the lots would either run sky-high or be rough stuff she didn't want to feed her flock. She thought of Annie and Clover and the others, waiting at home in her barn, and the dwindling stack of hay in her loft.

Karen raised an eyebrow at Melinda. *Keep going?*
Yes.

One bidder dropped out, then another. Melinda could hardly breathe. Both of the remaining competitors were on the other end of the crowd. She couldn't see who they were, but it didn't matter.

Karen elbowed her, and she elbowed back. *Don't stop.*

The auctioneer's call finally ground to a halt. He asked again, and no one moved.

"Sold!" He pointed at Karen. "Over here in the front. Number 54. How many?"

"Thirty."

A man behind them snickered. "Hobby farmers."

"Sixty!" Melinda blurted out. "We'll take sixty." She glared at the man, who looked away.

"I'm sorry," she told Karen. "We may need to make two trips. Or I'll call Ed; I know he's home."

"We'll figure something out. Take what you can get, while you can get it."

The auctioneer had already moved on and was picking up bids on the balance of the load. Karen and Melinda went back to the bidders' table, where the elderly woman in the shade of the large umbrella smiled at them as they approached.

"Good work, ladies! I was rooting for you." She made some notes on a pad. "Here's your ticket. Just take it into the office and they'll settle the payment. Some of the guys can help you load when you're ready."

Melinda swiped her credit card and tried not to look at the total when she signed the receipt. With the double load and the scattering of bales she'd picked up before, her barn would be well-stocked for some time. But the money from the iron bed was gone, and then some.

Ed was soon on his way over. Karen and Melinda went into the small cafeteria, where it was blissfully chilly, and splurged on sweet rolls and lemonade while they waited for him to arrive.

"You did it!" Karen cheered quietly, mindful of the morose farmers at the next table. "You're stocked up now, you don't have to worry."

Melinda put her hands over her face. "I never want to do that again. Thank God for John, I had no idea how hard it would be to get hay for my sheep."

Karen searched for something positive to say. "It's not like this when times are good; hay sales can be fun. And maybe the markets will turn around, before winter."

The thought of how many bales she'd need, week in and month out, once the snow started to fly made Melinda shudder. She had eighteen sheep now, not just twelve. What was she going to do?

"Anyway," Karen was saying, "eat up. It's not every day you see cinnamon rolls this huge."

19

Melinda looked out the kitchen's south-facing windows again, watching the lane for any sign of Chase's truck.

"He'll be here when he gets here." She went back to chopping vegetables for the salad. Two steaks were marinating in the refrigerator, ready for the grill. "I can't moon around like some lovestruck schoolgirl. The potatoes have to be wrapped in foil, I still need to set the table ..."

She smiled as she reached for the plates. They were her everyday dishes, but this was a sort-of-special occasion. She and Chase hadn't seen each other for almost two weeks, a stretch of time Melinda thought wouldn't bother her in the least. Yet when he returned from his business trip yesterday, and immediately offered to come down for dinner tonight, she'd been quick to agree.

While she added the glasses to the kitchen table, she stole another peek outside. But this time, Melinda only had eyes for her barn. Every time she approached its main door, or admired how proudly it sat on the south side of the yard as she drove up the lane, she was filled with relief and gratitude. Because inside its walls, stacked high in the haymow and piled on pallets downstairs, were the dozens of bales of hay that would help her sheep through this terrible drought.

Every dollar (or hundreds of dollars, to be honest) and every aching muscle had been more than worth it. But even with Karen and Ed's help, she'd thrown in the towel when it came to hauling every last bale up the haymow stairs. Between the larger load she'd purchased and the sweltering late-summer air, her friends had quickly agreed.

There was plenty of room to store some of the bales in an unused portion of the main floor, so they'd wrapped up their work earlier than expected and lingered in the air-conditioned kitchen, enjoying chocolate-chip cookies and ice-packed glasses of sun tea. The long day drained Melinda emotionally and physically, as well as financially. Once her helpers were paid and gone, she'd taken a hot shower and promptly fell asleep on the couch.

She reached into the drawer by the sink for the matches, and added them to her shorts' back pocket. As soon as Chase arrived, she'd run out and start the grill. She was thrilled to spend the night with her special guy, but equally relieved she never felt the need to impress him. It had been a long, crazy day at Prosper Hardware, and she was too tired to find a cute dress to wear or even think about doing her hair.

Between the overbearing heat, the lack of rain, and the county's continued mandates to conserve water, many of the store's customers were weary and cranky. And then today, Melinda witnessed something she thought she'd never see: Laid-back Mayor Jerry and easygoing Aunt Miriam, arguing over the fate of the handful of flower baskets still clinging to the light poles along Main Street.

Most of the other buildings' owners gave up on their planters long ago, and stored them away until next year. Only the containers in front of Prosper Hardware and the city buildings across the street soldiered on, thanks to Miriam and Jerry. But when the tiny community's water quota was cut to emergency levels, the tension between them began to build.

Miriam was desperate to keep the flowers alive, and promised she'd haul their water from her home on Cherry Street rather than pull from the lines serving the little business district. As a Master Gardener, Jerry wanted the impatiens to survive; but as mayor, he was supposed to urge residents to curtail their water usage. He'd finally put his foot down with Miriam that morning: The baskets were a frivolous use of water, and they had to come down.

Miriam countered that the flowers only required a few gallons a day. Sharp words were exchanged, despite Frank's pleas for reasonableness. Jerry finally stomped out of Prosper Hardware, marched across the sleepy street, and disappeared into city hall. He soon came out with a ladder in his hands and a scowl on his face and, while his friends watched from Prosper Hardware's front windows, jerked the city's three flower baskets off their chains and dumped them on the sidewalk.

More furious than Melinda had ever seen her, Miriam stormed outside and yelled across to Jerry that if he wasn't mayor, she'd have him charged with vandalism and littering. He ignored her threats, but soon returned with a bucket and broom to clear away his angry mess.

It didn't help when George, Auggie and Doc started laughing at the absurdity of it all. Bill scurried off to the woodshop, muttering something about a rush order. Miriam dropped into one of the folding chairs, her brown eyes snapping with anger, but then got an idea.

She hurried to the refrigerator case, pulled five of the biggest bottles of water from its shelves, and plunked them down by the front entrance. With the store's ladder filling her arms, she triumphantly asked Melinda to get the door.

It had been a silly argument about something of little consequence, but the heat had everyone off balance. Melinda just wanted to forget it ever happened, and the perfect distraction had just arrived.

"Hey, beautiful." Chase's easy grin when he came into the kitchen raised her spirits. He slipped an arm around her waist and kissed the side of her neck. She dropped the spoon for the fruit salad and properly returned his greeting.

"Am I glad to see you," she admitted when they finally came up for air.

"Long day?" His smile faded. "Everything OK?"

"Oh, I'll tell you about it later. Just little stuff, building up. And this drought doesn't help. Everyone's a wreck these days."

"Don't I know it. We've got some farmers already dragging their feet about settling their accounts on time. That usually doesn't happen until closer to harvest, when people have a better idea how their year's going to turn out."

He gave her another kiss and filched a peach slice from the bowl. "Anyway, enough gloom and doom for now. I'll go clean up and get the steaks on."

Melinda smiled when she heard Hobo give a happy bark.

"Hey, buddy!" she heard Chase say. "Glad you're staying cool. And there's Miss Hazel. Hello, Princess Grace. I see you're on your sofa throne, as usual."

The pipes rumbled as the water flowed into the downstairs bathroom. Melinda sliced the potatoes, added onion, and folded them inside packets of aluminum foil.

Chase reappeared in the kitchen, looking confused. "Hey, what happened to that fancy bed Horace had? Did you take it upstairs? I would've been happy to help you ..."

"Oh, I sold it last week." Melinda added a shrug for good measure as she turned her back and went for the steaks. "An antiques dealer in Clear Lake was dying to have it, so I decided, why not?"

"But, wasn't that Hobo's bed? And the kittens'? I thought you liked it, it had so much character. And the quilt ..."

"The quilt's upstairs, folded away, where it's safe." She looked at him long enough to offer a reassuring smile, but the questions on his face made her uneasy. "I'd never sell *that*. Besides, it really should go to Ada. Did you see that huge new pet bed I got for Hobo and the girls? They just love it."

Chase accepted the platter she passed his way, but didn't say anything before he carried it outside. Hobo was right behind him, and Melinda knew Sunny and Stormy had already stationed themselves under the picnic table. Any time Horace's little charcoal grill was wheeled out of the garage, there would be tasty scraps by the end of the evening.

She and Chase were both starving by the time everything was ready. He had left the office at five, but it took almost an hour to reach her farm. They chatted about this and that while they focused on their food. But once their plates were nearly empty, Chase put down his fork and gave Melinda a level stare.

"Your pasture's really getting rough." His blue eyes filled with concern. "It was the first thing I noticed when I drove in. How are the sheep doing? You've got, what, fifteen or so?"

"Eighteen, actually." Melinda chewed her bite of steak carefully, not returning his gaze. "But six of them are only half-grown. I sold Caesar to John Olson, so there's just little Clover and the other five lambs left." She motioned toward the counter. "There's some chocolate-chip cookies, if you'd like one."

Chase frowned and stared at his plate. "It's too bad you started naming them, babe. That's a bad habit, it makes it so much harder to ..."

"No one's going anywhere!"

Even Melinda was surprised by the sudden sharpness in her voice. She had nothing to be defensive about. They were her sheep, her flock to manage.

"Don't worry about it," she said softly by way of an apology. "I know the pasture's rough, but this drought has got to break soon. And I've got plenty of hay again now. That antiques dealer couldn't wait to get her hands on that bed. Karen and I went over to Eagle River on Saturday and ..."

Chase rubbed his chin. "Oh, no, tell me you didn't."

The tension at the table made Melinda start laughing. "I know: me, at a hay sale? Thank goodness Karen knew what she was doing. John and his family were at the state fair, anyway, and I know he's getting low himself, so ..."

"How much did you have to pay?"

She blinked. "What does it matter?"

"Melinda." He reached for her hand, but she pulled it back. "Why don't you just tell me? I mean, if you got such a bargain ..."

She looked away, out past the barn, out to where the sun was slowly sinking over the thirsty, stunted fields.

"That much, huh?" Chase sighed, but there was a hint of irritation in his voice that was like a hot poker to her heart. "I thought so, but I hoped I was wrong."

"OK, fine." She dropped her fork with a frustrated clatter. "None of this is any of your business, but I'll tell you."

Chase's jaw dropped.

"Don't look at me like that! You know how high prices are these days. But I got over eighty bales, when you count the odds and ends we picked up along the way. It's all decent, too, none of that rough stuff. And I'm stocked up now, for a good long while."

"And when you get low again, what are you going to do? What are you going to sell next?"

Melinda started to clear the table. "It's my money! None of this is your concern." She put the fruit in the refrigerator and turned to face him with crossed arms.

"Besides, isn't that what a farmer's supposed to do? Care for their herd, no matter what? I shouldn't have to tell you this, you should know, but things are getting bad around here. You should have seen the guys at that sale, the desperation on their faces. I wasn't the only one."

"You're right, a farmer's responsible for their animals." He took their half-empty glasses of iced tea to the counter. "But they're also responsible for making ends meet. I guess if you've got this all worked out, based on the futures market, and your balance sheet says you can make it work ..."

Melinda turned away.

"You can't be serious," he finally said, his voice low and cautious. "There's no balance sheet, is there? Oh, my God, you're just throwing money around, not projecting expenses and profits. And I'm guessing you didn't get much for their wool this summer, that market's been down."

"I didn't sell it yet!" she snapped. "It's up in the haymow, my mom's going to make scarves with it, once we find someone to clean it and spin it and ..."

"Will you listen to yourself? How is this going to work, then? The sheep just keep eating and eating, and you keep buying hay, straw and grain, and paying the vet bills and ... what? They just hang out?"

"Of course they do! I love those sheep. Horace did, too."

"Horace was a crazy old man, living out here all alone, with probably five bucks in his pocket. Puttering around in that beat-up old truck and ..."

Chase didn't realize it yet, but he'd just crossed a line.

"Don't you dare! You don't even know him."

"Yeah, maybe." Chase crossed his arms, his face turning red. "But I know plenty of guys like him. They're flat broke, practically going hungry themselves to pay the feed bill. They won't sell out and move to town, and they won't let go of their livestock, even if it puts them in the poor house. I thought you had more sense than that."

"I sure do! I'm smart enough to jump on an opportunity when it comes along. I needed that hay, I found the money to pay for it, and I got it done. This farm, my animals? They mean everything to me. Can't you see that?"

"You bet I can." Chase's eyes flashed with anger. "Absolutely. They're the reason you won't stay over, even one night! You always have to get home, you have to ..."

Melinda stared at him. "So, that's what this is really about, then. You?"

"No! It's about us. Why don't I see you more often? It's always this struggle, where are we going to meet that's halfway, when can you come to Meadville, when can I get down here. I'd question whether you care more about this farm than you care about me, but I can see that I've already lost."

Melinda threw up her hands. "It's not a competition! But I guess that's what you care about, huh? You're always angling for the lead at work, trying to beat the other guys month over month, prove to your dad that you're ready to take over the business ..."

"Hey, stop right there! Don't you ..."

"Don't I what?" Melinda started to cry, tears of hurt and anger running down her face. "Insult your life's work? Question your choices? Because that's what you just did to me."

She pointed at Chase, her voice low and cold. "And don't you ever, *ever*, talk about Horace like that again. Just because he's quiet, and doesn't throw his money around, doesn't mean he's stupid. He's the reason I'm here, the reason I'm still here. And just so you know, that bed came with the house, I didn't pay a dime for it. Horace will understand why I sold it, which is more than I can say for you."

"Maybe I should just go," Chase said quietly. "And speaking of beds, I think you've already made yours."

He swiped his wallet and keys off the counter by the back door. Then he turned around, his anger already replaced with concern.

"There's a reason why this life is so hard, why so many people don't make it. You're headed down a bad road. Financial ruin's not even the worst of it. This farm you love so much?" He pointed out the window. "If you don't pull yourself together, start treating it like the business that it is, it'll break your heart. And your spirit."

Melinda looked at the floor, then back at Chase.

"I'd rather you not go," she said evenly. "But it's up to you. I care about you, I really do, but ... I've got other things to care for, too."

"Oh, this place already has the upper hand. I can see that."

She crossed her arms and looked away. Chase's warning slid down her spine. As angry as she was, she knew there was a kernel of truth in what he was saying.

"You can't go on like this," he said sadly, "rolling the dice, over and over. Ask your dad and uncle, ask the guys at the store. The eighties were a nightmare around here. You think it's bad now? Wait until there's foreclosure sales at the courthouse every day but Sunday. If things don't turn around, and quick, it's going to happen all over again."

Hobo padded into the kitchen and leaned his head against Melinda's leg. She crouched down and wrapped her arms around him.

"I'm going to go." Chase stuffed his hands in his pockets. "Please, Melinda, think about what I said, about what you're doing. You have to be careful. I'll call you tomorrow, OK?"

When she didn't answer, he disappeared out the door.

* * *

Melinda sat on the kitchen floor for a long time, Hobo still at her side, as the day drew to a close. A storm raged in her heart, a confusing mix of sadness, anger, fear and regret. She remembered all those times Chase had turned up her lane, trying to sell her that aerial photo of the farm, the one she'd wanted so badly that now had a place of honor on the dining-room wall.

And then he'd wanted to see her again, and she'd found the courage to open her heart, just a little bit. What could it hurt? she'd decided.

"A lot. Everything." She wiped her face with one hand and leaned against the cabinet. Chase had come back into her life, and now he was gone again. Maybe for good.

Or maybe not. It was just an argument, the first real one they'd had. Surely things would blow over ... if she let them. How could a fifteen-minute fight undo everything they now shared? Melinda wasn't quite ready to say she loved Chase, but he did mean something to her. Much more, she now realized, than what she'd been willing to admit to anyone, even herself.

At the same time ... how dare he tell her what to do? This wasn't a for-profit farm; she had no illusions about that. Her sheep were pets, of course they were. The chickens, too. As for what he said about Horace ...

"Chase is a stupid fool," she told Hobo, who licked her hand in agreement. "You and I know better, don't we? Horace is smart, far more than most people give him credit for. He and Wilbur always found a way to make it work, to get by."

So what if Horace always drove an old pickup? Lizzie had seen better days, but she had a certain charm. So what if the house's clapboards could use another layer of paint or two? Horace's grandfather built this house, as well as the barn, and they'd both stood tall for over a hundred years.

Everything was now in Melinda's hands, and she wasn't about to let go.

As for why Chase cared so much about all of that ... well, maybe it was just because he cared about her. She hoped that was still true. But there was something else behind his pointed comments. She thought of Chase's almost-new truck, the one he polished every week even though most of its miles were marked on gravel roads, and Melinda was sure she had her answer.

Maybe Chase was too caught up in appearances. And it wasn't just that truck he was so ridiculously proud of, that set of shiny wheels his family's company had surely paid for. His hair was always just so. His teeth were flawlessly white. Even his house was spotless. Melinda had been relieved to never find a moldy towel stuffed behind the bathroom door, or food spoiling in the refrigerator, but she now saw everything in a different light.

Everything in Chase's life was ... new. Streamlined and expensive. Perfect.

Except for her.

She could never be that way. Didn't want to be. What little interest she'd once had in acquiring the newest and the best went out the window the moment she arrived at this farm. All she cared about now were her family, her friends, her animals and this farm. Was there any room in her life for someone like Chase? Was she tired of trying to fit him in?

Chase said he'd call her tomorrow. And she hoped he would. But were they too different to make things last?

* 20 *

"Come on, it's not that bad. It's just like before. Only colder."

"That's the problem." Auggie studied the insulated mug Melinda placed in his hands. "Coffee's supposed to be hot, warm you right through while it perks you up."

He almost took a sip, then gave her a wary look.

"You didn't put anything else in it? None of that fake flavored crap, or maple syrup?"

She rolled her eyes and pointed at the vintage sideboard's metal counter, which held only the cardboard canisters of plain powdered creamer and sugar. "Uh, no. We don't exactly have a full range of options here at the Prosper Hardware Coffee Shop."

Then she started laughing. "Maple syrup? You don't dump maple syrup in coffee. There's probably a special flavoring you could buy, but ..."

"Fall's right around the corner." George held his insulated mug away from his chest, as if he wasn't quite sure what to do with it. He was a coffee traditionalist, too. "Maple would be right in season. Melinda, you should look into that."

"First things first. Just give the iced coffee a try. It's almost eighty out there, and it's not even eight. How can you guys drink that boiling stuff when it's this hot?"

"Habit," Auggie muttered.

"Same." George finally took a small sip. "Hmm, not bad."

"I would think so." Doc laughed as he wiped his boots on the mat. "It's the same dang thing. Of course, I occasionally enjoy one of those iced concoctions from the coffee shop on Swanton's town square. But you have to be careful. Between the flavorings and the whole milk and the whipped cream, they can run to several hundred calories."

At last, Auggie lifted his cup. "OK, down the hatch. It's alright, I guess. Ow!" He knitted his forehead. "That hurts!"

When everyone stared at him, he chuckled.

"Oh, come on, I'm kidding. It's not cold enough to give me brain freeze. Really, it's sort of refreshing. But Melinda, aren't these insulated mugs a pain to wash? You know I don't have much time to clean up in the mornings, and the ceramic cups go quick."

"You're right," she admitted. "It's a trade-off. Maybe save the iced coffee for special occasions, then."

"Well, today might turn out to be one." Auggie reached for the creamer. "The weather's gonna break this evening, if we're lucky. All the models were in agreement this morning."

Eyebrows raised around the circle. Everyone stared out the windows, as if they could will it to be true.

"You don't mean ..." Jerry leaned forward. "Really? Are you sure?"

Bill reached for one of the blueberry muffins Jerry brought in. "You think it's going to *rain*? What's that?"

"I hope you're right." Doc crossed his arms. "It's tough out there. Yesterday ... and I'm not making this up, I swear ... I saw a tumbleweed north of town. Just rolling down the gravel, as free as you please."

"A tumbleweed?" Frank snorted. "It's dry, sure, but this is the Midwest, not the Wild West. Can we get our hopes up this time? Or is it going to be like Thursday all over again?"

George groaned. "I sat out on our porch for over an hour, just watching those heavy clouds roll in. And nothing."

Melinda nodded in sympathy. She had kept a hopeful eye on the sky that night, too, as she dragged a hose through her thirsty garden. And it was a good thing she watered the plants, as the dark clouds dropped only a few sprinkles before moving on.

"I'm not going to bet on it." Jerry rose from his chair. "Well, I guess I'll water the flowers before I head over to the office." He opened the refrigerated case and lifted out four bottles of water. That was Frank's cue to wrestle the ladder out of the corner and meet Jerry at the front door.

Prosper Hardware's four baskets of purple-and-white impatiens were the only ones still hanging along Main Street. They were surprisingly lush and bright, thanks to Aunt Miriam's determination and the water-bottle tab she paid out of her own purse.

With his conscience finally clear, Jerry had resumed his watering duties. Frank's feelings about all of this had never come to light, as he preferred to keep his mouth shut and maintain the peace between his wife and one of his oldest friends.

Bill topped off his mug before he started for the woodshop. "I'm going to look on the bright side. If we get a good soaker tonight, and a few more after that, we just might have this drought beat."

"Oh, the blind hope of the young." George shook his head. "We've got a long way to go to get ourselves out of this hole. But I'll take a rain cloud over a dust cloud any day, even if it doesn't amount to much."

He settled back in his chair. "This one day, summer of '39, I'll never forget. I was just a baby then, only two, and playing out by the pump when this black line appeared out to the west. Mother yelled for my older sisters and brothers to shut the windows, and Dad came running up from the barn ..."

Melinda and Doc exchanged weary looks. George's tales of long ago were usually welcome and often fascinating, but his memories of the tail end of the Great Depression were, well, depressing. Spirits were low enough around here.

"I think our chances are good today," Doc gently cut George off. "Even if this front's not a drought-buster, a little rain is better than nothing."

"I'm feeling good about it, too." Auggie shook his cup to redistribute the ice, and took another sip. "There looks to be some real moisture this time, and enough energy behind it to get the job done. There's a chance it'll push out some wind and hail, too, but who cares? We're desperate, so we'll take whatever we can get."

* * *

The hope for rain was the top story on the Mason City television station's evening newscast, whose coverage included a grim-faced farmer trudging through his stunted soybeans and an hour-by-hour prediction of when the showers would arrive. Several bands of moisture were brewing in Nebraska, the meteorologist noted with barely suppressed glee, so there was more than one chance for relief.

Melinda silently cheered the forecast, but decided to stick to her routine. As soon as the supper dishes were cleared, she pulled on her dusty sneakers, primed the garden hydrant, and hooked up the hose.

It was so humid, and so still, that moving from one row to the next was enough to make her break out in a sweat. She double-checked the rain barrel was ready, shooed the chickens into their coop, then started for the barn with Stormy and Sunny. Never wanting to miss a thing, Hobo soon dashed out of the windbreak and joined the procession.

"We need to bring the sheep in," she explained to her helpers. "I don't think it's going to storm bad tonight, but I'll feel better if everyone is inside." She shook a finger at Sunny and Stormy. "That means the two of you. Are you listening to me? I'm not going to lock you in, but this isn't a night for sleeping under the picnic table. Just look at those clouds!"

While most of the sky was still a clear blue, towering puffs of white were advancing from the southwest. The sun would set in an hour but, for the first night in what seemed like forever, its brilliant oranges and reds weren't likely to be visible. Even though the burnt grass was rough under her shoes, Melinda's steps were light as she crossed the yard.

The main barn door was already open, propped with a concrete block to funnel more fresh air to the box fans spinning in the corners of the sheep's living quarters. She filled a small bucket with corn, let herself through the aisle gate, and wandered out to the pasture. Although there wasn't much fresh grass to go around, the sheep still loved to spend their evenings outside.

"Hey, sheep! Here, sheep!"

By the second rattle of the pail, Annie was already on her way back to the barn. The others soon followed, as eager for nose pets as for the treats Melinda spread in their feed bunks. She latched the bottom half of the pasture door, then turned to admire the stacks of fresh hay on the other side of the aisle.

"It was worth it, every penny," she told Stormy, who supervised from the ridge of the fence. "No one around here is ever going to go hungry. I won't let that happen, I promise." She reached over and rubbed his gray ears. "Chase means well, but it's not up to him. This is my farm, and I have to handle things on my own."

Sunny joined his brother, and let out a "meow" that Melinda took as a vote of affirmation. "That's right! We'll find a way to make things work, won't we?"

Chase had called the day after their argument, just as he said he would. Melinda accepted his apologies and then made a few of her own, wincing as she recalled how she'd mocked his hopes to move up at his family's company. They'd met for dinner in Charles City the next evening, and things seemed to be back on track. But as she was driving home, long before nine and happily alone, Melinda realized Chase had never walked back his cruel comments about Horace. Her temper had flared again in defense of her friend, but she'd decided to let that slide. For now.

"I know you like Chase," she told Hobo as she latched the barn's main door. "I do, too. But I'm not sure where this is all going."

Hobo began to bark and ran off behind the garage. Melinda shook her head.

"At least one of us knows what they want. Hobo!" she called after him. "You leave those poor rabbits alone!"

Her garden was being raided on a regular basis, but she didn't have the heart to go after any of the wildlife that were to blame. Everything was just trying to get by. Her plot had so little to offer this year, she might as well share.

And it wasn't just the rabbits that were helping themselves; there was substantial evidence the raccoons were hard at work in the wee hours.

She hadn't seen the woodchuck again, but hoped it was also finding enough to eat. The birdfeeders were kept full, and she didn't mind when the blue jays, cardinals and sparrows flung some of their snacks to the ground. The deer were already chewing off her dried-out flowers; they might as well have a few mouthfuls of seed, too.

But maybe, tonight, the drought was finally going to break. She kicked her dirty shoes off inside the back porch, relished the blast of cool air that greeted her in the kitchen, and cut a generous slice off the watermelon waiting in the refrigerator.

By the time she went to bed, heat lightning was flashing in the west and the weather radar was filling in with beautiful shades of green and yellow. She drifted off to the soft rumble of faraway thunder, and those first wonderful tap-tap-taps of rain dancing on the farmhouse's steep roof.

She woke with a start, and sat up in bed. It was pitch-black outside, and her alarm clock glowed with the news that it was just after two. Cricket chirps echoed across the hall, a greeting coming from somewhere in the office or the bathroom.

Melinda rubbed her eyes and laid back down, too tired to chase the little insect around with a shoe. Besides, it wouldn't be long for this world once Grace or Hazel was on the hunt. Her pillow was fluffed and repositioned, and she was just about to close her eyes when a sudden "boom!" made her flinch. It rumbled away and, only seconds later, a sudden burst of light filled the room.

Was that what startled her awake? Was it storming? The wind was picking up, she could hear it sighing against the corner of the house, but the pitter-patter of the rain was nowhere to be found.

Another flash of lightning. "One thousand one, one thousand two ..." Melinda got to four before the thunder answered. Four miles away.

She went to the west window and pushed the thin curtains aside. The power was still on, and the yard light still glowed. A quick shock of lightning snaked across the sky, and she could briefly see a line of ominous, boiling clouds moving in from the southwest. Another flash came, faster than she had expected, and she jumped back from the window.

A weather alert had been issued for her county, according to her phone, but it was only for thunderstorms, not tornadoes. She was about to go back to bed when a new message scrolled across the screen.

The warning for Hartland County has been extended until 3 a.m. While only light rainfall is expected, significant cloud-to-ground lightning has been reported. Residents should be aware ...

"OK, that's it." Afraid to flip a light switch, she reached for the flashlight waiting on the bedside table. "Off to the basement, I guess."

The next bouts of lightning arrived before she made it to the bottom of the stairs, and the booms were now so loud and so close that they rattled the farmhouse's metal storm windows. Grace and Hazel crawled out of the downstairs bedroom, their stomachs nearly brushing the floor and their ears flat.

"It's OK, I'm here. But we need to get to the basement. Hey, where's Hobo?"

The new pillow bed was empty, and he wasn't hiding in the bathroom. Before Melinda could call for him, or make her way into the kitchen, several more flashes of light filled the house. This time, the thunder came before she even finished the first count. Less than a mile away.

A loud, long crackle echoed somewhere outside, and the sonic boom that followed was so immense she couldn't tell which direction it was coming from. Her bare arms tingled as she stuffed the flashlight in the pocket of her knit shorts and gathered up Hazel and Grace with both hands.

"Hobo!" she shouted over the thunder, which now rolled on with barely a break. "Hobo, where are you?"

The bursts of lightning were so close together, they showed her the way through the kitchen to the basement's entrance. She deposited the kittens on the stairway landing and, once they were safe behind the latched door, called for Hobo again.

And then, under the echoes of the crackles and booms, she heard several sharp barks on the back porch. The kitchen's doggie flap flew open, and Hobo launched himself through.

"Oh, thank God! Where have you been?"

Hobo was panting and frantic, barking and yipping as the storm rolled on outside. She grasped his collar with one hand and turned toward the basement door. Three more crashes of lightning, more answering roars, and the windows rattled again. During one second of eerie silence, Melinda heard the kittens howling on the landing.

Hobo barked again, then pulled away so fast Melinda's bare feet nearly went out from under her on the linoleum floor. In the second of suffocating darkness before the next flash of lightning, she felt his collar slide out of her hand.

"Hobo, come here!" She put a palm on the basement door, making sure it was tightly latched, then ran after him.

"Get back here! Don't go out there, you can't ..."

He was still on the porch, his barks raising in urgency and pitch. As soon as she came out of the kitchen, he jumped against the back door once, twice, then dashed out his doggie entrance before she could stop him.

"No! No! Hobo, don't!"

But he was already gone, and the roar of the thunder drowned out her shouts. She slipped on her old shoes and grabbed the leash. This was dangerous, she knew it, but she couldn't leave him out there.

The air was thick with ozone, the unstable clouds bursting with electricity but not a drop of rain. Hobo was nowhere to be found in the yard light's circular glow.

The sky was still rolling; it would be foolish to run out into the dark, with only a flashlight, until she had a better idea of where he might be.

She hovered on the back steps, pressed herself against the wall to keep the overhang above her head, and waited for another round of lightning to show her the way.

In the next flash, she found him. Hobo was just west of the barn, along the pasture fence.

Her heart thumping in her ears, Melinda took a deep breath and flew across the yard. An angry gust of wind slapped her face and, in one terrible second, she knew why Hobo was so frantic.

It was faint, but it was there: the unmistakable smell of smoke.

Somewhere, out in the darkness, something was on fire.

Melinda caught up to Hobo and pulled him away from the metal fence. She snapped the lead to his collar, her fingers flying from memory in the dark.

The acrid smell was stronger here, along the edge of the pasture. Another crack of lightning, another blast of light across the rumbling skies, and there it was.

Beyond the pasture, in the cornfield behind her farm, a spot of light. She blinked, but it was still there: a blob of orange, a flash of heat, maybe a quarter of a mile away. It was alive, and moving, and growing. Hobo barked again, leaping toward the flames with so much adrenaline that it felt like her arm would be ripped from its socket.

"Oh, my God! Yes, I see it, I see it! We have to go!"

When he didn't budge, she gritted her teeth and pulled hard on his lead. "I've got to call for help. Come on!"

One more tug, and he came. They raced back to the house, and she locked his outside entrance the second they got into the back porch.

She burst into the kitchen, her eyes scanning the darkness. Her phone was on the counter somewhere, but there wasn't a second to spare. Horace's old landline still hung on the wall, right inside the kitchen door.

"9-1-1. What is your emergency?"

"The field behind my farm is on fire! It's been struck by lightning!"

The gravity of what she'd just said made Melinda drop into a chair. She rattled off her name and address.

"I've got a crew on the way. Where are you in proximity to the flames?"

Another boom of thunder echoed through the house. "It's southwest of my place. Maybe a quarter mile? I think it just happened. My dog, he was barking and barking ..."

"Is he with you now?"

"Yes."

"Ma'am, I need you to stay in the house. Are you in the house?"

"Yes." She pressed her face to the kitchen window, trying to see out past the barn, but couldn't.

Her barn, with her sheep locked inside. And the hay. All that hay, the perfect fuel ...

The tears were coming now. "Oh, please, they have to hurry! That field is so dry, the pasture is, too, and the wind's blowing this way ..."

"They'll be there soon. Whatever you do, don't go outside. Is this the number where we can reach you?" She rattled off the farm's landline just as Melinda spied her phone by the stove.

"No, sorry, call my cell." Melinda gave her the number. "OK. OK. Thanks."

The wait between lightning strikes was longer now, but it was too late. She was pacing the kitchen floor, praying and crying, when her phone buzzed. It was Bill.

"Melinda, we're almost there!" He was shouting over the wail of the sirens. "ETA about five. We just turned off the blacktop. Are you OK?"

"Yes," she gasped. "I'm ... I'm in the house."

"Swanton's a few minutes behind us, they've got a bit farther to come, but they're bringing everything they've got. Eagle River's on the way." Bill faded out for a moment. "Doc's asking about your animals. Where is everybody?"

"The chickens are in their coop, Hobo and the kittens are with me. But the sheep are in the barn, and Sunny and Stormy ..."

"Whatever you do, do not go outside until we get there!"

She saw the engine's red lights first, and then Prosper's lone fire truck barreled up her lane and headed for the back side of the pasture. Someone jumped out and got the gate, and the rig was soon stationed halfway between the far fence and the barn. Melinda slipped around Hobo and ran out the back door.

The sky was still rumbling, even though the worst of the lightning had finally rolled away. Out there in the dark, beyond the beam of the yard light, she could see the fire rising into the sky, the flames wider and higher than before. Someone was hurrying in her direction, and they met up by the garage. It was Tony Bevins, Prosper's volunteer fire chief.

"We'll spray down your barn if it gets much closer," Tony shouted over the remaining rumbles of thunder and the traffic echoing from his radio. "Swanton's going to surround the fire, try to cut it off before it gets this far. Thank God no one lives between here and there."

Melinda nodded as she stared at the silvery emergency lights now flashing off to the southwest. A spotlight clicked on, far away, and plumes of white smoke were now visible over the angry red-and-orange flames.

She felt a heavy, gloved hand on her shoulder. Tony's face was grim.

"We're going to do everything we can. But you know how dry it is; that little rain we got a few hours ago is buying us a bit of time, and that's all." He looked over at the barn, at the browned pasture and lawn, and then at the windbreak of dehydrated trees lining the west and north sides of her property.

"I'm sorry, but you need to prepare for the worst. Everything out here? It's a tinderbox. The whole county is. If this thing gets away from us ..." He shook his head. "Do you understand what I'm saying?"

She put a hand over her mouth, and nodded.

More lights in the driveway. Another emergency vehicle and behind it, Ed and Mabel's car.

"My animals!" she sobbed. "Please, we have to get them out! If everything else ..."

"Doc already called John Olson," Tony said, "he's bringing his trailer. We'll get the sheep out, right away. Hopefully it won't get as far as the barn, but if it does ... well, it'll be too late by then. Doc said you've got two barn cats. Do you have any carriers? Will they come to you?"

Melinda ran toward the house. Mabel and Ed caught up with her by the back steps. "We can't let the sheep out yet," she told them. "But I have to get Sunny and Stormy, if I can."

She hurried inside for her two carriers and a second flashlight, and she and Mabel rushed to the barn. A chorus of panicked "baaas" greeted them when they appeared in the aisle.

The sheep were restless and frantic, their terror fueled by the faint smell of smoke that was starting to seep through the wallboards' cracks. Sunny and Stormy, huddled under the haymow steps, were too terrified to fight back as Melinda pushed them into the carriers and Mabel latched the doors. Ed met them by the grain barrels.

"John's here, he's backing up the trailer. Nathan's coming with his, too. I'll grab the fence panels while you take the cats up to the house."

With Sunny and Stormy stashed under the picnic table, Melinda and Mabel hurried back to the barn. Ed handed Melinda a bucket of corn, and she slid the latch on the gate.

The sheep bleated and stomped, and darted every which way. They were terrified, and she was, too. And not just because of the fire. For a split second, Melinda feared the sheep would bolt and run her down. But there wasn't time to be afraid. She pushed that thought away, called to her flock, and they finally gathered around her.

"I'm here, it's going to be OK." She got ahead of the pack, and rattled the pail. "We have to go! Come on!"

Most of the sheep fit into John's trailer. Nathan had backed in next to John, and the fence panels were moved to direct the rest of the flock his way.

"I count eighteen total," John called from the back of Nathan's trailer. "Is that everyone?"

"Yep." Ed latched the barn door closed. "They're all out."

Mabel had the foresight to call Roger and Diane, and they soon arrived. John and Nathan parked the trailers down by the road, then joined the exhausted, anxious group gathered around the picnic table. An unfamiliar truck soon pulled up the lane. It was the farmer who'd bought the Schermanns' fields from Horace and Wilbur years ago.

"I'm insured, of course," he said, blinking back tears, "and my crop's not going to be worth much this year, anyway. I'll be broke, no matter what. But my God, to see all that hard work, going up in smoke ..." He shook his head, and John clapped him on the shoulder.

There was nothing left to do but stand there, waiting and praying, watching the flames expand and advance. More lights appeared in the driveway, attached to one of Charles City's massive pumper trucks. A firefighter jumped out and hurried over to the group.

"You Melinda?"

She barely nodded.

"They've slowed the fire down, but it's still on the move. That's why we're here." He pointed into the field, where the number of emergency lights had doubled in the last few minutes. The pumper truck had already found its way through the back gate.

"Ma'am, we're going to soak the west section of your pasture and the edge of that field, try to snuff this monster out before it gets past the fence. Prosper's going to spray down the barn. We're fighting the wind, though. If this thing gets close enough to hurl any sparks at your barn, or the shed, or into the windbreak ..."

He peered under the picnic table, to where Sunny and Stormy cowered in their carriers, and shook his head. "If we can't keep the flames back, you'll all have about five minutes to evacuate."

Melinda suddenly felt dizzy. Diane put an arm around her daughter and lowered her to the wooden bench.

"We're going to do everything we can to stop it." The fireman's voice was firm, but his face was grim in the faint glow of the yard light. "But ma'am, I'd start thinking about what I absolutely have to save, and what I'm willing to leave behind."

* 21 *

Melinda rushed into the back porch, Diane and Roger at her heels. She knelt by Hobo and wrapped her arms around him. "We have to get ready to go, just in case. You stay out here with Dad, OK? We don't have much time."

Diane was already reaching for a stack of empty totes in the porch closet. "What will we do with Hazel and Grace? Sunny and Stormy are in the carriers."

"Cardboard box, I guess. I've got one in the basement that should work. But the chickens!"

Roger had taken Melinda's place next to Hobo. "If things get that bad, I'll run out to the coop and open the doors. They can make a run for it, at least."

Melinda and her mom hurried into the kitchen. Now that they were inside, Melinda noticed the smoke was embedded in her hair and clothes. The true threat of the fire, the possibility that she might lose her home, suddenly became all too real. She snatched one of the totes and turned to Diane.

"I'm going upstairs. I'll grab all my papers and my laptop, and the important things from the office. I want ..." She had only a few seconds to decide. "The pictures in the living room, and the clocks, too."

Diane followed her into the dining room and pulled down the wall clock, which had belonged to Roger's parents. "I'll get the one on the mantel, too. What about the china cabinet?"

"Yes! Whatever you can get. That vase there, on the top shelf? Horace and Ada gave it to me. It was handed down in their family."

The alarm clock on her nightstand showed it was now after three. Out her bedroom's west window, there in the darkness, Melinda caught a glimpse of the wall of flames pushing toward her farm. She tried to keep her panic in check by focusing on what she wanted to save.

There was a small, portable safe under the bed, filled with keepsakes and personal papers. Her jewelry box went into the bin next, and more pictures. In the office, she grabbed her laptop, some files, and Horace and Wilbur's sheep ledgers.

Just before she reached the stairwell, Melinda's sweeping gaze landed on the storage room's door. She shoved her way in and grabbed Anna's crazy quilt, which was wrapped in a clean sheet, off the top of the old cedar chest. As she ran down the stairs and through the house, her heart in her throat, a sudden thought came into her mind.

Anna, I don't know if you can hear me. But if you and Henry are near, if there's anything you can do ... please, we need your help. All the help we can get to save your farm.

Diane had already filled the other two totes and took them out to the porch. "I was just thinking about Anna. Where is her recipe box?"

Melinda blinked with surprise when her mom suddenly mentioned Anna, but there wasn't time to ponder that now.

"Ada took it home with her." She passed the final tote to her mom. "This is the last of it. I'll get Grace and Hazel."

The kittens had abandoned the basement landing for a better place to hide: under a bottom-row shelf in the canning room. Melinda grabbed the cardboard box, a pair of scissors and duct tape from the counter by the washer and dryer, poked in some air holes, and hurried back to where her babies huddled in a cobwebbed corner.

"The big boys have the carriers. I'm sorry, but this will have to do." Hazel was silent from fear, but Graze yowled and flung her paws about when Melinda picked her up.

She popped the kittens under the box's flaps, hurriedly taped the container closed, and tried to balance it as best as she could while struggling up the steps.

Diane met her in the kitchen, her face pale. "It's still on the move." Sirens wailed outside, closer now, as another fire truck roared past the kitchen's south windows. "They're leaving one crew to watch the back side of the fire, but moving everyone else up to the pasture. Tony thinks there's still a chance they can stop it before it reaches the barn, but he says it's going to be close."

And it was. Fed by row after row of parched corn stalks, the inferno blasted through the rest of the field and churned toward the pasture with alarming speed. Sparks rained ahead into the parched grass, and crews rushed to snuff them out before they could take hold.

The fire slipped through the fence, consuming the wooden posts as it went, but lost steam when it met up with the watered-down pasture. Firefighters had soaked the ground until it was a muddy mess and, with no fuel left in its path, the flames finally began to pull back.

But it still took two hours to beat the blaze into submission. The first streaks of pink were appearing on the horizon before the last of the flames were extinguished.

Her eyes gritty from smoke and exhaustion, Melinda stood at the side fence and studied the back quarter of her pasture, which was now only an angry swatch of scorched earth, mud, dirty water and ash. She was leaning against a post, tears of gratitude running down her smudged face, when Doc and Tony started her way.

"Thank you," she croaked, her throat sore from smoke. "Thank you," she said again. Those two words didn't seem like enough, no matter how many times she might say them. The barn was spared, and her farm had been saved.

Doc clapped her on the shoulder and pushed back his mask. "It almost got the better of us. When it burned through the fence, it was still so vicious, I was about to come up to the house and tell all of you to clear out."

"But then the wind suddenly died down, just like that." Tony made a slicing motion with one gloved hand and shook his head.

"That's when we really got it contained, knew we could keep it from reaching the barn or the yard. Once it mired down in that mud, we were able to wipe it out."

"It's a good thing you kept your sheep last fall," Doc said. "I know the pasture hasn't provided them much to eat this summer, but they've done a good job of keeping the grass chewed down to almost nothing. If they weren't here, and the grass had been much taller ..."

"We never could have put down enough water to smother the flames," Tony added as he reached inside his jacket.

He sighed, but he was smiling as he pulled out his phone. "Well, I'll call the county and tell them we don't need that all-hands bulletin issued. We can wrap things up on our own."

Melinda still hadn't been able to let go of that fence post. It was sturdy and straight, and had been rooted in that spot for decades. And now, it should be there for years to come.

"Hobo saved the farm, he ... he saved us all," she told Doc. "When the lightning started, I couldn't find him, I thought he was just on the back porch but, then he ran in, and ran back out ... I grabbed the leash and went after him and ..."

"He smelled it?" Doc's eyes were wide with wonder. "He showed you?"

"Yeah," she nodded. "The lightning was flashing all around, but I couldn't leave him out there. He was down here, barking and whimpering and jumping against the fence, staring out into the dark, out into that field. Then I could smell the smoke, and then I saw it, that ball of orange ..."

"And then you ran back in and made the call," Doc finished what she was suddenly too tired to say. He took it all in for a moment.

"I always thought Hobo was a special dog, but now I know it's true. He's a hero, Melinda, there's no other way to say it. If that fire had even ten more minutes on us, much less fifteen, or more ..."

Doc shook his head. "This farm? It'd be long gone by now. And we'd be evacuating half the people in this township. When it's this dry, who knows how far the fire might have spread?"

Three members of First Lutheran's women's group soon arrived, each carrying a hot breakfast casserole. One of them had retrieved a large-volume coffeemaker from the church, and soon had it percolating in Melinda's kitchen. The sun was up now, the skies a bright blue behind the lingering smoke, another scorching day on deck as if nothing had happened.

The firefighters gathered on the lawn, grateful for bracing cups of coffee and a few bites of breakfast. Many of them were volunteers, and had a long day ahead of them at their regular jobs.

The church's organist brought Melinda a square of egg casserole and gave her a hug. "God was watching out for you last night."

"That's for sure. I'm very lucky, and very blessed." She thought of Anna and Henry, of the plea she'd offered up as she ran down the stairs just hours ago. About how Tony said the wind had suddenly diminished, and the crew was at last able to get the fire under control.

Uncle Frank would open Prosper Hardware, and Miriam said she would cover the rest of the day with Esther's help. Bill insisted he could come in at noon, but Miriam refused. "A nap's not enough, I'm not letting him near that table saw today," she told Melinda. "You just do what you need to do, honey, and don't worry about the store. We'll get back to normal tomorrow."

Melinda called her insurance company's emergency line, and they promised to send out an agent that afternoon. The sheep couldn't use the pasture until the destroyed section of fence was replaced, but it didn't take long to secure a few fence panels around the barn and expand their territory into the back half of the building.

Getting the sheep back in the barn, however, was a far-more-difficult task.

Terrified from hours of sirens and shouts and smoke, the ewes and the half-grown lambs were timid and restless. They wanted out of those trailers, but the acrid fumes lingered in the barn and the aisle was crowded with strange faces. It took Ed and Melinda several tries with buckets of oats, as well as corn, to get them to fall in line.

Sunny and Stormy hid in the backs of the carriers, their eyes filled with fear, even after Melinda opened the doors and backed away. The cats finally made the two-yard dash to Hobo's doghouse, and she slipped bowls of kibble and fresh water inside and let them be.

A few of the bravest chickens were willing to explore their run when Melinda slid their hatch door to the side. Grace and Hazel accepted a few nervous bites of food, then hurried upstairs to the safe zone under Melinda's bed.

Hobo desperately wanted to be in the yard, mingling with the firefighters and neighbors and sniffing all the strange vehicles, but his doggie doors remained locked. Melinda was afraid to let him out of her sight, even though the time of danger was finally past. He enjoyed a special breakfast that included some bacon Diane fried for him, then promptly fell asleep in his new bolstered bed.

At last, everyone had left except her parents. Diane took the bag of breakfast trash out of her daughter's hand and pointed at the house. "We'll clean up, honey. You go in and lie down, you're about dead on your feet."

Melinda only made it as far as the couch. Her eyes closed as soon as her head hit the throw pillow and she felt, rather than saw, Hobo arrange himself at her feet. She quickly slipped into a deep but troubled sleep, filled with flames and smoke and frightened sheep and Hobo's shrill barks.

And then, someone was calling her name, shaking her shoulder. She opened her eyes.

"Hey." Chase brushed the hair out of her face.

"What ... what are you doing here? What time is it?" She looked to the mantel, but the clock wasn't there. Of course, it was still packed away ...

The terror of the night before rushed back, and she started to cry.

Chase helped her sit up, then slid in and pulled her close. "You've had quite the night, I hear. I'm just so relieved that you're OK, that everyone's OK."

He looked over at Hobo, who wagged his tail.

"Yeah, you're the big hero, aren't ya! Roger told me all about it," he said to Melinda. "He called the office, and they texted me. I got down here as quick as I could."

"I'm glad you came." Chase had been the furthest thing from her mind during all those hours of waiting and praying, but now? Her dad had made the right call.

"There's so much to do, but I'm just sitting here, waiting for the insurance adjuster." She wiped at her eyes. "The sooner the fence is fixed, the better. I've got fans running in the barn, and the tops of the doors are all open. But the sheep can't go outside."

"Well, I might be able to help with that." Chase smiled, and her spirits began to lift, just a little.

"A friend of my dad's over by Elm Springs has a construction company that does fence work. How about I make a call? I can't believe they're super-busy, with the economy slowing down. Maybe they could get out here in a day or two, get you an estimate."

"That would be wonderful." She reached for his hand, and looked him in the eye. "I know what you're going to say. You don't have to say it. I know what I have to do."

Chase touched her cheek. "I wasn't going to say a word."

She looked over at Hobo, and out to where a sooty haze still hung over her farm, and the tears were back.

"Everyone is fine, like you said, and that's all that matters in the end. But my pasture? It's not fine, and I know it. And it's almost September. Even if we suddenly get regular rains until frost, the grass in the back part won't really bounce back until spring."

"But you have hay." He raised an eyebrow. "Lots of hay, if I remember correctly. And you can get more."

She shook her head and looked at the floor. "I've been thinking about a lot of things lately, even before the fire. I ... I've taken on too much, with the sheep."

Chase looked shocked, and she held up a hand.

"No, no, I'm not going to sell them all, I couldn't bear that. But I have to ... downsize, I guess. That night we argued? You referenced a farm budget, a budget I don't even have. There's not as many projects coming in from Susan's firm, and the cost of hay and feed's going to stay high. Winter's coming, too. Something has to give."

"Oh, babe, I'm so sorry. I know how much they mean to you." He leaned in to kiss her cheek, and she let him. "You're smart to be looking ahead, but ... how are you ever going to decide who stays, and who goes?"

"I don't know." She covered her face with her hands. "I just don't know."

* 22 *

Melinda went into town a few minutes earlier than usual on Wednesday. After collecting her bucket of greens from Jessie, she started the coffee pot and set a blueberry coffee cake on Prosper Hardware's sideboard. Once the folding chairs were arranged in a circle, she pulled a manila folder crammed with receipts from her tote and powered on her laptop.

Auggie, as usual, was the first one in the door. "Look at you, all professional." He made a beeline for the cake and filled a mug. "Don't worry. If you're cutting any corners out at the farm, we won't rat you out to the IRS."

"Gee, thanks." She tried for a wry smile, but her heart was heavy. There was a sheep sale tomorrow at Eagle River, and she had to face the numbers and decide how many she could afford to keep.

It wouldn't do any good to drag this out until the next auction, which was in two weeks. She had to act now, or she might talk herself out of selling any of them.

"I doubt I've been doing anything wrong, tax-wise, since that's the problem. I haven't been doing *anything*. There's no budget, no projections. I just buy what I need to buy, when I need to buy it, and find a way to cover it when the credit card comes due."

"Oh, those credit cards." George shuffled up the aisle from the back. "Root of all evil, I say. That, and this online-shopping stuff." He waved it all away with one veined hand. "Nobody stays within their means anymore."

"Guilty as charged." Melinda set the laptop on the floor long enough to serve herself a hearty chunk of coffeecake. "At least, when it comes to the farm. I've pared down the rest of my spending in the past year. I rarely go out to eat, or buy new clothes, and I haven't missed most of it, most of the time. But tell me there's a hay sale at Eagle River, or show me some fancy new chicken waterers ..."

"You didn't." Auggie stared at her reproachfully. "I told you, the old pans work just fine."

Doc went straight to the sideboard. "Homesteading is an expensive hobby. All those magazines and websites don't help. There's a fancy gadget for everything, and a promise that your life will be more meaningful if you buy it. Believe me, most of the time, your animals can't tell the difference."

"Well, it's time for me to rein it in." Melinda cut more cake for Frank and Jerry, who had just arrived. "I need to sort things out, and fast. Tomorrow's my chance; John's going to ... he said he'd take them over for me."

She tried to blink back the tears. Frank reached for his coffee cake with one hand and put the other on his niece's shoulder. "How about I handle the receipts, so you can focus on the spreadsheet? Let's get this done."

The chickens, Melinda was relieved to discover, were paying for themselves (and then some) thanks to the demand for fresh eggs from both Horace's former customers and Prosper Hardware's patrons. Hobo and the cats weren't figured into the budget, as they were truly pets, and Melinda reserved the right to spoil them as she saw fit.

Expenses related to the sheep were larger than she remembered. But then, hadn't she tried to forget those costs as soon as the bills were paid? There was the hay and straw, vaccinations for all the sheep, initial exams for the lambs, the shearing bill, corn and oats ...

Auggie knew the futures markets up, down and sideways, and his worst-case projections for the coming fall and winter made her jaw drop. And of course, there was no significant sheep-related income to balance out any of their needs.

John paid her a fair price for Caesar, but that cash had quickly vanished into her feed bill at the co-op. So had the money she'd made that spring from selling Horace's sought-after "black gold," the rich, composted remains of the sheep's manure pile. The ewes' fleeces still waited in the haymow but, as Doc explained, they weren't worth much in their current state. If Melinda had the wool cleaned and spun and dyed, it would give her mom plenty of yarn for knitting projects. But it would take several retail sales to make back those production costs.

"I'm willing to lose money on the sheep," she finally said. "They're not a business. They're a hobby, and one I really enjoy. But this ..." She closed her eyes, shutting out the columns of numbers for a moment. "I have to face this. I can't let this go on."

Auggie nodded sagely. "So, the question is ... how much are you comfortable spending, and how many of them do you need to give up?"

* * *

Melinda said her goodbyes Thursday morning, and her face was streaked with tears before she ever made it out of the barn. John followed through on his promise to not only take the sheep to the sale, but to arrive at the farm only after she'd left for work.

Just before she passed Ed and Mabel's driveway, Melinda glanced in her rearview mirror and spotted a dark blob wreathed in dust that had to be John's truck and trailer. Sure enough, the dust cloud turned up her lane, and she quickly looked away. Just before she reached the blacktop, she pulled over to the gravel's shoulder and sobbed her heart out.

There were still eighteen sheep in her barn. But when she came home that evening, only eight would be left. Annie was staying, of course, and little Clover. Clover needed a young friend, so that meant her sister would remain. That left five spots to fill, a gut-wrenching decision Melinda agonized over with Doc and Auggie's gentle guidance. She ultimately picked from among the ewes, as she'd been caring for them for over a year and, when forced to choose, found she was more attached to them than most of the lambs.

Auggie had clapped her on the shoulder when they finished the list. With pride in his voice, he'd told her she was a real farmer now.

"Do real farmers cry this hard? I don't know how they do it." She found a tissue in her purse, brushed away the tears and took a deep breath. It would be another long day if she didn't get her emotions in check before she got to town.

As for the ten holes left in Melinda's heart, she didn't know how, or when, they'd ever heal.

But she tried to take comfort in the other numbers, the ones on her new spreadsheet. Even with figuring in worst-case feed and supply costs, the eight sheep she had left wouldn't put her in the poor house. She'd trimmed her flock, and it hurt more than she even imagined it would, but she shouldn't have to do it again.

She'd been parked on the gravel's shoulder long enough for the dust to start to settle. It was a beautiful late-August morning, just a shade cooler than the day before. The seasons were preparing to change, and she had to do the same. Melinda wiped her face again, squared her shoulders, and put the car into gear.

✳ ✳ ✳

Melinda tried her best to look ahead. And really, what else could she do? It was so hard to enter the barn, count noses and come up short. But now, when she studied her stash of hay, the fractions told her she'd made the right choice. The bales would last so much longer than before. As for the heartache, she'd just have to ride it out.

The proceeds check John dropped off was higher than she had hoped for, but she'd need every dime of it long before spring. John also brought a bit of good news: The sheep had been sold together, and he sort-of-knew their new owner. They were in good hands. The guy lived over north of ...

Melinda thanked her neighbor again, but kindly asked him to stop. It might be best to not know all the details. More than half of her sheep were gone, and she had to let them go.

The fire may have taken part of her pasture, but the rain that preceded it gave the garden a second wind. Even the lawn perked up a bit, with some brave green stems trying to push through the old, parched patches. The rest of the meadow might offer a few fresh snacks for the sheep, once the fence was replaced and they had their freedom again.

Melinda wasn't the only one trying to adapt. She'd come home Wednesday evening to find Sunny crouched in the dull grass just west of the barn, staring at the angry, black swath of scorched dirt and ash. The charred fence posts remained where they had fallen, tangled with the crumpled metal panels. The shocking width of the blaze was now easily seen, and the ugly scar spreading far into the cornfield was an eerie reminder of the terror of that awful night.

Sunny's nose took in the lingering scent of smoke as he studied the scene, and his ears twitched with what Melinda could only guess was a mix of annoyance and shock. His whole world had been turned upside down, and he was so distracted that he didn't even hear her steps across the crackling grass.

She wanted to run to him, wrap her arms around him and tell him that, someday, even if it took until spring, things would return to normal. But in the end, she decided to just let him be.

Sunday morning brought another change in routine. Instead of driving into Swanton to attend church with her parents, Melinda simply traveled two miles south to First Lutheran. During the time for announcements, she raised her hand.

She thanked the women's group for bringing breakfast the morning after the fire, and commended all the local emergency crews for the quick response that saved her farm.

In his sermon, Pastor Paul called for patience and hope, and shared a renewed faith that the drought would end soon.

There was another reason Melinda didn't go into Swanton that morning. Diane was already at the farm when she returned from church, and Mabel was on her way. This year's canning bee was going to be much smaller in scope, but they were determined to make the most of whatever could be preserved.

Diane was at the kitchen table, with two teenaged kittens competing for space in her lap. "Decided to just let myself in. Grace and Hazel didn't seem to mind."

"Of course not." Melinda smiled, and it felt good. "Grandma usually brings a few toy mice or treats, doesn't she?"

"I looked everywhere around the yard for Sunny and Stormy, but couldn't find them."

Melinda reached into a cabinet for three mugs. Her mom had put the coffee on, and the kitchen was already filling with that comforting aroma. "They're pretty scarce these days, the fire still has them shaken up." She told her mom about Sunny's sorrowful vigil a few nights before.

"Nobody likes to have their life rearranged." Diane shifted Grace and Hazel to the floor, which elicited several protesting meows. "That's interesting, what you said about Sunny. Hobo was doing the same thing when I came into the yard. I saw him before he saw me, even, he was so preoccupied."

"I know," Melinda sighed. "He's on watch all the time now. He went crazy when the fence crew showed up yesterday morning, barking and pacing. I had to lock him in the house before I went to work. Ed was eager to come by to give Hobo a midday potty break, and to evaluate how the work was going, of course." She gave her mom a knowing look. Ed was a great guy, but he could be as nosy as Auggie. "They had to drill down to set the posts, the ground is so dry and hard. But they got a good start, and I think they'll finish up tomorrow."

Diane shook her head. "Poor Hobo. He should settle down soon, I hope. He loves you so much, and this whole farm is a close second. He's a hero, no doubt; but it must have been terrifying for him, too."

Melinda set a platter of apple muffins on the table. A few small fruits were stubbornly clinging to the branches of the three apple trees on the edge of the windbreak. They were a heritage variety with an early season, and the apples were a little sour compared to last year, but she'd diced two of them and added more sugar to the batter.

"Hobo hasn't been himself, that's for sure. The other night, when I scrubbed up these canning jars?" She gestured at the counter by the sink, where the sparkling glass containers waited in neat rows.

"He didn't even want to help me bring them up from the basement, like last year. Of course, when I took the really nasty ones out to the hydrant for an initial rinse, he was right there."

"I saw those pots of cucumbers." Diane reached for a muffin. "So we're doing pickles, I assume?"

"Mabel said that's the best way to use them up, especially when they're so small."

Melinda wasn't terribly fond of dill pickles, truth be told. But her dad did, and a few of the Prosper Hardware coffee guys had expressed interest. Horace and Wilbur apparently loved them, as did Kevin and Ada. And after all those hot, sticky hours of watering and weeding, and praying for rains that too often hadn't come, Melinda wasn't about to let anything go to waste.

She'd scavenged just enough ears of sweet corn to almost make a batch of Horace's relish, and purchased extra corn, peppers and onions at the store to make everything stretch. The small basket of tomatoes was better than nothing, and Mabel was bringing what her garden had ready. They might get a dozen pint jars of stewed tomatoes out of all of it, if they were lucky.

Mabel soon arrived, her cheery face framed by a folded bandanna that held back her white curls. She set her totes on the counter and gave her younger neighbor a hug.

"How are you doing, honey? What a week you've had. If this dang drought hadn't slowed down my vines, I'd say this would be a good year to make some homemade blackberry wine."

Melinda raised her eyebrows in interest, and filed that idea away for next year.

"As for these pickles," Mabel said, "I'm glad I made it a priority to keep my herbs going. I've got plenty of dill, so we shouldn't run out."

"It's a good thing herbs are tough. I've got a little dill out there, too, along with basil and some cilantro for salsa. I'd love to say I'll be canning more tomatoes in a few weeks, but who knows what will be ready, and when?"

"There's always the freezer. Do a bag at a time as they come on. Not the same, I know, but ... 'desperate times' and all that." Mabel poured herself a cup of coffee and reached into the refrigerator for the milk. She dropped into one of the kitchen chairs with a sigh.

"It's been a mean season, that's for sure. There's always a dry spell here and there, but it's been years since I can remember it being this bad."

And then, there was an unexpected twinkle in her eyes.

"Ada called last night. She told me all about Horace, and his Maggie. Are they really going to meet, and right here at the farm? And to think, that's only a week from today! That must have been awful, trying to keep something like that under your hat, and for weeks!"

Thursday night, Maggie had suddenly informed Barb and Wendy that she wanted to see Horace. Everyone wondered what exactly had caused Maggie to change her mind, but no one wanted to ask for fear she would change it again.

Their plans had moved at a breathtaking pace since then. Ada and Kevin broke the news to Horace on Friday and, after more emotion than Ada had ever seen her brother show, he was on board for the long-awaited reunion. Ada had kept Melinda in the loop, but Melinda didn't allow herself to get excited until a date was set.

"Oh, I'm so glad I can talk about it now! You don't know how many times I wanted to tell everyone. I was dying to bring it up," she told Mabel, "on the odd chance you had any information that could help us. But I'd promised to keep it quiet."

"From what Ada's told me, I'm afraid I wouldn't have been much help. I didn't know Maggie at all, or her family. You found her, and that's all that matters. It sounds like Horace is thrilled, now that he's over the shock."

Diane raised an eyebrow. "I'm sure it was quite a surprise for him."

Melinda reached for a muffin. "It took a few minutes for it all to sink in, I guess. I worried he would be angry at us for keeping this from him, and for going through his personal things, but as you know, Horace is pretty easy-going."

He'd barely glanced at the letters, according to Ada, but the picture brought tears. Once he got his mind around the situation, Horace wanted to hear everything Ada knew. She didn't mention Maggie's baby, of course, but she did ask her brother point-blank why he and Maggie broke up.

Ada later told Melinda she was rather disappointed by his response.

"I guess he just shrugged," Melinda explained, "and told Kevin and Ada that Maggie wanted to go away to college, and he wanted to stay home."

"That's it?" Diane threw up her hands. "No angst-filled argument in the rain? No tearful goodbye at the train station? It's a good thing Horace decided to be a farmer. I don't think he would have had much luck writing romance novels."

"Horace has had a very long life," Mabel said once the laughter died away. "And, I would say, it's been a good one, even if it seems to have been rather uneventful. But I suppose, something that happened seventy years ago eventually loses its sting, over time. I would certainly hope so, at least. Melinda, what is it?"

She looked down. "I'm so glad Horace and Maggie are going to meet, and I'm happy to host them here, as it's sort-of-partway and they can have some privacy. But I have to say, I'm starting to get really nervous about this."

Diane leaned over the table. "You think there's something that Horace isn't saying." It wasn't a question.

"The thing with Horace is, there's always so much more beneath the surface than what he lets on. And Maggie's dragged her feet for weeks before finally agreeing to see him again. There's no way to know how this is going to go. I think we need to be prepared for just about anything."

Mabel shook her head in sympathy. "Horace must be reeling from this. I can't imagine. It has to be like a ghost from the past has shown up at his door. I've known him basically my entire life, and you're right. He doesn't always say much, but don't fool yourself into thinking he's oblivious to what's going on. He's far smarter, and more perceptive, than most people give him credit for."

Diane polished off her muffin with one last, large bite. "Well, I guess you just tidy up the house, bake something to serve your guests, and buckle your seat belt. Let's get started on these pickles."

Most of the cucumbers were so small, it didn't take many cuts to fit them into the jars. Fresh herbs were added, and the boiled brine was poured over the top. Mabel lowered a round of jars into the canner's boiling water, and the women started another batch.

"That didn't take long." Melinda reached for another bowl of cucumbers. "This is easier than making corn relish, or even canning tomatoes. I might have to make some of these next year, too. I've caught the canning bug, and I can't stop now."

"Feels good, doesn't it?" Mabel prepped another round of herbs. "Seeing those rows of colorful jars in the cellar is always so satisfying. There won't be as many this year. But, you know, it almost means more when it's a down year. Every jar is a reminder of all the hard work it took to keep the garden going."

Melinda stared out the south windows to where her barn still stood. It wasn't as full as it used to be, with only eight sheep calling it home, but it was still there. So was this house, and the shed and the chicken coop and the windbreak, and the rest of her dear animals. She was very blessed, yes; but just now, worn down from weeks of worry and uncertainty, she was so darn tired.

Diane read her daughter's face, and wrapped an arm around Melinda's shoulder. "Things have been tough, no doubt about that. But the hard times will pass, like they always do."

"The first batch is nearly ready." Mabel handed Melinda a set of potholders. "You know, it's sort of like these pickles. You can't enjoy them right away. Let them rest at least a week. Or even better, wait two weeks before you open the first jar. It takes time for all the flavors to come together."

✳ 23 ✳

Melinda had the back door open before Ada had a chance to park by the garage. Hobo spotted Horace in the car's front seat and ran ahead, eager to see his old friend.

"There's the conquering hero!" Horace tried to rub Hobo's ears, but he was wriggling with excitement. Melinda had to grasp Hobo's collar so Horace could safely get out of the car.

"You saved the farm, buddy. Oh, yes, you saved the farm! Careful now, don't get my new pants dirty." He pushed a vase of carnations into Melinda's free hand. "Here, take these flowers before he knocks them over."

"Those are so pretty. I'm sure she's going to love them." After so many weeks of trying to keep such a monumental secret, it felt strange for Melinda to even speak Maggie's name.

"Well, these flowers aren't the ones I wanted," Horace admitted as he grudgingly accepted the cane Kevin handed him from the back seat. "Not authentic, you see. But they'll have to do." He sported a new plaid shirt and pressed khakis, and his white hair was combed smooth. But his demeanor gave no indication this was anything more than a routine visit to his old home.

When you've waited seventy years, Melinda decided, *thirty more minutes maybe doesn't seem like much.* But to her, it felt like an eternity.

Ada was smiling when she came around the front of the car, but she seemed a bit nervous. Melinda wasn't the only one with her fingers crossed about what might happen this afternoon.

"I know you wanted tiger lilies, but the store didn't have them." She turned to Melinda. "He wanted us to stop along the road, root around in the ditches to get 'real' flowers, as he called them. It's too hot for that, and we're all dressed up, anyway. These would have to do."

The air was thick and humid, and the sun had vanished hours ago. The heavy skies held the promise of rain, the first real chance for moisture since the lightning storm nearly two weeks ago.

As Melinda checked the skies again, the bed of perennials behind the house caught her eye.

"Those coneflowers are tough, they're about the only plants holding on without much help from me. Horace, should I cut a few to add to your bouquet?"

He considered the offer, then finally nodded. "Sounds good. Maggie always did like purple."

Kevin followed Melinda when she went inside for scissors. "Can you believe this is really happening? I could barely sleep last night. I hope this doesn't blow up in our faces."

"They're both in their early nineties. I doubt there'll be much screaming and shouting if this all goes south."

"Or what if it's the opposite? What if one or both of them becomes so overwhelmed with joy that their heart bursts, right then and there? Maybe we should make Maggie's daughters sign a waiver or something."

Kevin gave a shocked whistle as they came down the back steps. "Just look at that pasture, at how close the fire came to the barn! I'm so sorry about the sheep. I don't know how you did it, how you were able to pick and choose like that."

"Desperation drove me to it," she said sadly, sifting through the coneflowers to find the best blooms. "But I couldn't keep them all, really, even before the fire. Guess I just needed a push to do the right thing."

Horace was waiting on the sidewalk with Hobo, staring at the barn and what was left of the pasture. He was silent, but she could see the tears in his faded blue eyes. The hand holding the vase had begun to tremble. She didn't know what to say. So she gently took the arrangement from his grasp and busied herself with adding the coneflowers, giving him the emotional space he needed.

"Nice fence," he said at last. "They did a good job."

Ada patted Hobo on the head. "You're a good boy, the very best. Melinda, I can't imagine how terrified you must have been. All that matters is everyone is safe, and the farm was spared. Let's get inside and out of this heat."

The house was refreshingly cool by comparison. Melinda had set out a few extra boxes of tissues as she'd straightened up the downstairs, and the coffee pot was already gurgling on the counter. There was iced tea, too, and fresh oatmeal cookies. Nothing too fancy, but Melinda suspected everyone would be too distracted to care.

Kevin shadowed Horace as he started for the dining room, with Hobo close behind. Melinda knew Horace preferred her reading chair, which sat in the spot by the fireplace where his recliner used to be.

"Well, we've done all we can," Ada said in a low voice once Horace was out of the kitchen. "And we never would have found her without your help."

"It was a lucky break, that day at the archives. Honestly, I was out of ideas."

"Oh, I don't know if luck was really the deciding factor." Ada tried for a smile as Melinda passed her a glass of iced tea. "I'd like to think this was meant to be, that the fates intervened to bring these two together again. I just wish she'd hurry up and get here."

Grace soon arrived out of nowhere, as cats are apt to do, and jumped into Ada's lap. "Oh, sweet baby Grace, am I glad to see you. Yes, come sit with me and make it all better."

Kevin appeared in the doorway. "I got him settled in your chair. He's asking for a cup of coffee."

"I'll get it." Melinda jumped up, eager for something to do other than wait. "You just sit with your mom and relax."

"Really? How am I going to do that?"

"I wish I knew."

Horace was staring into the downstairs bedroom, deep in thought. She handed him the cup, pulled the ottoman over so she could sit next to Hobo, and awaited the verdict.

"Ada told me all about it," Horace finally said. "Doesn't look so bad in there, with the bed gone."

"I'm so sorry, I hated to sell it." The words came out in a rush. "I'm glad you're not upset. I know you said it came with the house, and it was my choice, but I just ..."

"No matter. I would have done the same. It was fancy, but fancy won't keep the sheep from going hungry."

"Well, that's just it. I got a good price for the bed, but it wasn't enough."

"It never could be, not when you're trying to get through a drought like this one. And then the fire, too." He nodded at her, with understanding and respect in his eyes. "You had to scale back the flock. You did the right thing."

Under all her hurt, Melinda knew that was true. But hearing Horace say it made her feel so much better. She scooched the ottoman closer.

"So, I've been wondering ... You and Wilbur had sheep for years. But once you sold your last buck and stopped raising lambs, why did you keep the ewes? I mean, they can be expensive to care for, if there's not lambs to sell off. The price of wool's not so great these days. How did you make your money back?"

Horace let out a low chuckle. "Truth is, we didn't." He took a sip of his coffee, set it on the side table and leaned forward. Horace was often a man of few words, but he found them quickly when the topic kept his interest.

"Sheep are expensive lawnmowers, but they're some of the best critters to have around. They're pretty docile, usually healthy, and not big enough to hurt much if they step on your foot. Cows, now, they're a whole other deal. It was hard enough to let the cows go, but we decided the sheep and the chickens had to stay. Wouldn't be a farm without them."

Melinda felt the same way. "But it must have cost a lot those last few years. And I know you and Wilbur, well, you don't like to waste ..."

Horace cackled. "You mean, we're cheap."

She shrugged.

"Like I said, it didn't seem right to let them go. Farming was our life, all our life, but we knew we'd end up in a nursing home or dead, like everyone else. So we just bought the hay and straw and feed and never worried about it." He thought for a moment. "And I guess that's the difference between you and us. We were at the end, but you're just at the beginning."

Then he smiled. "You're just getting started, there's plenty of time to learn as you go. Remember that."

"I will. I promise." She turned to look out the picture window. The light was starting to change, the sky turning darker. "Maybe it'll rain after all."

Horace's eyes followed her gaze. Neither would admit it, but they were really watching the end of the driveway.

"I'd say rain's coming for sure." He rubbed his right knee. "My old bones tell me these things. So, how goes it with your young fellow?"

Melinda blinked. What? He meant Chase, of course. *I guess people who are fifty years behind you in life are always going to be young.*

"Ada told me about him. And that you had a fight."

She sighed. "Yes, we did. About the farm, actually. And the sheep."

"Did he show up after the fire? Come down and help you?"

"Yes. And he found someone to fix the fence, too."

"Sounds like a fine young man, then."

"Yes. We have our differences, but ... yes, he is."

Horace was especially chatty today. They were still alone with Hobo, as Kevin and Ada were talking in the kitchen and their guests had yet to arrive. Here was her chance.

"Horace," she whispered, "what really happened between you and Maggie? Will you tell me?"

He stared at the rug. Melinda studied his face, tried to find the young Horace behind all the age spots and wrinkles, but maybe it had been too long ago.

"You don't have to," she hurried on. "But if you do, I won't tell Kevin and Ada, or anyone else, if you don't want me to. Don't you want to talk about it, at least a little? She'll be here soon, and you must be so ..."

She waited. At last, he looked up.

"We were supposed to go off to Ames together. I was going to take engineering, you see. She was going to be a teacher. We had all these plans. And ... I loved her. Very much."

Melinda only nodded, and hoped her silence would keep him talking.

"And then one day, the week before we were going to go, I came home from town. Parked the truck by the barn, hauled in the bags of oats." He raised his chin with pride. "I could do that then, carry a fifty-pound bag over my shoulder like it was nothing. It was hot, like today, and it looked like a storm was brewing. So I went to put the truck in the shed."

He looked down at Hobo and began to pet him. But Melinda could see Horace was really trying to comfort himself.

"So, I ... I rolled the door open, and there was Wilbur. He was drunk. So drunk I could smell the booze on him from five feet away. Passed out cold."

"Wilbur was drunk? In the middle of the afternoon?"

"Oh, that wasn't the first time. Morning, night, whenever. He'd been home from the war for over a year by then, but it hadn't been long enough. He was still having those nightmares, you see. And his girl, she'd thrown him over while he was gone."

Kevin had found an old still in the machine shed. Family lore said Horace's grandpa started a side hustle to make ends meet, and Henry and his brother helped keep it going through

Prohibition. Horace had once mentioned that Wilbur revived the bootlegging operation for a few years after World War II, but this was a chapter of the story Melinda had never heard.

"The damn bottle was still in his hand." Horace frowned. "I took it away, the stuff was so strong any stray spark might have started the shed on fire. I knew right then, I couldn't leave. Wilbur was the oldest, he was supposed to take over the farm as Father aged, but how was he going to do it when he was like that?"

"Did your parents know?"

"I'm sure they did. But no one said anything. See, people didn't talk about things, not like they do now. Everybody's got their dirty laundry out on the line. But I don't know, maybe that's a good thing."

He paused for more coffee, the guarded look on his face now replaced with relief. Finally, after all these years, he could speak the truth.

"So, anyway, I go to the house, and I pass by the summer kitchen. Mother had been canning for hours every day, and she was exhausted. My younger brothers and sisters were helping, but keeping them all on task wasn't easy. And Father was lying down in there." He pointed into the bedroom.

"His back was going out on him, and he was trying to rest before chores. I'd already started packing my trunk, was counting the days until Maggie and I would leave, but ... I went upstairs and started pulling things out, throwing them on the floor."

He passed a weathered hand over his face.

"But it wasn't all Wilbur's fault. I wanted to leave, but I was uneasy, too. You see, this was the only place I'd ever lived. And I wanted to come back and farm, after college. That's the whole reason I wanted to go to school, so I could be the best farmer in these parts. But I saw that if I left, there may not be much of a farm to come home to."

Horace turned to Melinda with tears in his eyes. "The farm needed me, my family needed me. How could I leave? Even for Maggie?"

Melinda squeezed his hand. "Oh, Horace, I'm so sorry. What did Maggie say?"

"We fought, of course. She said I was weak, that I didn't love her if I wouldn't go. That wasn't true! I said, just because I wasn't going off to school, that didn't mean we couldn't be together. And then, she said she'd never be a farmer's wife. She never wanted to come back here."

Melinda checked the mantel clock. Shouldn't Maggie and her daughters be here by now? What if she had changed her mind again?

"Was that the last time you saw her?"

He looked down again. "That's the worst of it. She asked me to come to the depot to see her off. She was scared to go away on her own, I could tell. I knew I couldn't change her mind, I'd already tried, so ... I didn't go, and I've always been sorry. But it was over. I decided I just had to get on with life. What else was I going to do?"

Ada hurried in from the kitchen, her face flushed. "They're coming up the drive!" She glanced from Horace to Melinda. "Is everything OK?"

"It's fine. We're just fine." She looked to Horace for confirmation, and he finally gave a small nod. "Here, I'll get your coffee cup. Your cane's by the bookcase."

"Wilbur finally stopped drinking, a few years later," Horace said quickly once Ada left the room. "We had many good years here, before his dementia set in. I want you to know that. He's a good person."

"I know he is. The best. Next to yourself." She handed him a tissue. "Now, wipe your face and come with me."

There was a commotion on the back porch, bursts of chatter and nervous laughter as Ada welcomed their guests. Horace took in a sharp breath, and Melinda laid a hand on his arm. "Do you want to sit down?"

"Goodness no, I'm no invalid. She's upright, so I need to be, too."

He leaned the cane against the kitchen table and put a palm on its surface for a second of support, then reached for the vase. The purple coneflowers glowed among the cream and pink carnations, providing the pop of bright color the arrangement needed. "Maybe watch out for Hobo, though, so he doesn't knock her down." Kevin reached for Hobo's collar and guided him into the corner.

Wendy opened the kitchen door, a few tears mingling with her smile as she gave Melinda an encouraging nod.

"Mom, watch that threshold there," Wendy said over her shoulder. "Here, let me take your purse."

A slight, elderly woman shuffled into the room, pushing a walker. She was dressed casually, in a simple striped blouse and khaki pants, but had a bumblebee brooch pinned to her collar. Her lipstick was bold and carefully applied, and her mass of white curls looked perfect despite the heat and humidity.

Her brown eyes anxiously swept the kitchen before they landed on Horace. Then they filled with tears.

"Maggie."

"Horace. Oh, Horace, it's so good to see you."

At first glance, Melinda didn't find any resemblance to the vivacious young woman in the faded photo. But then Maggie smiled, and there she was.

It took Maggie and Horace a few moments to meet up, as neither moved very fast these days. Finally, they were face to face. Horace looked as if he longed to lift Maggie into his arms and swing her around, as he must have done seventy years ago. Maggie was crying harder now, and seemingly grasping for what to say next. With several decades' worth of catching up to do, where to begin?

"I brought you some flowers." Horace slid the vase under Maggie's nose so she could see them better and inhale their blooms. "They're not those orange lilies you love, but ..."

"Oh, Horace, they're just beautiful." She swallowed hard. "I'm ... I'm so sorry."

"For what, dear?" Horace's voice cracked.

"For everything. For pushing you away."

"I'm sorry I couldn't go with you."

"I know. I understand." Maggie looked around the kitchen, her eyes wide with wonder. "This house ... it looks so different, and yet the same. It was always a beautiful house. Your mother took such good care of it."

A shadow passed over Maggie's lined face when she mentioned Anna, and Melinda's stomach clenched. Edith was right, there had been trouble here that long-ago afternoon. Wendy turned pale and reached for Barb's hand.

Ada patted Wendy on the shoulder and stepped forward. "Melinda has been kind enough to bake us some cookies," she said brightly to no one in particular. "Let's all sit down. There's coffee, and iced tea."

Maggie and Horace didn't answer. They just stood there, holding hands, tears running down their cheeks.

"I'd love some tea," Kevin told Melinda, then turned to Wendy and Barb. "Have you heard about how Hobo saved the farm? He's quite the celebrity around here these days."

In the chatter and laughter that followed, it was as if the house, and everyone in it, let out a collective sigh of relief. This reunion was going to be a success. As for how much Maggie would tell Horace about her past, that would be up to her.

Melinda was about to move more chairs into the living room, but Ada waved her over. "Maybe the rest of us should stay in here," she whispered, and tipped her head at the dining-room table. "Might get a bit crowded in there."

"I'll help them get settled," Barb said, then lowered her voice. "They could use some privacy, I'm sure."

Wendy passed by with cookies for Horace and Maggie. "Believe it or not, it's cooling off outside. Melinda, I think I'd enjoy a little time on your screened-in porch."

Maggie and Horace were now side-by-side on the couch, with refreshments within easy reach on the coffee table. Hobo, who was wonderfully calm despite all the strangers in his home, had stretched out at their feet.

Horace reached for Maggie's hand. Her grip was feeble, but she didn't let go.

"Oh, Horace, I have so much to tell you."

"And I you. I'm as old as dirt these days, but I've got all the time in the world for you, Maggie."

"They'll be just fine," Barb whispered to Ada. "Let's go."

* * *

Wendy was right about the change in the weather. Melinda opened the farmhouse's front door to find a cool breeze rushing through the porch's screens, and the yard was wonderfully dim for a late-August afternoon. A gentle rumble of thunder echoed across the thirsty fields as Kevin and Ada brought out snacks and extra chairs.

Wendy started laughing after she took a bite of her cookie. "Ada and Melinda, I'd say everything has come full circle. You may not remember, but I served oatmeal cookies the morning you and Jen came to visit. Although these are better than mine, I must say. I'd love the recipe."

"Oh, that's right!" Ada shook her head in amazement. "I'm sure yours were good, but I wouldn't know. I was so nervous, I could hardly taste them. We had no idea how you were going to react."

"Everything worked out." Barb poured a glass of iced tea and handed it to Kevin. "I don't know if Mom will ever help us find our brother, but I'm so glad we've been able to reunite her and Horace. We've offered to drive past where she grew up, on the way home, and I hope she'll take us up on that. Maybe it would bring her some closure, if nothing else."

"I worried this would be too upsetting for her," Wendy said to her sister. "But she just blossomed when she saw him! And I can't remember the last time she smiled like that."

Grace and Hazel had joined the procession out to the porch. Grace was already in Kevin's lap, and Ada patted the space between her and Wendy on the porch swing. Hazel didn't have to be asked twice.

"The sheer joy on Horace's face!" Ada shook her head. "I swear, the minute he saw Maggie, he looked twenty years younger."

Wendy's eyes filled with happy tears. "Mom's hearing is surprisingly good, so they'll be able to talk on the phone. And the drive's not much more than an hour, we'll bring her for a visit as often as we can."

Melinda reached for a cookie. "Horace is sort of a homebody, but I'm sure he'd love to come to Cedar Falls once in a while." She peered out through the wall of screens. "Am I hearing things? Is that what I think it is?"

Everyone was still for a moment, listening and hoping.

Another soft *splat* on the porch's roof, then several more. The tapping turned to a drumming and then, all at once, the heavy skies opened. The gravel road was soon lost in a haze of rain, and water poured over the maple tree's tired leaves and washed the dust off the dull grass.

"Oh, thank God." Ada pressed her hands together. "A real rain! It's been so long."

"Thirteen days," Melinda told Wendy and Barb. "Thirteen days since we've had even a drop, and weeks since there's been a soaker like this." She threw up her hands.

"The rain barrel! I was going to check it this morning, make sure it's ready. But I was so distracted, I forgot all about it. I'll be right back."

There wasn't an umbrella handy, but she didn't care. She burst through the screen door and flew down the steps, a refreshing blast of cool water greeting her once she was out of the protection of the porch's roof. She kicked off her sandals and ran, barefoot and jubilant, around the house.

The grass was still brown and dull, but now it was damp, too, and it felt wonderful under her feet.

In the garden, the plants turned their leaves toward the sky, as if offering a prayer of thanksgiving for the rain that poured down around them.

Melinda cheered when she saw the water splashing over the rain barrel's rim and through its screen. Her hair and shirt were soaked by the time she jogged past the front porch, and her guests' laughter started before she came through the door.

Kevin handed her a kitchen towel. "The best I could find on such short notice. Our lovebirds are deep in conversation. I didn't want to head for the bathroom and get in their way."

"Thanks." Melinda rubbed her hair and dropped back into her chair. "I'm soaked, but so what? It feels wonderful!"

"I was just telling Ada," Wendy said, "this house is so beautiful! I can see why you fell in love with it, Melinda. All that oak woodwork, and those bookcases. That fireplace! How could anyone not feel at home here?"

"And this porch." Barb nodded with approval. "I just love this swing, and Ada says you found those wicker chairs at a consignment shop? They're perfect. It's so lovely out here, like something out of a magazine. But the best part is this ceiling! I don't know when I've ever seen a prettier shade of light blue."

Melinda looked up and smiled. All those superstitions surrounding the "haint blue" paint, and its ability to keep spirits away ... Well, she could see it was a special color. But in her mind, the legends had it all turned around.

She liked to think this blue could bring back the long-ago lives tied to this farmhouse, that it was a symbol of healing and forgiveness. One person from the past was here, right now, in the living room with Horace, and very much alive. She thought of Anna and Henry, and how the wind had suddenly calmed the night of the fire and allowed their farm to be spared. And what if Anna had played a role in bringing Horace and his lost love back together?

Melinda believed it was possible, but it was so hard to explain. All she wanted to do, right now, was enjoy this special afternoon, its long-awaited rain, and the friends that filled her farmhouse.

"I'm glad you like the color. It's so soothing. Sitting out here can make all of your worries disappear." She reached for the pitcher. "Would anyone like more iced tea?"

WHAT'S NEXT

"Turning Season": Autumn is probably my favorite time of year! Refreshing days, foggy nights and the beautiful colors of the changing landscape will all be found in Book 7, along with some Halloween hijinks, of course! Read on for an excerpt from the book.

Recipes: Three more special dishes have been added to the collection on the website. My great-grandma was known for her home-canned pickles, made with fresh dill from her garden, and they're so easy to make! You'll also discover a hearty calico-bean casserole and a no-bake citrus cheesecake.

Stay in touch: Be sure to sign up for the email newsletter when you visit fremontcreekpress.com. That's the best way to find out when more titles will be available for pre-order.

Thanks for reading!
Melanie

Sneak peek: Turning Season

September:
Prosper Hardware

The parking spots in front of city hall and Prosper Hardware were already filled when Melinda arrived in town that morning. The side door on one van slid open, and she spotted three carriers inside. "Good morning, kitties," she sang out. "Today's the best day of your life."

Karen's monthly clinics for community cats were so popular, she and Doctor Vogel now planned to offer a second program in both October and November. There was a long waiting list for the reduced-fee services, and the threat of sudden snow and ice would make it difficult to plan clinics for the winter months.

Melinda usually had the gravel lot behind the store to herself at this hour, but the commotion on Main Street had driven Auggie, Jerry and Frank to park behind the store. A gust of wind threatened to lift the aluminum foil off her apple-pie bars, but she welcomed the changes the cool breeze promised.

It was a little early to break out the sweaters and the slow cookers, since the afternoon highs had only dropped into the low eighties. But the seasons were about to turn again, and she couldn't wait.

"You must have found a place to park." Auggie's eyes lit up when he spotted the pan in Melinda's hands, but he was fascinated by the scene outside the plate-glass windows.

"Oh, look at that one!" He pointed at the humane trap one woman carried. "That long coat, brown with white. He's a big boy, for sure. Bet he's never gone for a ride before."

Jerry and Melinda exchanged amused glances. Auggie had always claimed to not care about cats. That all changed when he was adopted by the two former strays now presiding over Prosper Feed Co.

"I'm glad the cat clinics are so successful." Jerry reached for a treat. "But they're just one more reminder that we need a real community center. Performing veterinary procedures in the scrubbed-down council chambers is far from ideal."

The coffee was ready, and Uncle Frank reached for a cup. "You're right. But what's the answer? Other towns have tried all sorts of things, from reclaiming rundown properties to erecting new buildings on vacant lots."

Auggie shook his head. "Well, we've got plenty of the first. But we all know the drama that comes with properties changing hands."

"And none of the latter," Jerry sighed. "Or at least, no empty lots owned by the city. There's just a few around, but they're all on residential streets."

"A community center means congestion," Frank warned. "Who'd want to live next door to that? But it's an issue we'll have to take on. Jake says he's going to address public use of city space as part of his mayoral candidate platform."

Melinda poured herself some coffee. "Jerry, here's an opportunity for you to beat Jake at his own game. Policies are fine, but when there's so little public space to fight over, it makes him look short-sighted. How about you put something on the next council agenda? Beat him at his own game?"

"Good idea."

"Whew, it's almost cold out there!" George came in from the back. "I might need to pull out the long-sleeve shirts soon. Do you think Doc will give up those khakis and light-colored tees? Makes me do a double-take every time. Never seen him in anything but jeans, until this summer."

"Never seen it so blasted hot, either, as it was the past few months," Auggie reminded George. "A man's gotta dress for the job. I'd rather Doc look like a preppie, than have him keel over out on a call."

"Especially when he's one of our first responders," Jerry added. "We need all the volunteers we can get."

Melinda went behind the counter and reached for the dust cloth. Two stuffed-fabric pumpkins were already on display next to the register. "Hey, there's another plank for your platform. How about a plan to recruit more firefighters and EMTs? Public safety is a major issue for voters."

"Yeah, I'll add it to the list." Jerry crossed his arms. "This platform's going to have so many planks, I could just about build a community center from scratch."

Auggie twisted in his chair, his eyes wide.

"What?" Frank nudged him and chuckled. "See a ghost? It's a little early for that yet. Give it a month. I can't wait to get our Halloween decorations out. I'd love to add one of those inflatable pumpkins, but I don't know if Miriam ..."

"Now, that is just eerie." Auggie hurried to the door. "Here we were talking about the emergency crew, and I swear, Tony's truck just pulled up. He usually has to be in Swanton by eight, you never see him in town this time of day. What's going on?" Tony Bevins worked at one of the area's banks, since serving as Prosper's emergency management chief came with only a small yearly stipend.

Jerry joined Auggie by the windows. "Hey, he's got Doc with him. Guess Tony's having coffee with us this morning. Good thing we've got extra chairs."

Doc and Tony wore big grins as they wiped their shoes on the mat.

"I don't have long, I have to get to the bank." Tony's ruddy face was alight with ... something. Maybe excitement? "But I wanted to tell everyone, right away. Melinda, take a seat."

"Me? What ..."

"You're smirking like crazy. Both of you." Auggie eyed Tony and Doc. "What's the deal? Spit it out, already!"

"Hobo's a hero!" Doc clapped and hooted.

"Well, yeah." Frank furrowed his brow. "Everyone knows that. He saved Melinda's farm, saved the whole township from ..."

"No, no, for real!" Tony shoved his phone into Melinda's hand. She blinked twice, trying to process the email there on the screen. Happy tears sprang into her eyes.

"Wait ... is this for real? Hobo's getting an award?"

A national organization had chosen Hobo to receive one of its highest honors, an award granted to animals showing bravery during emergencies. A certificate and medal were on their way to Prosper, and the group would make a one-time donation in Hobo's name to any non-profit that helped animals in need. Melinda would choose which one.

"We were talking about Hobo, the day after the fire." Doc rubbed his hands together. "I told Tony, it was worth a shot."

"I filled out the form online right away." Tony accepted Jerry's high-five. "The paperwork and everything will come later this week."

Uncle Frank clapped Melinda on the shoulder. "Looks like we've got another agenda item for next week's council meeting. So, how well does Hobo handle crowds?"

She cringed, thinking of Hobo's first visit to Horace and Wilbur's nursing home. It was probably his last.

"He's ... unpredictable. But if I bring him in the back door of city hall, and we can be in and out in ten minutes, I think we can manage it. Oh, this is so exciting!"

"Turning Season" is available in Kindle, paperback, hardcover and large-print paperback editions.

ABOUT THE BOOKS

*Don't miss any of the titles
in these heartwarming rural fiction series*

THE GROWING SEASON SERIES

Melinda is at a crossroads when the "for rent" sign beckons her down a dusty gravel lane. Facing forty, single and downsized from her stellar career at a big-city ad agency, she's struggling to start over when a phone call brings her home to Iowa.

She moves to the country, takes on a rundown farm and its headstrong animals, and lands behind the counter of her family's hardware store in the community of Prosper, whose motto is "The Great Little Town That Didn't." And just like the sprawling garden she tends under the summer sun, Melinda begins to thrive. But when storm clouds arrive on her horizon, can she hold on to the new life she's worked so hard to create?

Filled with memorable characters, from a big-hearted farm dog to the weather-obsessed owner of the local co-op, "Growing Season" celebrates the twists and turns of small-town life. Discover the heartwarming series that's filled with new friends, fresh starts and second chances.

**FOR DETAILS ON ALL THE TITLES
VISIT FREMONTCREEKPRESS.COM**

THE MAILBOX MYSTERIES SERIES

It's been a rough year for Kate Duncan, both on and off the job. Being a mail carrier puts her in close proximity to her customers, with consequences that can't always be foreseen. So when a position opens at her hometown post office, she decides to leave Chicago in her rearview mirror.

Kate and her cat settle into a charming apartment above Eagle River's historic Main Street, but she dreams of a different home to call her own. And as she drives the back roads around Eagle River, Kate begins to take a personal interest in the people on her route.

So when an elderly resident goes missing, she feels compelled to help track him down. It's a quest marked not by miles of gravel, but matters of the heart: friendship, family, and the small connections that add up to a well-lived life.

A TIN TRAIN CHRISTMAS

The toy train was everything two boys could want: colorful, shiny, and the perfect vehicle for their imaginations. But was it meant to be theirs? Revisit Horace's childhood for this special holiday short story inspired by the "Growing Season" series!